DRAGON
OF THE
DEEP

DRAGON
OF THE
DEEP

STEVEN ARMSTRONG

atmosphere press

For Kels. You saw this book before I did.
For Fred. This one is yours.

CAST OF CHARACTERS

Skylet, raised by Séya the sorceress, and Jessie the dragon

Jessie, the dragon, surrogate mother to Skylet and other dragons

Séya, sorceress, and surrogate parent to Skylet

Oros, a former Dragonhunter; kin to Skylet

Ulonae, a dragon youngling

Solen, escaped prisoner

Arca, kin to Skylet

Henricks, high ranking knight of the King's Court

King Rondal, monarch of the kingdom of Ondriten

Layona, an official from Selnes on the hunt for criminals

Oberon, veteran Sentinel, and her partner

Holera, captain of Selnes army on the mission

Gonden, one of Holera's men

Delsce, one of Holera's men

Sebastian, a mysterious sea dragon

Ulysus, water colony elder

Aria, Sebastian's son

Floren, Sebastian's son

I.

The storm winds blew just off the coast of the massive Gyenola Island as vicious and angry as an agitated wild animal that should have been left alone. The rain was merciless; the lightning and thunder engaged in a spirited call-and-response conversation with each other, neither letting the other have the last word. In the midst of this, every form of life seemed to have taken shelter among the beautiful chaos. Yet, something moved in the darkness, crawling upon the sludge of uneven earth. Its head protruded from bushes, revealing itself to be a large dragon of a golden brown hue, like newly turned fall leaves. Though, on that night, it was covered in thick layers of mud in an effort to disguise itself.

On his belly, he traveled deliberately, slowly rolling around in the sludge. He repeatedly covered himself in it whenever the rain washed too much away from his body. He would only stop advancing if he heard the slightest movement from his surroundings.

A hint of salt in the air tapped tentatively at the dragon's nose as though it might be a trick of the mind. But this was no trick. The ocean was near. He was certain; it was the only unique scent among that of the wet earth and rainwater. Lest he got too excited and risk exposure, he had to stay himself until he was sure it was safe to move.

It had been two days since Solen escaped from the far end of the large island. He had been doing well enough evading soldiers with the aid of his natural camouflage ability, which had strengthened since the soldiers had forcibly removed his wings. Yet after two days of hiding, without food, water, or even rest to replenish his body, his abilities were weakening. Now, he had to rely on his surroundings to keep him safe. All he needed to do, he thought, was reach the ocean and try to swim to the closest landmass he could find away from the island. He hoped it would be enough, at least until the storm passed. Then, he could figure out what to do next.

A faint rustling of bushes in the distance brought him back to himself. Alert, as though ready to pounce upon an unsuspecting victim, the dragon kept still and held his breath. His eyes narrowed, looking straight ahead with a focus that couldn't be described. Could they have gotten so close to him? How was he not aware enough to allow that? *I let them gain on me,* he thought. *I shouldn't have lingered yesterday.*

Solen cursed himself but quickly put the thought aside. Nothing could be done about it now. What mattered was making it to the ocean. Just then, another very faint shuffling sound reached his ears. He took a moment to appreciate how close they had gotten, slightly smirking to himself. *Very good,* he thought.

There was no question that they were near now. No doubt that after the first day and a half, the soldiers employed the talents of the most elite tracking team that could be found in the region. For next to the highly trained Dragonhunters, only the scouts could have had a real chance at managing to pick up his trail. Bolder ones might even employ tactics to capture, though that task typically was reserved for the hunters.

A chemical secreted by a dragon's glands betrayed Solen, which the trackers probably latched on to during the hunt. The untrained nose would never pick up the scent, but the Dragon Scouts had studied the beasts for centuries to hone that technique in service to the work of hunters. Solen understood this. If the scouts and soldiers were about, who was to say there wasn't a Dragonhunter nearby also playing a game of cat and mouse alongside them? He had no desire to find out. It was time to move.

Solen felt sitting too much longer in his position would undoubtedly seal his fate. Were he captured again, nothing short of death would be in store for him.

He pressed himself into the mud, even flatter than he had already been. Using his large hands to slowly dig and move heaps of earth closer to himself, he carefully and quietly covered what he could of his body to mask the secretion coming from him and hid from sight. Once he felt covered enough in the short time he gave himself, Solen prepared to move. Taking one deep breath, he closed his eyes and slowly exhaled.

He took off. Moving as fast as he could, his body felt like it needed a few strides to wake up after long periods of moving so slowly. Sure enough, the rustling behind him told Solen that the soldiers and scouts were on top of him. "There!" a soldier whispered loudly.

The scouts, however, were silent and stealthy. They needn't have been told where Solen was. This was their job, and they did it well.

Through the brush and woods, the dragon ran. He jumped over boulders and scattered underneath downed trees. Solen ran as his heart pounded against his chest like a blacksmith's hammer. He couldn't stop, or he would be finished.

A moment later, the shore appeared in the distance beyond the woods. The sight strengthened Solen's resolve. If he could just reach the ocean, he could escape. He leaped over a tall bush, bumping his head against a high bough from a nearby spruce tree. He grunted and quickly rubbed his head as his body plopped on the shore's edge. No sooner had he landed than two scouts appeared feet away from him. They threw special darts to slow him down, but he was too quick for them. Straight ahead, he ran toward the ocean, and just before he could jump in, he was hit in the tail and the hind leg with a series of darts. Solen roared in pain and frustration but forced himself up and continued to push toward the water. *Come on*, he thought to himself. *Come on!! Get to the—*

His body gave out, and he plopped headfirst with a splash, barely making the water. His mouth and hands were partially submerged. All was quiet save for the raging storm and the screaming ocean; all worked up.

One of the scouts turned to face the woods where they all came from and removed a pocket-size torch from one side of his belt and a rock from the other. Striking the two objects and covering them with one hand, he lit the small torch to signal that the hunt was finished. They had subdued the dragon.

The scouts closed in as calmly as they had during the chase, barely winded. The soldiers were more visibly pleased, shaking hands in their triumph. Just as they got within range to collect Solen, the sea became agitated as the thunder and lightning continued to hit.

A few of the men had begun to try and drag Solen away from the water, and one noticed something out of the corner of his eye. A wave, slightly larger than they had seen previously, was approaching fast. Barely visible by the flashes of lightning, his stomach sank. "Grab the dragon!" he exclaimed. "HURRY!! THE WATER!!"

Within a few moments, a fifteen-foot-tall wave was upon them. They all heaved as best they could, pulling an unresponsive Solen deeper inland, but they wouldn't get far before the wave crashed down, pushing them all back with unimaginable force. They slammed against the edge of the woods where the land ended and dipped into the sand, desperately trying to regain themselves and maintain control of the dragon.

As the water returned to the sea, claiming a downed Solen as its prize, the head of something large emerged from beneath the surface. It grumbled so loudly that a couple of the men shrieked. "Monster!" one man called out, coughing up water. "MONSTER!!"

Lightning flashes in the dark of night revealed the silhouette of a giant creature much larger than Solen. Standing at least thirty feet tall, it leaned forward to get a closer look at the men. Its eyes, narrowed in anger, were like that of two rich blood moons, a dark red and golden color with more than a suggestion of fire in them. They glowed in the darkness, a particularly unsettling sight. "RUN!" one of the soldiers screamed. They all tried to scatter about in a flurry, but their wet armor significantly hindered the speed with which they could move. They frantically began removing articles of clothing and gear to give themselves more flexibility.

The sea dragon leaned back and drew in a deep breath, its wings unfurling brilliantly in the storm, and before anyone had time to think, the creature expelled a massive streak of fire. It had a sparkly quality never seen from the element, which one might have appreciated from a distance on a different night. But nothing of the sort would take place for the men. There would be no reverence for the beauty of this particular release of fire because something beyond fear clutched their hearts in the storm that night.

Soldiers screamed and scurried, falling and rolling along the hot sand as they burned in a heat so intense the rain had no effect. The scouts, on the other hand, silently met their punishment. There was simply no chance of calming the flames from the dragon that emerged from the deep.

2.

The faintest breeze worked its way over Skylet's shoulders from behind like a blanket made of cool silk. Yet, she barely felt it as she stood in an opening in the cave, looking down at what little could be seen of the dark mountainside lit by the moonlight. After the dream she had about Jessie and her dragon siblings, she barely felt anything these days. Three months had passed since the battle in Selnes that resulted in Jessie's death, and still, it felt like no time had passed. It seemed all she thought of was that dream, whether she spoke to it or not.

With each passing day, she seemed more and more consumed, carving the names of her dragon siblings into different cave walls where she would spend time thinking. *Arca, Tithla, Beresay, Eagan, Solly*. She scarcely ate and rarely considered anything that wasn't about the dream. She looked forward to sleep, hoping to have another vision that would continue what she believed was as real and true as anything she encountered in her waking life.

She tried interacting with Ulonae, who was walking on her own now and had attempted to form words, but she mostly babbled. It was one of the few things that provided

Skylet some comfort. The young dragon had shown how much she had grown and come to understand in a few short months. While Skylet was surprised each day by the new things she noticed the little one discovering on her own as she moved about, in the end, the youngling was too painful a reminder of Jessie and the other dragons. Hence, she limited her time with Ulonae to mornings, mesmerizing the little one with handmade fire.

Séya noticed the change in Skylet's behavior since she had the dream, yet there was little the sorceress could do to quell what burned inside the young woman she helped raise, especially since she was coping with Jessie's death in her own way. It pleased her each day to spend time with Ulonae, training her in dragon ways. The youngling seemed awed by her own body. She played with her tail and examined as much of her little wings as she could reach, making Séya smile at her small discoveries.

Soon, she would be ready to learn about her ability to breathe fire. Each morning, Séya took time to help Ulonae stretch her body, training the muscles needed to perform at its peak for when it was time to control that ability, which wouldn't be too much longer. Having spent much of her life around dragons, Séya learned a thing or two about their physiology. She also wanted to make sure if the youngling was ever in trouble, she knew how to fight to survive and escape any potential traps in the world.

Yet, Séya realized it was still too soon to go that far in preparing the young dragon for life in a world that would see her dead. In thinking of protecting Ulonae, her mind inevitably wandered back to her old friend Jessie and what the dragon was missing with the youngling.

It warmed her heart to see Ulonae developing. She

swelled with great pride watching Skylet continue to mature, and she felt an ever-growing affinity for Oros as he was adjusting to his new, more stable living arrangement. Jessie was missing everything, and Séya was missing a piece of herself.

Meanwhile, Oros rested in the circular patch of grass he had grown accustomed to. Wide awake, he lay thinking and listening to the perpetual song of the waterfalls. After a few months of sleeping there, Oros was just beginning to feel comfortable among such sounds, especially since he was used to moving about often and sleeping wherever a place could be found in the wilderness, accompanied by the night creatures that always had something to say. He never needed to speak back to them, yet there was always some wisdom they gave him, some comfort he enjoyed.

He would rather speak to Skylet, but that became more challenging since they had returned to Mysteya with Jessie's death hanging so heavily upon them. Oros understood this too well, having lost nearly his whole family. Yet, he was surprised by how much more he was beginning to feel about the loss of Jessie, only knowing the dragon a short while; he hadn't anticipated the impact she would have on him. Since they met, Oros found himself understanding Jessie and her significance in the lives of Skylet and Séya more deeply.

Oros gradually recognized how Skylet and Séya seemed to regress and withdraw into themselves in their own way, seemingly moving about as though they were mindless souls with little direction. Each day, the interactions felt more and more devoid of something, less open than they once did. They sat and played with Ulonae to the point where it seemed, from what Oros could tell, that the young dragon was being used as a shield to hide from each other and not address what they all were feeling.

The group gathered in the cave for meals, discussing trivial things like the weather and what people were talking about in the Town's Heart. Topics ranged from news of a new Town Master stepping in to manage Mysteya's affairs to who was getting married in town to conversations about the battle against the military forces of Selnes and a recent dragon attack off the coast of a distant land.

"Are you sure you heard right, Séya?" Skylet asked, looking up from her plate during lunch one afternoon. Her body perked up with the most interest she had in a while as she cut a corn muffin in half.

"I'm sure, girl," Séya responded, her tone exasperated as she sipped her tea. "I've heard enough mentions of the attack from enough people in town to be certain."

"But how does anyone know it was a dragon?"

"I don't know," answered Séya. "No one has seen anything, far as I can tell. Yet, something tells me that there is truth in the whispers."

The space fell silent as if to allow room for Séya's thought to sink in.

"Given the commotion in Selnes when we escaped," Oros began thoughtfully. "Might it be possible that other dragons have resurfaced?"

"I wouldn't have entertained that thought before," Séya said. "There had been fewer and fewer mentions of dragons in the recent years beyond The Dragon Purge. But after finding Ulonae, I think anything is possible."

"What if it's the others?" Skylet asked. "Maybe they felt..." She trailed off.

In the silence, Ulonae rolled and played on the floor

near them, completely amused with herself.

"It has been too many years, dear," Séya said softly.

The old woman took one last sip of her tea and removed herself from the large tree trunk table, leaving the group.

Oros and Skylet sat alone quietly as Ulonae approached them, leaning against Oros' leg. He went to pick her up, trying to think of something comforting to say to Skylet, but nothing came to him. He felt his sister's defeat, her body hunched as she sat at the table. Ultimately, Oros thought that simply sitting with her might be comfort enough.

Ulonae nestled herself deep into his arm, her tiny talons pricking his skin like blades of grass. They sat together, listening to the waterfall reverberating off the cave walls.

Skylet suddenly looked as though she were in a trance. Her gaze was trained straight ahead of herself, never looking at Oros or Ulonae. She seemed to bear witness to something no one else could see. Skylet exhaled and turned from the table, leaving Oros and Ulonae alone. Her corn muffin untouched.

3.

Ulonae was quiet, nestled up to Oros. Perhaps she expended most of her energy frolicking about and was ready to nap. As he looked down at her, feeling the warmth of her body against his arm, Oros noticed how soft she still felt. Most dragons he encountered in his time had rough, scaly skin from years of rugged living. Yet, the youngling was smooth; he found himself appreciating that.

Oros let his mind wander; he saw the dragon once she reached maturity, how the texture of her skin might change, how much coarser it would become. An older Ulonae stood near the edge of a tall hill overlooking a village as the sun rose. She sat up straight and still as though she were waiting for something. The dragon was calm and meditative. Her eyes were focused, like she would fly off and strike something at a moment's notice. The image reminded him of another dragon.

A flash of the face of Arca suddenly distorted his vision of a mature Ulonae. Oros wondered how the two dragons might have gotten along before another thought occurred to him: he wanted Skylet to have some interaction with Arca, and it saddened him that that couldn't happen.

Perhaps she would feel differently if one of the bravest dragons he knew were present then. They would all be a happy group, content to take care of each other in all the days of their lives. The thought comforted him. Not for himself but for Skylet, especially when she seemed so lost.

He stood up slowly, trying not to disturb the resting young dragon in his arms, and exited the cave. Oros walked down the mountainside, and the sun warmed his face as he trekked forward. He noticed how quiet it was in the afternoon after all the birds and other wildlife went about their day. Oros wound around spruce trees and followed a trail that led him to where Skylet sat, her back against another tree. He saw her in the distance, lost in her thoughts, and he remembered: this was not far from where, only months before, he kidnapped her and took her away from Mysteya, consumed with anger, desperately trying to find answers about Jessie, the dragon.

Now, he was holding a little one he was growing fond of, returning to a place connected with a painful memory to find Skylet, not as an enemy, but as her brother, with the intention of continuing the healing between them. The irony was not lost on him as he slowly approached her.

Hearing gentle footsteps get closer brought Skylet back from her thoughts momentarily to turn and acknowledge Oros before she looked again beyond herself. He stood before her, careful to make sure he wasn't encroaching upon her personal space. At first, he said nothing. Instead, he looked in the same direction as she did. Oros composed himself, preparing to sit on the ground near Skylet. He cradled the baby dragon in one arm like Séya had once taught him. Except now, Oros had become quite adept at the act. It was as though he had handled younglings and babies forever. "It never ceases to amaze how peaceful she is in this state," said Oros genuinely.

Skylet turned to witness the sight, and she softened enough to reveal a slight smile. "Yes," she replied before looking back beyond them.

"You know," began Oros. "I can still remember when you were like this."

Skylet scoffed to herself.

"I was thinking," he said, pausing to figure out how to continue the next piece of his thought.

"What about?" Skylet asked.

"Your dragonkin."

She turned to look at him, waiting for him to say more.

"You believe they are still alive."

She said nothing.

"I am not certain," he said. "But Jessie showed me things..." he trailed off.

"Séya doesn't think it could be true," Skylet said glumly, rubbing the edges of her cloak.

Oros nodded. "I felt it in my spirit. Everything she showed me," he said. "I think your dreams are worth exploring."

Skylet blinked.

"Something else I had been pondering on was your brother."

"Arca," she said as she looked down.

"Yes," Oros replied. "How would you like to pay him a visit?"

4.

Skylet took a breath and said nothing for a moment. Oros looked at Ulonae, examining her face as she rested. His eyes moved down, looking at her wings and how they wrapped around her body, noticing the tiny scales on the surface of her skin.

"Where is he?" asked Skylet, breaking the calm silence.

Oros looked up deliberately from the dragon and into the face that reminded him so much of his mother. "He is buried just outside of this town."

Skylet looked off again as if pondering whether she wanted to go. Perhaps she was thinking of whether or not she was even ready to make such a trip. She hadn't seen him in years and couldn't know how she might feel about visiting his resting place. The thought of her brother taking her to see the brother she grew up with was strange, but something about it was also oddly comforting. "I would like to go and visit him," she said finally.

Oros took a moment to take in her response. "And I would like to take you," he said. "Perhaps afterward..." He looked down at Ulonae and continued. "We can talk more about the others. If you like."

***

Séya prepared herself to head back to town. She realized Ulonae was running low on food, and a quickly growing dragon without food was not something she was willing to experience, knowing all too well how destructive dragon tantrums could be. While on that subject, her mind wandered to searching for other abandoned dragon eggs once again. She had been so preoccupied with Ulonae and managing her feelings about Jessie's absence that she'd scarcely had the energy to plan for being away. Besides, Jessie was gone, and with her, the notion of a dragon mother for orphaned hatchlings.

Séya knew enough about dragons to teach them of dragon ways and how to stay safe, but she felt, even in rearing Ulonae, that being around a seasoned dragon for a youngling was of the utmost importance. There were nuances that Séya could speak about, but there would never be that deeper, silent understanding that an elder could exchange. The thought made her sad.

Séya tied up her wavy hair, which had gotten longer in the months since the events in Selnes, and wrapped herself in her gray robes. She then slipped on her boots and breathed deeply before leaving the cavern where Jessie used to sleep. She climbed down the entranceway and stopped to look around, noticing the cave was empty and quiet save for the running waterfall. Figuring that everyone had gone just outside, Séya thought she might find them.

She exited the mountain cave and felt the slight breeze against her face. For a moment, it reminded her of the night she found Skylet while on her walk. Séya took deliberate steps down the side of the mountain until she heard rustling beyond her ahead, followed by voices she recognized speaking in hushed tones. Soon, Skylet and Oros were approaching. "There you are," called out Séya.

Oros nodded as he handed Skylet the baby dragon.

"Where are you headed off to?" Skylet asked, glancing up at her from Ulonae momentarily.

"That little one is running low on food, and so are we, I noticed," said Séya. "I thought I would make my way into town and collect some. Is there anything either of you might be interested in me bringing back?"

"Not particularly," said Oros.

"All right. I will return."

As Séya turned to leave, Skylet spoke. "We're leaving too, Séya."

"Oh? Where are you going?"

Skylet and Oros shared a look.

"To see Arca."

Séya blinked.

"We are going to his resting place," Oros interjected.

"Oh," Séya said. She took a moment to compose herself. "Perhaps we can all go together," she added. "We can go to town, and when I get through there, we can meet and go see Arca. How does that sound?"

There was silence between them. Oros looked at Skylet as he massaged his wrist, something he hadn't caught himself doing since he was a child.

Skylet looked at Séya, seeming to communicate something silently.

"All right," said Séya. "Let us go."

5.

Commotion swept through the village of Carmona on Gyenola Island. The talk was fierce about the recent deaths of Dragon Scouts and soldiers by some mysterious force during a storm. Speculation was rampant that a monster or some other unknown creature was to blame. Panic and fear spread across the areas closest to the island's shores.

Messengers from Gyenola's monarch, King Rondal, didn't help matters. Troops of young men traversed throughout Carmona and neighboring villages, spreading the word to villagers to be careful while out near the ocean on the beach. They urged everyone to keep a watchful eye for any mysterious creatures and to report anything unusual.

A team from the King's Court had arrived just behind the last wave of messengers who had investigated the area. They stationed themselves where the attacks occurred and fanned out across the beach. All of them were stoic and serious, speaking in hushed tones, poking at the burned-marked ground with sticks.

There was one among the group who was particularly serious and did none of the things that his colleagues did.

He was older than the others, tall and slim, like the trees in the distance behind them. With his arms behind his back, he stood as if to survey the larger picture before him and the ocean beyond. He wore a high collar, and his overcoat was long and dark brown like his eyes were. He brushed a hand across his forehead, grazing a scar above his left eye. He watched quietly and then took a deep breath. "Dragon fire," Henricks said to himself.

He looked out to the ocean, his eyes narrowing. He had a strong feeling that he knew what had happened, declaring the whole case closed in his mind. He turned away from the scene and headed further from the group of men as they continued their investigation. Henricks stepped through the nearby brush and came upon another group of men from the King's Court who stood conversing with one another. "What say you, Master Henricks?" asked one of the men. "What should we report to the king on this matter?"

Henricks stood and looked at the brown-haired man of average height, dressed in the court's official blue and silver garb. "Nothing," replied Henricks. "I will report this to the king myself." He nodded at the man, looking at him thoughtfully. "Take your men and return to the court. I will follow behind shortly."

"Very good, sir." The man nodded, putting a fist to the center of his chest and bowing slightly.

Henricks returned the gesture and turned to walk away.

The further he got from the beach, the more he regressed into himself. Each step took him back to his more vibrant youth when dragons were his life. He was once a Dragonhunter, and a reasonably good one, particularly during the years of the Dragon Purge. Having reached the third stage of his study, he was well-accomplished.

Henricks possessed a dedication that rivaled few others, except perhaps one – Servalan, one of the greatest hunters of his generation. Many fellow students of the discipline and peers alike admired him, including Henricks.

Every so often, Servalan would travel to areas with a local guild to lecture hunters and those in training about the importance of the respect of dragonkind. Hunters from distant lands traveled just to hear even a single word uttered by the great Servalan. Such was his influence. Those lectures often included various tricks and reminders that hunting dragons should never be done for personal gain in any way. This did not stop many from forgoing the ideals of the Dragonhunter and doing just that, which accelerated dragon deaths in the Purge. Still, Servalan always made a point to impart upon listeners to recognize the majesty, beauty, and complexity of the creatures they were hunting.

Henricks allowed himself a small smile while walking for the slightest of moments. He became more serious when other, more haunting thoughts associated with that time in his life seemed to rush back to him. Few who have had any experience hunting dragons find themselves without memories that bring out feelings of regret. He felt himself becoming sentimental, and before he was too tangled in the reveries, he pulled back and firmly planted himself in the present by stopping his walk.

Henricks knelt and touched the soft earth beneath him. He was grateful he wore the fingerless gloves to feel the textures of the still-damp dirt road. Running his fingers across nearby blades of grass as a slight breeze picked up, he stood and took a moment to compose himself, then continued his walk along the pathway.

6.

Midday in the kingdom of Ondriten was as busy as always. People ran every which way to one destination or another; merchants went from area to area, selling items to anyone passing through. When Henricks arrived in the street, hopping off a horse-pulled cart just beyond the royal grounds, he stumbled across a few colorful characters entertaining children with toys and juggling items.

The activity didn't faze Henricks. He was so used to the various shades of sounds that defined much of his early time in Ondriten when he once patrolled the grounds. He walked along stone streets through crowds, heading directly for the king's quarters in the Castle of Purple Roses, named so for the various patches of richly hued flowers lining the front of the castle. Henricks passed guards and others who greeted him by placing a fist to the center of their chests, bowing slightly. Even those who did not serve under him recognized Henricks as one worthy of respect.

Entering the castle, he marched purposefully up the stairs on his way to the king when a young man carrying a large pouch of messages stopped him. "Master Henricks, sir!" the boy exclaimed. "A message for you!"

Henricks turned to find Pesh, the messenger boy, slightly winded, his wavy hair disheveled. He held out a rolled piece of parchment. "Ah," said Henricks, collecting it from the boy. "Thank you, Pesh."

Before Henricks could turn away from him to continue his journey, Pesh made an audible sound that caught Henricks' attention. "Oh," began Pesh. "One other thing, sir." He reached into the deep pouch and pulled out a small beige bag tied shut with string.

Henricks took a moment to look at the parcel sitting in the palm of the young man's hand. It might have seemed as though he tried to guess what was inside, but there needn't have been a guess at all. Henricks was sure of what the bag contained; he could almost see through it. He knew the shape of the item so well, and it made his heart sink a little more at the thought of what that meant.

"Sir?"

Henricks blinked and glanced to the side as though considering something other than the items Pesh presented to him. He returned to the present moment and looked warmly upon the young man. "Yes, of course," he said. "My thanks to you, Pesh."

Henricks gingerly took the bag from the boy as though it contained the most delicate and fragile thing, like something was alive inside it. He bowed slightly.

"Master Henricks," said Pesh. He put his fist to the center of his chest and heartily bowed before running off to deliver more messages.

"My best to your parents," called out Henricks.

Pesh half-turned and waved as he moved swiftly, like the wind.

Henricks stood holding the parchment and the small

wrapped bag in his other hand. He let out a deep sigh and placed the bag in his overcoat pocket. Unraveling the parchment, he saw a note in a most elegant and precise script. There could be no mistake of the intent, no misreading of the message. It read:

I am not in need of anything from you.
-L

Henricks carefully folded up the parchment and placed it in the inner pocket of his overcoat as if to keep it close to his heart. He took another deep breath; his head hung slightly for a short time while activity within the castle went on around him, seemingly without a care that he was there, standing midway up the stairs.

7.

Skylet, Oros, and Séya, with Ulonae in tow, approached the forest edge that led to town. They all walked in a silence punctuated by the sounds of wildlife that called the forest their home, twigs and dead leaves crunching beneath their feet. In the months since Jessie's death, the air of sorrow surrounded them all, and yet, some trace of her could still be felt somehow, making it all the more painful that her physical presence was not there. Skylet was seldom without the cloak made of Jessie's skin, whether she slept, whenever she could sleep, or when awake and moving about.

It was as though she hoped she could somehow go inside of it and see the dragon and feel the warmth of being wrapped in Jessie's large hands. Skylet wished to feel the dragon's wings envelop her whole being, pulling her into Jessie's bosom. Reaching up, she gently clutched the talon necklace that once belonged to Oros. She needed the dragon's measured voice to give her some sense of direction. Skylet rubbed her fingers over the surface of the long jet-black piece of Jessie for several steps along the journey. Then she remembered again: Jessie had already given her a sound sense of direction as far as she was concerned. The dream about her other siblings, whom she hadn't seen in years, sat strongly upon her heart like a boulder she could not lift with her own strength. She just couldn't believe that they were gone as Séya did.

The idea of visiting Arca's resting place seemed like something she couldn't place, a feeling she couldn't describe. She wasn't happy about it, nor was she sad. She was in between feelings about Arca, to whom she was so close, yet she was beyond them. She missed Arca still; she continued to wear the boots made of his skin shedding. Meanwhile, Oros still wore the onyx cloak from Arca, so the headstrong dragon was close to them in a way. Still, thoughts of Skylet's other siblings were just as potent for her, overriding anything in the form of emotion.

Séya, meanwhile, held the weight of life without Jessie as best she could. Every step closer to town reminded her that she would eventually take those same steps back to the mountain cave, and when she returned there, the dragon, her deepest spiritual companion, would not be there to greet her. Her mind wandered to Arca, and she realized that visiting his resting place would probably lead her to experience some feelings. Before she could examine anything within herself about that, the group had arrived as close to the edge of town as was safe for them with a dragon in their company. When Séya stopped moving, they all stopped. "I don't expect to be long," she said. "Is there anything, in particular, I might collect before I continue on?"

Skylet and Oros shook their heads.

"Thank you," Oros said, still carrying a silent Ulonae.

"All right. I will return soon," she said.

Séya turned away and began to make her way into town.

8.

When Séya arrived in the Town's Heart, it was abuzz with activity. She threw her hood over her head so as not to be noticed by anyone and made a direct approach to the market area, which she could see was already getting crowded with people. Casually preparing her makeshift bag made of an old bedsheet, Séya stepped under one of the covered stands and placed food into it.

As she made her way from one stand to another, collecting what she needed, she noticed two men in dark uniforms approach one of the market merchants at a stand nearby. At first, she paid them no attention and went about her business. When she stopped in front of the fruit, she happened to glance up again. Her eyes landed upon the uniformed men once more. Séya's body suddenly tightened when she recognized where she had seen similar-looking garb: Selnes. The two men were soldiers, or at least high-ranking ones. She remembered the ordeal that resulted in Jessie's death. Before she picked up anything else, she made her way on instinct behind a group of other patrons as the men walked along.

They were talking to one of the merchants casually, yet

it seemed to Séya that there was an overtone of serious-
ness in how they conversed. No one smiled or laughed. It
was very business-like.

One of the men pulled out a tattered piece of parchment and began reading something aloud to the merchant.
Séya couldn't make out everything, but she did catch the
words "witch" and "dragon." Her heart sank to her stomach. They couldn't be looking for her. Could they? They
could, and she decided they were. As far as she understood,
there was only one person she knew to be called a witch,
and spent extensive time with a dragon. She needed to
take extra special care to escape this predicament unseen
by the men.

Séya had been so consumed with Jessie, and feeling as
though she was floundering adrift in the sea of her anguish
without the dragon to anchor her, that she had almost forgotten that feeling of fear that had been with her those
months prior. Her immediate concern was getting back to
the group and getting out of sight, but something nagged
at her. A slight feeling urged her to see if she could catch
the nature of the conversation. Why was it that she was
being searched for? And yet, she knew the answer. She
needed to understand the extent of the search.

Séya saw the merchant at the nearby market stand
point off in the distance, as if directing the men to where
they should go for answers. They exchanged nods, and the
men from Selnes stepped away from the merchant, walking along the edges of the market as though curious about
what every stand had to offer. Except there was no stopping to examine the various items. They moved with purpose.

Keeping an eye on them while picking up a few more

essential items, Séya went up to the merchant woman, who she had seen often at the market, to pay for her things.

"Hello, Séya," she said.

"Hello." Séya's tone was serious, but she tried masking it with warmth. She took out the coins to pay the woman, looking away to catch where the soldiers were going.

"Intimidating looking men there," the merchant woman said.

"Oh yes," Séya replied. "I hope no one is in any sort of trouble."

"Hard to tell," the woman responded, helping collect Séya's items.

Séya kept looking off, occasionally making eye contact with the merchant across from her.

"I thought I heard one of them mention a dragon," the woman said. "Whatever might that be all about?"

"I haven't the faintest idea," replied Séya. She sensed the men would be out of sight soon, and she would miss learning more about this visit from them. "My thanks to you," she said.

"Be well, Séya."

"And you, dear."

Séya nodded and was off. She worked her way along the edges of the various stands, just close enough for merchants to recognize that she might not be interested in browsing or purchasing anything from them but far enough that they needn't try to get her attention. She kept her eyes focused on the men, who were now even further away. Séya tempered her steps to avoid moving so quickly while trying to maintain a certain degree of cover as she used other patrons to shield her from sight. Few who saw her thought anything of it, assuming Séya was being her usual odd self.

The men stopped at an herbalist stand that was seemingly abandoned. They stood and waited, calmly and stoically, like mature guard dogs on alert. Younger dogs might cause a commotion and make a scene, barking and hollering aggressively, announcing to any potential enemy that they should be taken seriously. Wiser dogs might not behave in such a way. These two officials from Selnes stood upright a few feet apart, hands behind their backs, surveying the stand.

Moments passed, and all the market commotion shuffled around them before an old man with a long white beard and no hair on his head exited a small tent within the covered stand. He used a walking stick to assist him with one hand and carried a small jute sack in the other. He stepped very deliberately, looking down at the ground to make sure he didn't trip over any loose items that might have made their way to his stand.

Séya was far enough away to maintain her sight of the men, yet close enough to hear any words exchanged. She hunched under her hood, being careful not to stray too far from the crowd, keeping her ears pricked up.

The old man raised his gaze, noticing the two officials standing ahead of him. "Might I be able to interest you gentlemen in anything here?" his voice had a touch of hoarseness.

One of the men unrolled the parchment he carried, looking down at it to reference why he was there. "Not today," he replied. His tone was firm. "We come from Selnes with important business to discuss."

"Ah, Selnes," the old man mused as if tapping into a fond reverie. "Such a wonderful place that was. You know, I lived many years there. Seems like a lifetime ago now."

He chuckled to himself.

"Yes, well, we are here searching for any information on a witch, who came to Selnes a few months ago," the soldier paused.

"A witch, you say?" the old man asked.

"Correct. She brought with her a terrible dragon, damaging many homes and displacing more than half the residents in the Dax County of Selnes.

The old man perked up, nearly dropping his jute sack. "I've been hearin' the whispers around here about that. Couldn't believe it might be true."

"And who might you have heard these 'whispers' from?" the soldier asked.

"My daughter," replied the old man. "She and I manage this stand here. Takes good care of her old dad."

"We must speak with her at once," the second soldier asserted forcefully. Séya sensed that he could barely contain himself, desperate for answers.

"What is the meaning of that?"

"Do not become an obstacle, old fool," the second solder spat.

"Now, young man—"

"Owneras," the first soldier cut in. "We will not receive cooperation by resorting to that sort of behavior."

Owneras huffed and looked askance.

"You must excuse our shortness," the first soldier said. "We do not have much time. We must visit many other towns as we look for answers."

"Looking for answers, you say? Well, seems to me you carry a question or two."

"Yes," the first soldier replied. "Many men fell at the hands of the dragon and the witch who unleashed it. We must find them and bring them back to Selnes to pay for their crimes."

He stepped closer to the old man and held up the parchment. "Do you see anything familiar here?"

"My eyesight isn't what it once was, I'm afraid," the old man said. "When you live as long as I have..." he trailed off. "My daughter might be of some help. Wait here." With his walking stick and jute sack, the old man shuffled off into the tent.

The soldiers stood, composed, hands behind their backs. Owneras shrugged his shoulders every few moments, as if trying to rid himself of excess energy.

Séya struggled through the increasing volume of commotion around to hear clearly as she watched the exchange. A moment later, Séya saw a full-figured older woman appear from inside the tent along with her father. Her head was covered with a silk scarf, and she had on a long-sleeved dress with a thick waist strap.

The old man nodded his head upward, "You showed me some parchment before. My daughter will be sure to answer any questions about it." He turned to his daughter. "Do you suppose you might help these men?" He touched her shoulder with a free hand.

"How can I help you, gentlemen? I'm sure Father kept you entertained."

To Séya, it seemed that the woman would rather be engaged in any other task than standing where she was across from the soldiers.

"He is a hundred years old, you see," the woman said. "All this excitement with soldiers is more than enough adventure for the day."

"Mistress," the first soldier began. "We come from

Selnes in search of answers."

"Might your presence here have anything to do with the witch and the dragon?"

"Yes," Owneras replied.

The first soldier held out the parchment. "Do you see anything familiar?"

The parchment had text that noted they were searching for a witch and a dragon, but it was the lower half of the parchment that intrigued the old woman: there was a sketch of a person in robes and a pretty good sketch of a dragon.

"Sure, I do."

"And have you seen anyone who looks like the sketch before you? Have you seen this witch and her companion?"

"I don't know about any witch or dragon," she said. "But, the woman looks like a resident I have seen around here from time to time. You might consider stopping in the neighborhood a little less than a mile from the foothills of the mountains."

"And why there specifically?" the second soldier asked. "Who is this resident you speak of?"

Séya's heart pounded inside her chest like punches. She hoped to the skies she would hear details so misaligned that there was no way soldiers could connect her to the incident at Selnes.

"A rather odd one who may not be as... 'present' as the rest of us," she said. "You see her at your own risk."

The men shared a confused look.

"What is she called? Her name?" The senior soldier asked.

"She's known around the neighborhood as Silly Old Séya."

9.

Séya froze, dropping her bag of groceries. Neither the soldiers nor the old man's daughter noticed, with all the activity around. She stayed herself a moment longer as the realization caught up to her. Now, the soldiers had a name to go with the image on the parchment. It would not be difficult at all if she were to be spotted right then. She needed to collect herself and move. Casually kneeling to pick up her bag while simultaneously turning to leave, she caught one last bit.

"What is it you intend to do with her when you find her?" the old woman asked.

"We... just need to ask her a few questions," Owneras responded. His tone smacked of an undercurrent of unsavoriness to Séya.

"She is harmless. All the kiddies love her, but most everyone else thinks she's batty."

"And what do you think of her?" the first soldier asked.

"I don't have too many dealings with her. I occasionally see her around here in the market, but that is all."

And with that, Séya was off, maneuvering through the crowds of people as though she could do it in her sleep.

She clutched the bag of groceries tightly so as not to drop it and slow herself down. That would be a bad deal should the soldiers come upon her in a moment of clumsiness.

Soon, she was through the worst of the crowds and at the edge of the Town's Heart. Séya thought of the old man's daughter, Ellava, whose family has deep roots in Mysteya. Distant relatives were responsible for creating the infirmary that Séya once led, a place where she was so well respected. Ellava's great-grandmother, whom she was named after, was one of Séya's early teachers. Never had there been a time when Séya would have shared that, at least not without getting into the real story about what happened following the terrible plague that ripped through Old Mysteya. It was best, Séya thought, to go on being an acquaintance.

The elder Ellava opted for Séya to assume the position of infirmary leader. And though they never discussed it, as the sorceress got older, she was almost sure that Ellava suspected that young Séya was different. Whether or not it was apparent that there was magic about her pupil, it seemed that whatever it was that set Séya apart from her peers and instructors alike, it was of no consequence to Ellava.

In thinking of her old instructor, naturally, her mind wandered to Jessie. In many ways, the dragon had occupied a similar role in Séya's life. It was as if she subconsciously called upon memories from a simpler time in an effort to escape where her spirit seemed to be. It felt heavy, and Jessie was not around to help her carry the burden.

Séya continued on her way until she reached her small home. She quickly climbed the stairs and looked around to see if anything out of the ordinary warranted her being more concerned than she had already been. Quickly, she opened her door and entered, shutting it behind her. The home felt almost foreign since she had barely been back a handful of times following Jessie's death. Séya placed the groceries on the small round oak table in the main room and grabbed clothes, vials, and small bottles to pack. She had a feeling she wouldn't be back for another extended period. Yet, she wouldn't be back at the cave either. Séya didn't know for sure why she felt that, but with soldiers from Selnes now looking for her and Jessie gone, nothing felt certain anymore.

Everything she gathered fit in a large pouch that she threw over her shoulder with a strap before grabbing the bag of groceries and quickly leaving her home, locking the door behind her.

10.

Oros and Skylet sat on large boulders, watching Ulonae tumble and fumble about. Never before had she been out of the cave for as long as this; there was something pleasant about witnessing the innocent little creature exist in herself without a real concern aside from eating and sleeping.

Skylet looked at the dragon and then at Oros. She noticed his expression while watching was intense. What was he thinking? she wondered. He seemed split between two planes of existence.

Oros stood from his place on the boulder, looking out into the woods. He released a deep breath and placed his hands on his hips, something he suddenly remembered his father doing. "I wonder what it is that seems to be keeping her," he said. "Does it seem to you that she has been gone for longer than we expected she might be?

"I suppose," replied Skylet. "I'm sure she is just being careful about what to pack."

"Of course," said Oros.

"Can I ask you a question?"

Oros turned to face her. "Of course."

"What...?" Skylet began. She seemed to be searching for how to ask the question in a way that didn't embarrass herself or make her feel too vulnerable. "Can you tell me about our mother?"

Oros' face softened, and he dropped his hands to his sides. He took a breath and responded. "I can do my best."

Oros walked over to a nearby oak tree and leaned against it. "What would you like to know about her?"

"Whatever you can remember."

"Hmm." Oros stroked the stubble around his chin. "I wonder, what makes you ask such a question."

Skylet looked away from him; her face contorted slightly into an expression that Oros could see was one of pain. "Jessie showed her to me," she said. "Through a memory."

"I see," said Oros. "I can attest to what a powerful experience that must have been for you."

"She was beautiful..." Skylet trailed off. "I felt so much love from her."

"Yes," said Oros. "She was full of love." He slid down the side of the tree and sat with his arms wrapped around his knees, hands clasped together. "I was beginning to forget what she looked like; it had been so long since I had seen her face."

He lowered his gaze at the earth and continued. "She enjoyed much of the things you might expect from most mothers, such as cooking and keeping a clean house. I can remember how pleased she seemed when everything was to her liking and how upset she became whenever father came home." Oros chuckled to himself. "He would track mud or whatever filth he came into contact with through the entire place."

"I saw a little of him in the memory Jessie showed me,"

said Skylet. "He was a Dragonhunter too?"

"He was. That is, until he lost his lower leg in a fight with two dragons. A sight that was not for the faint of heart. Mother and Uncle tended to that injury as though they were born to do such things. I can remember being impressed as I watched them. Uncle held the wound while Mother attacked the process of wrapping it up. There was so much blood, and she never flinched. Not once."

Skylet cringed at that detail. "No one shielded you from the sight?"

"Of course not," Oros scoffed, looking up at her. "It was understood that I was to be a Dragonhunter one day, and as far as they were concerned, the sooner I was comfortable with such sights, the better."

"She sounds like a strong person."

"Oh, she was," said Oros. "Mother had as much heart as most anyone I had known in my short life. Certainly as much as Father and Uncle."

Skylet looked at Ulonae and saw that she was wandering too far off, in danger of tumbling down a nearby hill. She stood up and grabbed the youngling from the ground to hold her. "Did she have any friends?"

"Did she?" Oros smiled. "She was quite popular in town."

"Really?"

"She was. She was a talented artist and a council member in Selnes at one point before meeting Father. Notable since she was one of the youngest ever to be appointed. There always seemed to be someone from that time around the house for dinner or some other gathering, which no one complained about since she cooked so splendidly. And she enjoyed the company, especially at times when Father was away with Uncle."

As soon as he finished that thought, Oros paused and noticed her face. "You seem dissatisfied with that."

"I suppose I wondered if she had any friends she was close to."

"Oh, I see. Well, she did, as a matter of fact."

"She did?"

"There was one woman, easily Mother's closest friend. They were like sisters. She always had a treat for me whenever she would visit. Always kissed my cheeks when she left."

Oros looked down and smiled to himself. "I didn't see too much of her in the nearly two years before the start of my training, but she and a few others were among Mother's dearest people."

"Do you suppose any of them survived..." she trailed off.

"I cannot say. The destruction was heavy."

After a while of quietly cooing and murmuring to herself, Ulonae started getting antsy in Skylet's arms.

"Shh, please, girl."

The dragon squirmed and wiggled around before turning and reaching her hands out to Oros.

Skylet looked across at him. "It seems she wants a change of hands. Are you up for it?"

Oros glanced at the little one; the urge to turn away from her was strong. Yet, the charm of the youngling was no doubt growing inside of him.

"I suppose." He got up from his place against the tree and walked over to take the baby dragon, which quieted her.

Oros grabbed a pouch from his belt with a free hand

and held it out to Skylet. "Might you unravel this for me?"

Skylet took the pouch and undid the tied string wrapped at the top of it. The fragrant smell of citrus fruit and nuts escaped the bag, greeting her nose, and the gentle breeze only served to permeate the air with the aroma. She returned the pouch to Oros, who took it into his palm.

"Thank you," he said.

Skylet nodded and then stood from her sitting place to walk toward the oak tree. "She seems fond of you."

"Perhaps," said Oros as he began feeding Ulonae some of the citrus fruit and nuts.

"Do you think our mother would like her too?"

Oros grew somber. "If she had come across a youngling like this, she might have tried to keep her. Though Father might never have approved."

"Hm," Skylet managed to say before turning away from them and looking into the forest. She hoped to see Séya hurrying through, but still, there was no sign of her. Skylet now began to wonder what was taking so long. She hoped Séya was okay and half thought to go and look for her. However, she reconsidered that since her cape might attract too much attention. She didn't want to part with it, yet the idea of going into town would mean she had to remove it; out of the question. Plus, Séya would be exposed.

Leaves and brush dropped from the trees and blew past her line of sight. Chirping birds flew about, and squirrels scurried through the woods on an otherwise lovely day. Skylet wanted to allow herself to enjoy the moment of calm, surrounded by such life, but a heat returned to the pit of her stomach. She wondered how she would feel about seeing Arca's resting place. A part of her really wanted to be there in order to feel as though she could actually say something meaningful to him, but a part of her also wanted to just get on with finding her siblings, who she believed were alive. But they could not move without Séya. Where was she?

II.

Séya walked cautiously but kept a consistent pace, returning to Skylet, Oros, and Ulonae. She didn't want to arouse
any suspicion that she was trying to escape something,
and she didn't know who else might have been sent to
Mysteya in search of her. Keeping that in mind, she tried
her best not to get lost in her thoughts.

Soon, the beginning of the forest was in range. Séya
could see it beyond the hill she came up to. When she
reached the top, she noticed people standing outside their
homes, unsure why. Then she looked to her left and understood.

Two uniformed men with armor plates stood just outside the door to a home she recognized well. These weren't
the same men she had seen at the market before, but Séya
knew that they, too, were from Selnes and were no doubt
questioning residents on her whereabouts over the last
few months.

She slowed down and inched closer to get a good view
of the area and how far she might go before possibly being
recognized. Séya glanced again to see the door open, and
out came a familiar face. Clean-shaven these days, Willard

stood and faced the two men at his door. Séya's mind flashed back to when she saw him while trying to escape into the woods with baby Skylet so long ago. Her knees felt weak at the sight of him now. Were it not for his broad shoulders and general bearing, Séya almost might not have recognized him.

Séya slowly stepped backward, clutching the shoulder strap to her bag with one hand and grabbing the sack of groceries tighter with the other. She couldn't make out the conversation, but she saw one of the soldiers open the parchment and show it to Willard, who, not having stubble to stroke, made do with an exposed chin as he contemplated a response to the men.

Séya felt her heart pounding, threatening to burst from her chest. Nearly everyone in town knew where she lived. As the village loon, she didn't have too many interactions with anyone outside of children occasionally. While little ones found her charming and fun, there was nothing whatsoever stopping any adult from directing these men from Selnes to her.

Séya continued to watch while trying to devise a plan to escape the area.

Willard nodded and then placed his hands in his pockets as he listened to the soldiers' explanation. He pointed in the direction of Séya's home. She felt a wave of heat in her stomach, which made her turn around and begin walking back the way she came. She looked to her left and right, searching for a pocket where she could hide, but found none. Instead, she saw homes and fences that surrounded some of them.

Séya stopped just before she came to the small hill and turned around. The sudden increase in incoherent speech from other neighbors suggested something she wanted to be aware of.

There were two more soldiers present, talking to neighbors across from where the others were talking to Willard. Séya hadn't the slightest idea where they came from. One of them, she could see, was a woman, as evidenced by the fact that she was smaller than her male counterpart. Her dark golden hair protruded from the base of her helmet and came down the center of her back in a single neat braid.

Séya looked across to Willard's place and saw that he was still occupied with the soldiers at his door. The thought occurred to her to try and make a clean break for the woods just beyond all of them straight ahead, but she knew that wouldn't be smart. She needed something to distract everyone from spotting her. The only thing she could think of was using a spell. Still, she had to be careful not to do something so big that it would take away too much of her energy since she still needed enough to slip past the group of soldiers and the neighbors who were now alerted to the fact that Séya was a person of interest.

She knelt, removed the bag from her shoulder, and sat it beside her, along with the grocery bag. Séya placed one palm on the surface of the earth and held out her other hand, palm facing upward, connecting herself to the ground beneath her and the air around her. Her spirit needed to be open, her mind clear from the concerns of her current predicament. This was paramount if she were to escape.

Séya closed her eyes and bowed her head before taking a breath. She whispered an incantation and waited a half second.

A calm draft emanated from around her. Holding her hands in their respective positions, she pressed her palm more firmly into the ground. Then she turned her upward facing palm away from her toward the soldiers and neighbors before gently pushing her palm forward as though she were brushing back a thin veil.

The breeze swept along smoothly and consistently until Séya released a slight breath. At that point, the draft became a powerful gust of wind, moving in the direction Séya needed to go. She opened her eyes and looked up; the result of the strong winds was undeniable. Neighbors quickly found ways to end their conversations with the soldiers, as the breeze was so intense that they could no longer stand up straight without losing their balance.

It was the diversion Séya needed. She calmly grabbed her bag of groceries and belongings and put the strap over her shoulder as the wind swept through the area. She began moving, and when she felt she was close enough that onlookers might see her, she pretended to be moving as though the gust affected her. Séya clutched her items and robes close and wobbled along.

She saw members of the Selnes army scatter about, trying to keep their helmets on, holding tightly to the important parchments they carried with them.

Just as she passed Willard's home, she stopped and noticed him scrambling back inside as she pretended to block her face from the intense wind. Right before closing his front door, they locked eyes for a half second. Through the breeze, Séya could see his hardened face as he held the door for a moment. She shook her head ever so slightly at him as if to communicate something. He seemed to understand it because his face softened, which she saw before turning away. Willard shut his door and went to the nearby window, watching Silly Old Séya continue on the pathway, stumbling her way deeper into the forest.

<h1 style="text-align:center">12.</h1>

The high winds persisted. Séya continued to feign struggle as she traversed through the woods. She was deep in but didn't feel safe enough to drop the charade. Upon reaching a divergence in her path, she glanced at the ground before stepping over a big rock. Near it was the back of a parchment from one of the soldiers. It had been blown into the woods, now blocked by a thick fallen tree branch.

She knelt to pick it up, turning it over to see the information on it. She didn't bother reading the text, but even as the parchment ruffled in the winds, she caught what she thought was a decent sketch of her and Jessie. Séya sighed deeply, thinking of the last time she saw the dragon in the Selnes prison. She rolled the parchment up and placed it into the grocery bag before continuing on her way.

As she moved along, she stopped pretending that the wind made walking challenging and resumed as she usually would. Jessie was at the forefront of her mind now. Séya could almost feel the dragon's embrace.

She went step by step, wrapped in her thoughts of the adventures and conversations with the dragon. She smiled to herself, remembering one such discussion from Séya's relative youth about love and whether either would go off to be with someone else and live a life of marital bliss.

"I've only ever loved one other," the dragon once told her. "That is, enough to consider devoting the rest of my existence to."

There didn't seem to be anything more she wanted to share, and Séya didn't push. Besides, by that point in time, the Dragon Purge was in full effect, and what mattered more than anything else was preserving dragon life.

In those days, there were other dragons already in her care. Some were of mature age, while others were waiting to hatch. That was where Séya began learning about helping to rear and raise hatchlings. Those of age neared when they would leave Jessie's care and go on to find another place to ride out the storm of impending extinction. Some of them paired up in couples, some going so far as to participate in a bonding ceremony, equivalent to what humans called a wedding.

She didn't always do it, but Séya would act as the Bonder, whose job was to lead the ceremony. Those were times when conversations about love and partnership came up strongly between Séya and the other female dragons, and some males even reveled in such discussions.

There were only ever a handful of bondings she participated in over her time around dragons. Those who did placed their palms together and turned in a circular motion to signify the unbroken cycle of their love. Three times, the two partners would turn, each one denoting a phase, the birth of their courtship, the life of their connection, and finally, the crossing of their spirits as one to the ether where their love continued. Or so it was believed.

At the end of a ceremony, the young sorceress would

conjure a sparkly dust to celebrate the union. Those were happy times amidst the turmoil surrounding them outside the mountain, and the memories made her miss Jessie even more than she thought she already did.

Séya kept moving in a haze, surrounded by the feelings within her from those happier times, and she began to feel a calm come over her. The strong winds began to die down as she made the last stretch to her destination in the heart of the woods, where Skylet, Oros, and Ulonae awaited.

Séya made another turn toward a dip ahead of her, then another reflexive turn around a thick oak tree through a space between it and a large boulder. Shaking her shoulder to avoid a broken trunk that stuck out, she didn't realize that one of her scarves had fallen out of the bag containing some of her belongings. The remainder of the wind spell she cast had just enough force to pull the garment out and push it against the base of a tree.

Séya persisted, coming back to the present moment. After passing the area where the land dipped downward, she kept curving around more trees and rocks until, finally, she could see Skylet and Oros in the distance. Séya noticed Ulonae napping in Oros' arms; he sat on a boulder looking off through the woods and then up to take in the richness of the mountain ash trees.

Skylet stood looking at the ground before Séya came in range of her sight. Her eyes worked their way up to the old woman's face, which she could see was contorted into a slight scowl. "We were beginning to worry," said Skylet.

Oros turned to see Séya passing between the two trees that seemed like a gateway to their safe area.

"I apologize, dear," Séya replied. "I was worried myself."

"Are you all right? What happened?" asked Skylet.

Séya dug into her grocery bag and pulled out the parchment, handing it to Skylet.

"What is it?" Oros asked. His tone suggested he knew the answer.

"It is good that we will be on the move," Séya said. "It appears we are remembered."

Skylet cursed under her breath. "What does this mean?"

"The army of Selnes must be here," Oros responded. "No doubt they will want some recompense for the losses they sustained during our... visit."

"Yes," agreed Séya. "How did you know?"

"I recognize that parchment type; it is closer to the more expensive vellum."

There was a pause.

"Which means?"

"They spared no expense. No cost is too great to complete their assignment."

"There is more," Skylet interjected, now closely reading the parchment.

"What do you mean, dear?" Séya looked at her.

"It says that a Dragonhunter was in the company of the witch and the dragon, and should he be apprehended, he will be tried and sentenced."

"It won't take them long to figure out who I am." Oros turned his head away from them, looking out to the woods.

"What?" Skylet asked.

"My uncle was the last known hunter who survived the destruction. He took an oath, and I, along with him. We did so among the council and survivors to rid the areas surrounding Selnes of dragons." He paused. "There was no one else."

"Then we must keep moving," Séya said. "We will go to

Arca's resting place and continue from there."

Oros nodded and looked back at Séya. His eyes darted to Skylet; her hands dropped to her side in exasperation. She gripped the parchment tightly. "Then let's not waste any more time," Skylet said.

13.

Henricks made his way to the king's quarters. Four men stood guard on either side of the blue and silver edged carpeted pathway leading to the door.

They turned to acknowledge his presence, putting fists to their chests and bowing their heads.

Henricks nodded. "Allow me to visit with the king," he said, stopping just before the door.

"Master Henricks," one of the men began. "Be warned that His Majesty is... unavailable at the moment."

"Understood," replied Henricks. "I will suffer whatever the consequences."

The soldier nodded to the others across from him, and they all returned to their previous positions facing each other.

Henricks stepped to the door and struck it twice; he waited to hear a bell that would ring from the inside, indicating it was approved for anyone to enter. There was no ringing of the bell. Instead, the door opened slowly, and two women exited the quarters. Though they were mostly dressed, Henricks noticed one of them struggling to get a slipper on her foot while the other was finishing putting on a forest green tunic over her chemise.

"My dears," a booming voice called to them. "You mustn't use that doorway. The other would be much more suitable. Oh, be sure to help yourself to any dish you like when you reach the kitchen."

"Many thanks, Your Highness," said the woman with long blonde hair tied with a bow. She turned and shot an appraising glance at Henricks, who nodded and looked down at the floor.

The other woman with deep scarlet locks never took her eyes off Henricks, smirking at him. He could feel her staring but did not return her gaze. "Master Henricks," she said to him.

"Mistress," he responded, finally looking at her and giving her a slight bow.

She turned around and bowed deeply to the king before following her companion to a door at the far end of the room leading to a stairway.

"Ah, Roman!" King Rondal exclaimed as he finished putting on a beige shirt and navy blue and silver robes. He outstretched his arms as though taking in the morning sun.

Roman was the nickname given to Henricks after rescuing the king from certain death amid a skirmish with rouge members of a rival army several years earlier. He took the name from the leader of a small militia that existed when Ondriten first emerged as a formidable territory nearly two centuries before. The Crimson Wings were the elite force established by Roman to protect the kingdom against outside threats. He became the king's most trusted servant and ultimately sacrificed himself for the crown.

Similarly, Henricks sustained severe wounds to protect King Rondal, all while demonstrating a prowess on the battlefield that devastated the opposition. From that day forward, Henricks was seen as strong and dominant, like the noble Roman, leader of the once-feared Crimson Wings.

As Henricks closed the door behind him, the staircase door behind the women shut. The sound of both echoed through the room. His back facing the king, he took a breath, allowing the monarch time to finish dressing before finally turning to meet him.

"You do not approve?" The king said heartily, a boyish smirk on his face.

"It is not my place to offer advice on the matter, Your Grace." He paused. "That position is already filled."

"Come now, Roman," replied the monarch. "Ondriten has been without a queen since Armana left. Why should I not indulge myself in a bit of... frivolity?"

Henricks turned his head to the side at the mention of Armana. "What you indulge yourself in is yours to manage and yours alone."

After learning they shared the same hometown, Armana and Henricks became fast friends. It didn't hurt either that they were closer in age than she and the king, the monarch being several years her junior. Henricks tried not to think of her too much, still carrying sadness behind her leaving the kingdom some years before. Her name coming up now reminded Henricks that Armana was one of his only real connections since arriving in Ondriten, and he missed her.

King Rondal strolled over to a nearby desk, and before he sat, he gestured to a chair across from him. "Join me."

The king poured two glasses of a fragrant beer and pushed Henricks' across to him. "I trust you've brought news of the attack."

"I have," Henricks took a seat. "Thank you."

"And?" King Rondal sat and took a drink of his beer.

"A dragon was responsible for the attack."

"Of course, you are certain."

"I am."

"I trust your judgment."

The two drank in silence for a few moments.

The king looked toward the window and spoke. "Any thoughts on how to proceed?"

"Hmm," said Henricks, scowling at the center of the desk. "Direct approach isn't the most prudent."

The king turned back to face Henricks with a smirk. "The hunter in you still lives."

Henricks looked up from the desk to face the king. "We might wait a while... see if any further reports of attacks arise."

King Rondal raised an eyebrow.

"There is too much conversation on the matter of a monster at present. What happens next might be best handled as quietly as possible."

The king sighed in mock exasperation. "Aw, it appears the hunter isn't as fun as he once might have been. No bait to smoke out the beast? No men at the ready to mount a surprise attack? You know, we could use another dragon since the other escaped."

"If I may, Your Grace," Henricks began. "There is an excess in supply from the dragons already within the kingdom walls. The army is quite well resourced."

The king leaned over the desk toward Henricks. "And

would you have other forces gain an advantage over us here?"

Henricks didn't respond.

"More is more, Roman."

"Perhaps, but trouble is all that awaits should we go about this the wrong way. The people of this kingdom should be considered."

"The people," King Rondal scoffed. "You're always thinking of the big picture. Perhaps you should be in my position rather than a boring and thoughtful Court Knight." He chuckled, taking another drink of his beer.

"Perhaps when you reach my age, Your Highness, you will see that life is a great teacher if you care to take in the lessons."

"Aw, you aren't too far from your prime!" The king laughed. "Where is the hunter's sense of adventure?"

Henricks looked down at the table again, recalling some lesson from his past. "It has been replaced with maturity. I'm afraid my hunting days remain behind me."

"Nonsense!" the king slapped the desk. "To restate the sentiment of an old instructor I once had as a young prince, 'a hunter once, shall remain so.' "

Henricks waved off the sentiment.

"Hunting is in your essence, Roman!"

***

Oros led the way on their trek, holding baby Ulonae as they traveled. Having long left Mysteya behind, they traveled through a vast space of misty woods. It was twilight and getting near time to stop and camp for the night. He slowed his pace and looked around.

"Why have we stopped?" asked Séya.

"We will need to rest soon."

"Thank goodness," Skylet said, almost under her breath. "I don't know how you traveled as much as you have on foot."

"Rigorous training," replied Oros, with no sense of irony.

"Where are you thinking we should rest then?" Séya asked.

Oros was silent as he peered out further. "Up ahead," he said. "I recall a decent place somewhat out of the way that isn't much further." He turned to Séya, handing a sleeping Ulonae to her.

The group continued their hike. Séya cradled the youngling as they traveled. She glanced at the little one occasionally and suddenly felt overcome with sadness. The old woman turned to Skylet. "Would you hold her for a while, child?"

Skylet gave a slight nod, grabbing the edges of her cloak and wrapping Ulonae in it as she held the dragon like a newly baked treat she had just removed from an oven, afraid to damage it.

Soon, night had fallen, and a chill swept through the dark woods like a specter of some sort. Luckily, they were coming upon the area Oros had mentioned earlier where they would camp for the night.

"There," he said.

They reached the inwardly curved wall of a hill to their right. Just above, at the top of the mound, loomed thick birch trees, towering over the area like ancient watchers.

Oros walked toward the center of the curve and took out his sword, placing it on the ground there. He reached his hands out to Séya, and she handed him the bags she carried. He put them on the floor in a neat pile and turned to address Séya and Skylet. "I will gather some wood for a fire."

"Can you see well enough?" Séya asked. "We barely reached this area without killing ourselves, falling over things in the darkness here."

"I will be fine. Just rest here and stay aware."

"That training must come in handy," Skylet said in a tone that registered to him as sassy.

Oros tilted his head, though he wasn't sure she could see him clearly. "Well, yes, as a matter of fact, it does."

Silence entered the conversation before Oros took a breath. "Try and get as comfortable as you can. I will return shortly." Without waiting for a response, he lowered himself to a crouch and went further into the darkness.

Séya plopped onto the cool earth and leaned against the curved wall, exhaling.

Skylet knelt with Ulonae and leaned herself against the wall near Séya.

"How are you feeling about this, girl?" the old woman asked.

"I don't know," Skylet's voice was low.

"Well, we will meet it together." She reached out and caressed Skylet's thick hair before turning and looking ahead of herself. "I never saw him before he left. I imagine visiting Arca's resting place might be healing for the both of us."

"Of course," Skylet said, looking at the shadowy outline of the baby dragon in her lap. She thought of asking Séya about the feelings she needed help sorting through, about why it seemed the old woman didn't believe that there was a possibility that the other dragons could be alive. She didn't know how to work herself up to it just yet. Skylet could see that Séya was trying as best she could to be present, but she could feel a block. Something she never really felt from Séya. Ever.

Skylet couldn't pinpoint what it was, but she understood enough for it to feel palpable. She suspected that while Jessie's death might be a factor, she couldn't ignore the feeling that something deeper could be amiss. As her imagination ran wild with possibilities, she ultimately returned to how disjointed everything felt. Skylet could only imagine what lay in the abyss of thought and feeling for both of them. She wasn't sure she was ready to find out what revelations might be there.

After several moments of silence, listening to each other's breathing and the sounds of the night creatures in the woods, Oros returned with timber and stones to make a fire.

He placed the materials in the center of the floor and began assembling the station. When he finished, Skylet could hear the sticks sliding and lightly tapping together in Oros' hands as he prepared to make the fire. "Can I do that?" she asked him.

"Are you certain? It seems the little one is comfortable in your lap there."

"I don't mind," she said. "I haven't made a fire in a long while."

"All right. I will take watch when you build the flame."

Skylet slowly stood, still holding the baby dragon wrapped in her cape. "If you wrap her up like this in your cloak, that might be nice. She can be warmer."

"I will try that." Oros exchanged sticks for Ulonae and carefully knelt, settling himself with the young dragon.

Because she hadn't yet matured, Ulonae was not able to generate the inner warmth that older dragons could, which kept their body temperature regulated in colder climates. They can calibrate based on their environment well enough, but she still had a long way to go before she could do that.

Skylet knelt and began rubbing the sticks together and blowing at the base. She continued the process, remembering when Séya patiently taught her the steps as a child, Jessie watching nearby, smiling warmly. She was so excited at the notion that she could use her hands to build a fire with such simple items as sticks and her own breath. No, she could not expel fire, but like her siblings, her very breath could make the difference between a living flame and nothing. Only Arca seemed impressed, though he teased her mercilessly about how much longer it took to produce.

'Snails-a-flame,' was the nickname he called her on such occasions as when they traveled to hidden places and huddled around each other to tell stories. "Hurry up, Snails-a-flame!" he would say. "You know, I'll bet even a snail could build one faster than you!"

Skylet expelled a light huff, hearing his voice echo in her head, thinking fondly of those times. Soon, the low light of the flame appeared, and before long, the fire was alive. She tossed the two sticks she used into the wood pile and looked up as the light from the flame began to brighten and illuminate the area. She noticed Oros looking down at Ulonae before he looked at the fire and then at Skylet. The girl's eyes looked at Séya, who seemed to be staring off somewhere else, her hood over her head. The old woman's eyes met hers, smiling.

Skylet hoped that by making the fire, she would feel close to Séya, but instead, she felt close to the woman Séya used to be. At that moment, Skylet realized that the woman who found her in the river those many years ago was not with them at the fire. At least not now.

She looked down and stared into the flame.

"That is quite impressive how quickly the fire came together," Oros said.

Skylet looked up from the flame at him, her expression slightly contorted, trying to figure out how to respond. She was keenly aware of how quiet Séya was. She had no proud response to let him know that it was she who taught the girl how to produce a fire.

A different sadness latched itself onto Skylet's heart, and the best she could muster to Oros was a hushed-toned "Thank you."

14.

The morning hours brought with them the sounds of birds excitedly conversing with each other as though the notion of a new day was a novel concept. It was barely daybreak, and Skylet awoke face-to-face with baby Ulonae rolling around, making soft cooing sounds. The aroma of salted jerky and bird eggs cooking over the flame pleased Skylet's nose. She inhaled deeply, letting the scent permeate her being and fill her lungs as she stretched her arms and legs out.

"You're awake," Oros said to Skylet. "Good morning."

"Yes, good morning," Skylet groggily replied. She looked over at Séya, who lay just beyond her feet, curled up, her back facing them.

Oros noticed Skylet's gaze trained on Séya in the dim morning light as he turned the eggs over on the cooking sheet. "I thought we all would eat breakfast and then continue on our way," he said.

Skylet nodded and sat herself up, leaning against the earthy wall.

Ulonae suddenly began to get testy as she tapped her hands against the dirt. Then she stamped her feet, grunting.

"In the pouch over there," Oros began, nodding in the direction he wanted Skylet to look. "There is a citrus fruit and some nuts in there. Might you feed some of that to her? I am not certain, but she could be hungry."

Skylet crawled over to the pouch at the far end of where Séya lay sleeping; the dark bag sat a foot away from her head. Collecting it, Skylet loosened the tie around the opening and crawled back over to where Ulonae was in the middle of her pouting session. "Come, girl". She took out pieces of the citrus fruit and some nuts to feed the dragon. Ulonae stepped closer to Skylet and laid her head against the girl's knee, sighing. Something about that touched a tender spot in Skylet's heart. She picked up the youngling and began holding out some of the food. Ulonae started eating, and Skylet caressed her face.

***

Oros and Skylet sat and ate their breakfast in silence. Ulonae tapped at the dirt, attempting to squish some flying bugs nearby attracted to the food. She seemed to revel in not actually killing them since it kept her amused to play with them. Séya still slept; her breathing seemed so consistent that it felt to Skylet as though it was a natural part of the forest soundscape.

The sun peeked through the thick heads of the trees that surrounded them. Oros looked up and noticed the cascade of the sun rays, reaching a hand out in an attempt to touch one. He was just out of range, given the sun's current placement.

Oros could tell that it was still early enough to leisurely prepare for their continued travel, but they would need to pick up if they wanted to make their destination before nightfall. His mind also went back to the soldiers from Selnes and how they were likely searching all areas near and surrounding his hometown. If they weren't safe in a place like Mysteya, they certainly were exposed in the lands between established borders such as where they were. They would need to get going, and very soon.

Coming back to the present moment after finishing off a slice of an apple, he looked at Skylet and then over to Séya. "We will need to continue soon," he said. "I don't like the thought, but we might have to wake her."

Skylet nodded, wrapping the last piece of jerky into a slice of bread with egg and taking a bite.

"A few moments more of rest, and then we'll wake her," Oros said almost to himself. He turned to Skylet. "I hope you approve of breakfast. It isn't much, but it was what could be found around here."

"It is just fine," Skylet said. "Better than I've had in a while. Um, thank you." She was still working out comfortably interacting with him. And he with her.

"Of course."

"Did our mother teach you to prepare food like that?"

"Uncle did, actually," Oros said. "He was such a lover of food. Mother was too. They would sometimes cook together with Father, though that was very rare. Uncle mostly trained and studied."

Skylet looked down at the pile of ash that was once the fire she had started while Séya shuffled in her resting place upon the smooth earth. Skylet and Oros looked over at her before Oros turned his attention upward to look at the sun rays again. They had shifted slightly, which made him anxious. He stood up and stretched his body for a moment since he had been sitting for so long. He took a couple of steps beyond the area where they all gathered and looked both the way they had come and the way they would be continuing to move. It was still a relatively peaceful morning.

Oros turned to see everyone. Séya's back still faced the group. Skylet scanned the ground aimlessly, and Ulonae circled the ashes while occasionally sniffing a black wrapped up pouch the size of a small melon. The leftover breakfast portions for Séya seemed enough to pique the young dragon's curiosity about what was inside. Perhaps she, too, believed the smell to be pleasant.

Oros came back to the group and knelt next to Séya. He grabbed the bag of food he had prepared for her and held it. Leaning in close, Oros held the bag over the other side of her where her hands could reach it more easily. He placed it on her shoulder with his free hand and spoke in a hushed voice. "Are you awake?" he asked.

Séya didn't respond.

"I have prepared breakfast for you. Won't you have some before we get moving again?"

Slowly, Séya held her hands up as though she were cupping a drink of water from a river. "Thank you," she said, not turning over to look at him as the bag was placed into her hands.

"Take as much time as you feel you need," said Oros. "But you should understand the sooner we leave, the earlier we will arrive at our destination."

"How long until then?" asked Séya, her voice sounding tired. Not at all like she might have usually been in the morning.

"At least a day's journey."

Séya sat herself up and leaned against the wall behind her. "Good morning, dear," she said to Skylet.

"Good morning."

Ulonae made her way to Séya and nestled herself against the old woman's leg. "Oh! Hello girl," she said, stroking the dragon's back before unraveling the string from the bag in her lap. She reached in and pulled out one of the pieces of jerky, chewing while slowly preparing to stand up. Thinking about what Oros had told her about them moving on, she dusted herself off and picked up her bag of belongings. Séya then tied it up with the breakfast and placed it in the larger bag that carried some of the groceries. She bent down to pick it up and walked a few steps away from the group just outside the curved wall.

"We do not have to leave just yet," said Oros.

"Of course," Séya replied. "I just wanted to move around a bit to wake up my body. Besides, we should remain vigilant with the soldiers searching for us."

"Yes," said Oros.

"Do you think they can find us?" asked Skylet.

"It is very possible," Oros replied. "Most of the soldiers are likely the grounded piece of a more cerebral entity: The Sentinels. It is *they* who no doubt devised the plan to assist the soldiers in searching."

"How can you be so sure?" asked Skylet.

"It is their job to hunt down criminals as it has been for nearly a century."

***

It was dusk. The bright beacon of the Scarlet Edge in Mysteya had long since lost its reflective light for the day.

Now, the trees' leaves were a maroon, black cherry hue.

Three sentinels, followed by three Selnes soldiers, walked along near the Scarlet Edge, passing the few people moving around, going in and out of taverns and eateries.

"We should be more aggressive with these people here," one of the Selnes footmen said. "That's what Commander Brawns would have wanted."

"He would have," another man said. "What I would give to have him here with us now."

"Then we wouldn't be here," said a woman soldier in the group as she took the dark golden braid of her hair draped over her shoulder and tossed it behind her back.

There was silence among them for a moment as they slowed their pace ever so slightly to put just a little more distance between them and the sentinels who led them.

"Right," the first soldier said, lowering his voice even more. "And as we are here for him, justice must be served, Holera. We have been here the whole day and have yielded nothing for our efforts. We must press harder."

She turned to address him. "Gonden," began Holera, her voice nearly at a growl, "We —" she was cut off by the voice of a stern woman in the group ahead of them, who stopped walking to turn and address the Selnes footmen and woman.

"Let us remember that our priority is to gain information," she said. "We will not obtain that easily if we become impatient with the people here. We are not to make enemies."

Everyone was quiet. Footsteps and chatter of the locals around them began to die down.

"Commander Brawns is dead," Gonden spat. "Would

you have us not fight to see justice done?"

"I understand your frustrations," said the woman. "But aggression will lead to fear and distrust. And we need people from every place we visit on this search to trust us. All of us."

"Stuff your trust!" he growled, anger seeming to seep through his teeth like venom. "Don't mistake this 'arrangement' we have to be a permanent one, Principal. You do not command us."

"On this search, and by order of the council, I do. And as such, I expect nothing less than your respect of that fact."

"You stubborn stick," Gonden said. "Aimlessly poking around, beating the rugs, walls, and dirt, picking up only dust. There will come a time when we won't be at your service."

"Gonden," Holera stepped in and touched his breastplate. "We are working toward the same goal. We are collaborating." She turned to face the woman leading them through Mysteya. "What would you suggest at this juncture, Principal?"

Layona took a breath before she responded as if to shake off the tension of the conversation. "We continue as we have done, Captain," she said. "Let us split. Take your men and begin questioning at the tavern and neighboring places. We will continue down the road."

"Understood. We'll reconvene at the end of the road."

"That is fine," replied Layona.

The six of them broke away into two groups. Layona led the sentinels toward the nearby establishments, and Holera walked along with her comrades.

The captain turned around to make sure she was

out of earshot of Layona and her team before looking at Gonden as they walked. "We are not sentinels," she said. "We are soldiers like Brawns was. When the time is right, there will be a place for us to fight. We just cannot do it the way we want around them. When we find the witch and the dragon, that is when we will strike. But not before. Understand?"

"I understand."

"We will see justice done," Holera said. "We just cannot go forward as he did. His impulsiveness was ultimately his downfall. Do not make that mistake."

The sentinels stopped in between two establishments, surveying the area around them. "You two go there, and I'll see about the next couple of places," Layona instructed the woman and the man with her.

They nodded and did as she said. Layona stood and watched them, allowing her mind to wander as she pulled out the information parchment from her waist. She couldn't wait until all of this was over so she could get back to the more routine activities of her work.

Since the death of Commander Brawns, and the subsequent conversations about what to do moving forward, the tensions between Selnes' army and the sentinels were at a high no one had seen since the destruction nearly two decades ago. All the talk about the resurgence of dragons, what to do about the lack of hunters, bringing a witch to trial, and the like overwhelmed her. However, as the Principal Sentinel of the search, she had to manage a little longer.

It had been three years since her return, and yet, she was just now beginning to form stronger bonds with her birthplace, having left it with her mother not long after the dragon attack. She was just a child then.

Now, in some strange way, she had an opportunity to do right by the town she had few pleasant memories of; she felt compelled to make the most of it.

Layona stood and looked around, her eyes resting upon an establishment that wasn't marked in a way that made it obvious for passersby to know what it was. One had to be a local to possess such knowledge. She decided she would go inside. When she opened the door, Layona stepped into a cube of a space, noticing boxes stacked from the floor to the ceiling. The scent of herbs greeted her nose when she heard a voice speak.

"Can I interest you in something, young lady?" a white-haired old man in a white shirt and brown vest looked up from a book he was reading to address her.

"Thank you, but I'm afraid what I am interested in isn't anything you might have for sale."

"Well, how might I be able to help you, Madame Sentinel?"

Layona smiled warmly. For a brief moment, she forgot herself and what she was there for. Something about the man warmed her spirit in a way that felt paternal, and it pleased her. She quickly pushed away the thought, approaching where he sat behind a counter, looking intently at her with a welcoming expression. She noticed the many lines on his face, which were much more visible when she got closer to the groups of lit candles on stands near him.

Layona held up the parchment and unrolled it on the top of the counter. "I wonder if anything here looks or sounds familiar to you at all."

The man grabbed one of the candlestands and brought

it closer to the parchment to see it better.

Just then, a woman entered the room through a curtain dividing the main area from another. She held a cup of tea and walked it over to the counter. "Tea for you, dear," she placed the cup before the man. "Oh! Hello!" she said upon noticing Layona.

"Hello to you."

"Would you care for some tea as well?" the kindly old woman asked.

"No, thank you," replied Layona. "I won't be long here."

"Well, aren't you lovely," the merchant's wife gushed.

"Dear, she is a working sentinel. This isn't the time for talk among the ladies."

"Oh, sit yourself there and hush up," she chuckled.

"It is no trouble," Layona allowed herself a smile but remained poised. "Mistress—"

"You can call me Calinan, dear," the old woman said.

"Of course... Calinan. Would you mind looking at this with us?" Layona gestured to the parchment that her husband was examining.

She came around the side of the counter and stood over her husband's shoulder to look over the document. "Word traveled here about the Selnes attack not long ago," Calinan said. "Here is where the other boot drops, right?"

"We just want to bring those responsible to justice."

"I'm afraid I haven't seen or heard anything about a witch around here," said the merchant. "Can't say I know the woman."

"Nor I," said his wife.

Layona took a breath and looked at the floor before another question occurred to her. She leaned over the counter, closer to the merchant and his spouse, as if preparing to share a secret. "What about hunters? Anyone like that ever come around here?"

"As a matter of fact," the old man began. "There was a Dragonhunter in this very place a few months ago. He came here looking for a dragon."

"You never told me that," Calinan playfully slapped his shoulder.

"I did, dear," the merchant said, still looking at Layona. "He seemed like an honorable lad, preoccupied with his mission."

"Oh?"

"An intensity was about him. A focus."

"And did he purchase anything?"

"He sure did. Just some herbs and maybe some spices. Does this help some?"

"Yes, sir. It is very helpful."

"I hate to think he got mixed up in any trouble," said the man.

"Look, dear," his wife said. "You must have missed this piece mentioning a presumed hunter who was seen with the witch." She pointed to a section near the top of the parchment. "Is he in trouble?"

"No one is certain of that just now," Layona replied. "Apparently, he had been seen with the witch following his battle with the dragon."

"Ha," the old man chuckled to himself. "So, he found that dragon. Seemed to me that he would succeed if not get real close to it."

"According to witnesses, he did," said Layona. "Did he give any indication of his destination once he left here?"

"I'm afraid he didn't."

"No matter. This has certainly been the boost we needed following a day of scouring nearly the whole of this town." She reached over slowly and collected the parchment, rolling it up to place it in a sheath that sat at her waist. "I thank you both for your time and conversation on this matter. I will regroup with my company."

"When you see him," the merchant began. "Do give him my regards. Tell him the old merchant sends him peace. I hope he is more settled than he was when I met him."

"Of course," Layona replied.

"It seems ironic to me that yet another hunter comes here to a place that deals in herbs." said the old man.

"What do you mean, dear?"

Layona looked quizzically at the man.

"Well, that young man was here hunting a dragon, and now it seems he is being hunted."

"We just need to ask him questions about the events that resulted in a fair number of deaths."

"Well, we hope you find him well," said Calinan.

"As do I," said Layona. "A good night to you both." With that, she turned and left the place, thinking about what the man had said.

Of course, she was hunting the hunter. It was one of the tasks of a sentinel when anything that looked like a crime of some kind had been committed. To make matters increasingly pressing, she had been tasked specifically by the council to make finding the hunter the priority of her team. Meanwhile, the agenda of the Selnes army was to ensure the witch and dragon were apprehended. Conflicting goals at the core of the efforts of both sides would be enough to make anyone wash their hands of it all. But Layona had a duty.

She could only hope that it wouldn't be too much to handle when she found what she was looking for. Layona walked out to the middle of the pathway and waited for the group to come and meet her.

15.

It was now the middle of the afternoon into another day of travel, Oros leading the way. The group traversed along the outskirts of different towns, moving through the woods. They were on schedule and steadily closing in on the area of Arca's resting place. Opting not to stop for a rest earlier in the morning likely benefitted them, or it would be much later than they would like.

Oros stopped as he reached a curve on the pathway that led to his right and up a hill, turning to address Skylet and Séya. "At the end of this trail, beyond another turn, is where we'll end," he said to them.

They didn't respond. They only nodded.

Séya adjusted her bag of belongings, which included baby Ulonae, and kept pace with Skylet.

Oros allowed them to pass him, and they walked up the long hill. It would be a long while before they slowed down. Oros made his way to the front once more, and as they came to the plateau, they could see to the left of them several feet away that the hill they traversed along ended and led to a cliff, which went down a slope. At the very bottom lay an extensive valley of grass, spotted with trees, and in the distance beyond the valley were the beginnings of a pathway toward a town and mountains after that.

Oros could see the familiar area and remembered his trek to find Jessie, which led him here. His stomach felt a flash of heat as his mind went further to Arca's intense expression in death. He shook his head slightly, coming back to the moment.

"Here," he began. "We are nearly there." He kept walking past them as if now guided by some force that was not the will of his mind.

"Just beyond this next turn coming?" asked Séya.

"That is correct."

They walked until they reached another curve in the road. In the distance, there was a mound to the left side of the road, fresh grass growing on and around it.

"There," Oros said, pointing to the mound. He didn't recognize the grass there, specifically around the burial site, concluding that the earth had begun gaining nutrients from Arca's body; the juxtaposition of life and death made plain in one instance.

They all approached the mound; Oros was careful to keep a few feet away, wanting to respect the time and space for Séya and Skylet. He understood very well that they were the dragon's family and wanted them to feel as though they could gain a sense of connectedness.

Oros looked out beyond the hill over the valley. He knelt and got himself into a meditative position.

Skylet and Séya dropped to their knees in silence, looking at the mound. Skylet noticed several small daisy flowers across various parts of it. A strange mixture of thoughts entered her mind, shifting between the beauty of the image in front of her and the grief of Arca's absence, knowing that his decomposed body was just beneath. She placed her palms directly onto the surface of the grassy mound and closed her eyes as if trying to connect with him. All she could see was darkness, and it reminded her of the color of Arca's skin at dusk. Skylet's mind trailed from there to the darkness of the night, which he flew out into the last time she saw him. She felt nothing. She could see nothing of him, and it made her angry.

Skylet gently patted the surface with a palm as though making a sandcastle on a beach somewhere, and then the tears came. She leaned over the grave and laid herself face down, blanketing it. It was as though she could wrap her arms through the earth that now cradled her brother in his slumber from which he would never wake. She desperately wanted to hold him, and laying out over the mound was the closest she could get to that. She cried hard into the dirt, imagining her tears seeping into the soil and touching his heart to make it beat again.

Skylet knew nothing would happen, yet she wished so hard against what she knew. Hearing his voice, even hearing him tease her, would bring her so much pleasure. Instead, his voice echoed in her mind. "Arca," she sobbed. "I miss you." She clenched her fingers, ripping up some of the fresh grass.

Séya kissed her own palms, placed them on the grave's surface, and bowed her head. Eyes closed, she cried silently. A deep pain intruded her chest, hearing Skylet's sobs that seemed almost overwhelming for the girl. The old woman held her position; the grass around her hands slowly began to dry up and turn yellow, dying. For a moment longer, she didn't move, letting her emotions take her where they might. Séya remembered Arca as a youngling following

Skylet around when she started walking as a child. She recalled him mischievously zipping around the cave, picking up flight before the other dragons.

Séya opened her eyes, sniffling. She noticed baby Ulonae had slipped out of her bag. The young dragon was awake, alert, and seemed to understand the energy between Skylet and Séya. She made soft sounds, trying to get herself comfortable as she laid herself near the center of the mound, her eyes silently watching as the old woman and the girl expressed themselves.

Séya, while still on her knees, moved closer to Skylet, who was still face down in the dirt sobbing. She placed a hand on one shoulder, stroked Skylet's hair with her free hand, and said almost in a whisper, as though putting him to sleep, "We love you, beautiful Arca."

16.

It was mostly quiet on the hill. Oros remained sitting, facing the valley, his eyes closed. Sniffles from Skylet and Séya shook his soul. He couldn't help but feel a deep sense of guilt. The thought of soldiers from Selnes entered his mind, and he almost wanted them to catch him now, bring him back to where everything began for him. He hadn't anticipated how visiting Arca's resting place would trigger such feelings. Oros envisioned himself punished in Selnes for his association with Séya and Jessie, and that, somehow, felt like it was what he deserved.

True, he didn't kill Arca, but as far as anyone else was concerned, he thought, he may as well have done it. Even though he struggled with his feelings at that moment, he believed it necessary that they were all there together. Everyone needed something from visiting the grave.

Oros suddenly thought about what a loss it would be if they were all caught and what would happen to baby Ulonae, whom he was beginning to feel even closer to. She would certainly be locked away, her blood harvested. If there were a way for the Selnes soldiers to collect Oros without the others, he would explore it even if it were his last option.

Having only gained his sister back for a few months, he wanted desperately to develop a real bond with her. As hard as they tried, it had been challenging for them to genuinely connect. He felt that suggesting a visit to Arca's grave might help create a firm foundation, a more level ground on which both he and Skylet could stand as they began building their relationship anew.

Oros looked over occasionally at Skylet and Séya on the mound and wondered if the thought of Jessie and Arca being together was of any comfort to them. After a while longer, he stood up. Looking out over the valley, Oros lost himself in its vastness. Off to his right, further away, he could see where the ocean started and imagined himself standing at the beach looking out over it.

Ulonae cooed softly. Séya caressed Skylet's back as she lay on the mound, getting up on one knee to stand. She walked over to Oros and looked out over the valley.

He turned his head and looked in the same direction.

"I do not know how she will tell you," the old woman began. "But I can say for myself, I... am grateful that you have led us here."

Oros nodded.

Séya touched his shoulder and looked at him.

He turned and met her eyes, barely able to hold the sight.

"Thank you," she said genuinely, her voice cracking. "This can't have been easy or pleasant for you to be back here."

Oros looked to the ground.

Séya took a breath. "I suspect we will need to get moving again soon."

Oros did not respond.

"I will collect her." Séya turned, made her way to Skylet, and knelt, carefully placing her hands on the girl's shoulders. "We must prepare to leave soon, girl."

Skylet didn't respond, keeping her palms planted on the surface of the dirt. She slowly sat on her knees, staring off somewhere, the tears still trailing down her face. Her hands felt warm, having held them against the grass for so long. She thought nothing of it at first until she looked down and saw Ulonae lying near her. She reached out to touch the youngling, who slightly recoiled when Skylet made contact with the dragon's head. "Oh!" she said through a sniffle. "I am sorry."

Séya's head tilted at the sight. She watched Ulonae get up from her spot and walk down the mound near her. What made the little dragon jump back so?

Oros turned and noticed Skylet beginning to stand herself up. He approached the group, careful to stay a few feet away. He didn't look at Skylet, and she didn't look at him.

Séya sensed the discomfort between them. She looked down and saw the youngling walking half circles around her legs, considering whether or not she wanted to pick up the dragon.

Ulonae patted Séya's shin with her tiny hands, and eventually, Séya gave in. She knelt to pick up the baby and put her in the bag of the clothes she had brought from home.

"Are we ready?" asked Oros.

Séya nodded. "Do we continue ahead?"

"Yes."

Séya nodded again. Adjusting her bag so the baby felt more comfortable, she walked past Skylet, leaving her standing at the mound of Arca's grave.

Oros watched.

He stood for a moment or two, observing Séya get three steps beyond Skylet before he finally moved. When he got to within range of Skylet, she suddenly turned to him and shoved him backward with both hands. Her tears came harder.

He stepped back, half surprised. A part of him expected something from Skylet; he just wasn't sure what.

Séya turned around to see if her suspicions about what she heard were correct.

Skylet stepped closer to Oros and pushed him back again, releasing an inaudible grunt.

"Skylet!" Séya exclaimed. With that second push, it was almost as though she could feel strong tremors of the girl's frustration through the very earth they all stood on.

Skylet let out a deep sigh, staring at Oros. She grabbed the edge of his cloak and tossed it at him.

Oros put his hands up, looking at her. "It is all right," he said.

The girl put her head in her hands and let another tidal wave of emotions wash over her.

With her face hidden from him, Oros looked at her. He felt great sadness and guilt, wanting to reach out and touch her, perhaps embrace her like he used to do when he was a young boy. But after she shoved him, it seemed even more unlikely that any sort of bonding between them would happen. Maybe it would be different another time, but at that moment, Oros couldn't see it.

When Skylet looked up from her hands, Oros didn't look away this time. Their eyes met, and the cloak on Skylet's back instantaneously reacted, flapping and flailing around. It wrapped around her, expanding and contracting as Séya and Oros dodged around to avoid being hit by its sweeping motions.

Skylet couldn't control what was happening, so she did her best to give in and let the cloak guide her to where she felt it was pulling her, and that was back down to the mound of Arca's grave. She thought to place her palms upon Arca's grave and close her eyes, which she did. At first, she saw nothing. And then, after a second, she began to see a vision that reminded her of the dream she believed Jessie was using to communicate with her.

She saw a large dark chamber made of stone, cut in the shape of bricks. Daylight from windows located high up barely lit the room, so the base of the chamber was much darker. At night, wall-mounted torches were the primary source of light. At the very back of the center space of the room, Skylet saw four large cages inside. Each was shrouded in darkness as if they were empty. And though she couldn't see any shapes or figures, Skylet knew they were there: the other dragons.

As soon as she recognized this, the vision shifted, and she saw a mountainside. It was as though she were standing so close to it that she couldn't see the full view. Suddenly, the land on the hillside began to crack and slide down, revealing the large yellow eye of what she knew to be a dragon. However, she didn't recognize this one. The land around it fell some more as it continued shuffling. She was overcome with fear.

The vision shifted again to Arca being slammed on the ground not far from where she, Séya, Oros, and baby Ulonae were. He was battered, and she could tell that he had severe injuries. She saw how stoic he was, knowing no matter how badly he was hurt, he would let no one see.

But Skylet knew it as though she were inside of him. She looked down, the vision placed her above him as though she were standing over him, and that's when she saw the large shadow of a dragon getting smaller. It seemed to be flying away from her. Her sight was soon blinded by a light that was like the sun, and she could see only the brightness.

The vision ended, and suddenly, she was floating above Arca's grave. She was no longer in control or even aware of what was happening. Her hands held out as though she were carrying something large and heavy from the bottom, like a boulder. She had nothing of the sort, but wisps of smoke rose from her palms, heat from them emanating with such a force that Séya and Oros could feel it. Ulonae ducked her head deeper into Séya's bag.

They were stunned to see Skylet not only floating in midair but the sight of her eyes, which looked like they had been replaced. They glowed red and orange with the light and heat of a fire. Small flames flickered and danced around, bleeding outward and above to the base of her brow.

"SKYLET!" Séya shouted.

The cape flowed outward and expanded like the sails of a sea ship. Séya looked on, realizing she didn't understand what forces were at work that resulted in what was happening to Skylet, so the old woman resorted to using magic to get to the bottom of that. She opened her hands and directed them at Skylet in the air, closing her eyes. Séya attempted to scan the girl with her ability, moving her hands up and down slowly as though massaging the space between them.

She figured maybe Jessie was behind what was happening. But how? And if the dragon was now in control, why would she make it so that Skylet had no control over herself? More importantly for Séya, why would the dragon not reveal herself?

Séya changed her strategy and decided to search for and try to contact Jessie. She outstretched her arms as though being open for a hug from the dragon. Bowing her head, she spoke from the depths of herself, "Jessie, my friend. What magic is this?"

Almost immediately following her words, the edges of Skylet's mantle flapped and whipped around the girl, and up she went. The whipping force broke Séya's connection and knocked her backward, nearly falling onto the ground.

Oros stepped in quickly to catch her. Higher Skylet went until she flew off over the valley toward the ocean.

Séya and Oros looked at each other before he helped her stand up, and they went quickly in the direction Skylet flew off in.

17.

They traveled as fast as they could down the other side of the hill, Séya keeping pace as well as expected. "Don't wait for me," she huffed. "We must not lose her."

As it was, Oros maintained sight of her as they went along but knew he would lose visibility as they reached the woods when they came upon more level ground.

"If we need to separate, then let us do that!" Séya said, some distance between both of them. "I will find you; go and collect your sister!"

Ulonae made squeaking sounds that suggested excitement. The young one seemed to enjoy bouncing up and down in Séya's bag as she jogged along.

Oros turned and nodded as he kept trotting, careful not to tumble down the hill as they reached a point where the earth beneath their feet declined. "Take your time as you make your descent!" he shouted back.

Séya waved him off, and then she stopped to catch her breath.

Oros continued on his way.

Ulonae almost immediately threw a fit, squirming in the bag.

"I just need a moment, child," Séya said.

The little one didn't let up, squealing and pounding her head against Séya's side.

"Well," she said sternly. "That is not nice at all. No."

Ulonae pushed some more, forcefully stretching her body outward in the bag to the point where her hands and feet began tearing through it.

Séya saw this and calmly knelt, taking the bag from over her shoulder and placing it on the ground before her. She took the squirming youngling out of the bag and put her down. The old woman threw the bag back over her shoulder and watched the dragon quietly.

Ulonae fussed, jumping up and down, crying. Tears streamed as she quickly shook her head. She screamed so hard she started cackling. A brief burst of fire shot from her mouth, which surprised her enough to be still. The dragon stopped her tantrum immediately and looked up at Séya, her eyes wide in astonishment.

Despite being deeply concerned about Skylet, in that brief moment, Séya forgot about her fear and couldn't help but smile warmly at the dragon. She chuckled. "Are you ready to be calm?" she asked.

Ulonae whimpered and turned around as though trying to catch her tail.

Séya reached out and touched the youngling, which seemed to calm her. The old woman scooped her up and cradled the dragon in her arms. "Be calm now," she said, leaning in to kiss the top of her head.

She stood and looked out ahead, noticing Oros was far away and would reach the beginning of the woods below soon. "I realize," she said to Ulonae. "There is another way to get ourselves down there."

Séya opened her hand and stretched it outward, palm facing down. She swiped her hand to her left, and suddenly, a small cyclone surrounded her, reaching her ankles. Séya crouched and leaned forward, allowing the wind to push her ahead. She held her hand out to maintain the spell's power, and off they went, hovering down the hill after Oros.

*****

The river water was brisk, like the morning air when Layona doused her face with it in the early hours of the day. Awake before the rest of her company, she couldn't help thinking, figuring. Always, her mind was on finishing the task before her. She splashed more water on herself and looked at the sky, noticing it was brightening. The water from her face ran down her neck, where she wiped some of it away, brushing over the edges of a scar from an old injury that went far below her uniform. Rarely did she even think of it, but when she did, it seemed like the memories surrounding the injury belonged to someone else.

Layona stood from her position at the river and quietly walked around the group sleeping nearby. When she arrived at her resting spot, she collected her belongings, which included a dagger and the container she kept the parchment with the search information on it. As she prepared for the day's travel, she thought of the hunter she was expected to find. There had not been very many in Selnes for a long time. In fact, she had only ever known maybe three in her life.

As a child, she remembered hearing of the greatness of Servalan, but she learned just before embarking on her current task that Servalan had one in his tutelage at the time of the Great Destruction, according to the old records. She initially assumed she might be searching for Servalan since no one in Selnes had seen him since he left to fulfill the town's wishes, taking his pupil with him. However, after her conversation with the herb merchant and his wife, she was positive now that she was searching for Servalan's student, who, from what she could tell, would be the right age, for the merchant called him an 'honorable lad.' She spoke nothing of her deepest internal thoughts on the subject, reasoning that it might create more complications and raise more questions than she was prepared to consider.

Layona walked over to a nearby bald cypress tree and leaned against it, wondering exactly where the hunter might be, imagining what sort of conversation they might have when they met and what would happen after that.

***

Elsewhere in the forest edges of Mysteya, a group of Selnes soldiers, partnered in twos, scoured the area. They weren't sure what they hoped to find, yet the order was given to search nearby hiding places in the woods. Legends had many believe that forests were places where witches and other magical entities could be found. As the sun rose, one of the soldiers looked to the ground and saw something half-covered in dead leaves and dirt.

Kneeling to pick it up, he saw more clearly that it was a scarf. The man stood, holding it, rubbing it between his fingers, appreciating the softness of the handmade fabric. He rolled it up and slid it over his belt, letting the edges hang from his side as he rejoined his comrades in searching for the dragon and the witch.

18.

Séya hadn't slept all night. She thought it best to stay within the woods just enough not to feel the full extent of the chilled air so close to the ocean while on the beach. Most of the night, she sat watching baby Ulonae, who lay wrapped in one of her scarves near a fire that was dying out. Now that it was morning, Séya wondered whether she should make contact with Oros but decided to wait a little longer to give the dragon more time to rest.

***

Oros found himself looking out over the ocean at the beach as morning arrived. He sat on his knees, dejected, wondering where Skylet could have gotten to. Had she flown across the sea? He hadn't the slightest idea. Forgoing sleep the night before, he spent much of the evening trying to catch up to Skylet. When he couldn't find her, he sat in the sand and waited.

Soon, Oros found himself beginning to doze off. Without missing a beat, he stood up and approached the cold water.

He knelt and threw his hands in, cupping out and splashing several helpings upon his face. Oros did this a few more times before taking another look around the beach as the day brightened. Moving back to his earlier position, Oros pulled his blade from the sheath behind his back and stuck it into the sand, using it to support his weight as he dropped to one knee.

Looking at the grains, he tried hard not to despair, but the emotions were coming. He felt tears forming; it was like Skylet was lost from him all over again. He hadn't any idea what to do when it came to sorting out other ways to find her, giving in to the thought that he had failed. Oros delved into feeling the worst things about himself until he remembered. He had tracked her before. Standing from his position, Oros put his blade back in his sheath. Suddenly, he was full of hope again and cursed himself for having forgotten what he knew in his sinews.

Oros took a moment and closed his eyes, inhaling air through his nose. He took two deep breaths, a technique hunters used to sort through the various scents around them as they tried to focus on a particular fragrance from the subject they were tracking. It was challenging, surrounded by the smell of salt water, wet sand, and seagull excrement. Yet, he persisted until, at last, he caught the scent of baby Ulonae, but it was jumbled together with the smell of Skylet's cloak. It was faint, but Oros calibrated each inhalation to hold on to the trail as best he could, as though trying to maintain hold of a fragrance that took him back to a pleasant time from his childhood.

Oros reasoned that being in such turmoil and worry inside himself over Skylet, and since he was no longer a hunter, the actions he would usually take, the skills he would use to hunt, were pushed out of himself, at least in one way. Since reconnecting with Skylet and living his new life with her and Séya, and now Ulonae, he had spent the past few months making space within himself for a new way of being.

Yet, as fate would have it, some of the old ways of being would not leave him fully anytime soon. Suddenly, the ocean water rose in the form of a wall, breaking Oros' concentration. The beach rumbled.

Oros opened his eyes, taken aback by the sight of the height of the wave. He hardly had time to adjust and react before something else, something more concerning, revealed itself as the waves from the ocean crashed down, pushing Oros back. A large light blue, almost white dragon with a tremendous wingspan rose from the water like a mountain, looking down upon Oros with an expression of immeasurable anger in its eyes.

19.

Oros couldn't remember the last time he had felt the emotion he understood as fear. Proper fear. Except for the day he watched his uncle Servalan die.

Though he had seen and engaged in battles with dragons alongside his uncle, he was never really afraid. Not until they came upon Jessie. He was genuinely scared for his uncle. Beyond that, he had been so consumed by anger that he scarcely had room for any other feeling. But now, since he had been afforded time to begin learning about other facets of himself, the fear within him was more than palpable. And in the presence of the towering dragon, he was afraid.

The eyes of the sea creature shook him to his core, resembling a rich moonlight tinted with brilliant red hues.

On instinct, Oros reached behind his back and pulled out his Moonbeam Metal sword, standing in a defensive position.

The enemy wasted no time. It took a deep breath and released a thick, flowing trail of solid fire toward Oros.

The hunter grabbed the edge of his cape with his free hand and blocked the flames. The fire did not dissipate upon contact as he had assumed would happen. Instead, it was continuous. It seemed as though the dragon could exhale quite a breath. Oros quickly turned out and away from the force of the onslaught and engaged in a combat roll away, barely getting himself on his feet for the split second he needed to dive further out of range of the intense heat.

The dragon crouched, partially submerging itself in the water. It twisted its whole body in a full circle, then quickly rose, its wings widely outstretched for less than a blink before they flapped once and powerfully. The force resulted in a giant wave being pushed toward Oros as he tried to move further out of harm's way.

As fast as he was to avoid much of the water crashing down onto the beach, he did not get away unscathed. Enough had caught him at the end of the wave to push him further back.

Oros howled in pain, surprised that the water was hot enough to scald him. He was lucky he missed the full force of the wave, for the damage would certainly have been much worse.

The attack slowed him down, but Oros managed to get up and shake himself off. He had the fleeting thought of how quiet the dragon was, like a stealthy killer. It didn't grunt, growl, or release any sound that might have hinted at any emotion whatsoever. His history with such dragons, particularly those from specific territories like the water or the woods, reminded him that the manner of their attacks was strictly executed to protect both living arrangements and offspring or other family members.

Oros ran further toward the right side of the beach, his eyes trained upon the dragon. He watched as the reddish moonlight eyes of his enemy locked on to him and followed his moves.

Oros jumped into the water, which was much cooler at that area of the beach. He went in just deep enough to submerge himself to take the edge off the burning sensation he still felt from the hot wave of ocean water.

The dragon seemed surprised by this because it leaned backward for a second until it got low enough so that its massive head was submerged in the water up to its nose.

Oros stood in the knee-deep cool water, sword still in hand, and waited.

The dragon charged ahead, Oros directly in its path; the threat of being rammed with the full force of the giant adversary was imminent.

Rather than strike, when the sea creature was within range, Oros dived out of the way to his right, splashing in the water.

The enemy whipped its head in Oros' direction; water splattered everywhere.

Oros stood himself up in the shallow waters again, but this time, calming himself, he stood up straight, no longer in an offensive or defensive position. He looked into his enemy's eyes and stuck his blade into the water. Only the hilt remained just above the ocean surface. Oros dropped his hands to his sides.

Disregarding that the hunter had conceded defeat, the dragon, its body still low, stalked closer to Oros with intention, pondering all the ways to destroy him.

Oros stood and studied the creature. He took note of the unique silvery blue hue of its skin, which was rare to see in dragons of the water. This one was undoubtedly unique when compared to others he came across.

The dragon stood upright, preparing to take another deep breath. But before the creature could release, something stopped it. It just looked at Oros for a moment with an expression of frustration. Or perhaps confusion, Oros thought.

Suddenly, Séya appeared on the beach from out of the woods, holding baby Ulonae in one arm, her free hand outstretched as if she could hold off the dragon. "OROS!" she called out, seeing them facing off.

It turned around to look at her, and upon registering the youngling with Séya, something seemed to shake the sea dragon. It whipped its head around to see Oros again in the same position. His eyes trained on the creature, a blank expression on his face. Oros huffed to catch his breath.

The dragon turned away toward the open ocean and submerged itself, swimming off as quickly as it arrived.

Oros watched as the tumultuous waters returned to a more peaceful state and then turned to share a look with Séya, who stood frozen in shock.

20.

Skylet came to lying flat on her stomach, sprawled out on the sand of the beach, one side of her head kissed by the current of the ocean as it pushed and pulled back and forth. Slowly, she began moving to sit up, and as soon as she did, Skylet realized she didn't know where she was. Worse still, she was there alone. Her breathing quickened. She looked around frantically, anxiety growing within her as the ocean waves greeted and receded from her. *"Séya!"* she called out, looking to her right. She thought back to the last thing she remembered, how after shoving Oros back, she felt that after a brief absence, Jessie had returned to show her more about the location of her siblings. She felt the dragon's essence surrounding her so strongly that she began to wonder if the connection somehow became stronger after some time of no interaction and no notable recent dreams.

Skylet couldn't be sure. She doubted the thought as it came to her since she had just become aware of herself and her surroundings after awakening. Skylet concluded that her head needed some time to clear itself. It worried her that she hadn't the faintest idea of how she got to the beach, and she began to wonder where to start figuring out how to reconnect with Séya, Oros and the Ulonae.

She positioned herself on her knees and turned around, noticing how far back the beach went away from her. There were deep and rich woods beyond that, and to her left, the mountains stood in the distance. Just as she was beginning to stand, she felt something disrupt her thoughts, a kind of tremor that translated into a faint, and then a sudden wave of heat in her stomach that went away as quickly as it came. Something was growing from the unconscious space of her mind. Some kernel of an idea slowly rooting itself in the recesses of her head, only to sprout tendrils of lively electric images that tried to have itself be recognized by Skylet's conscious mind. A voice. It wasn't entirely clear yet, but she began to understand that it was as palpable as anything else outside herself.

It attempted to speak to her, and at first, Skylet was confused. The sounds she heard were muffled as though coming from underwater. The timbre of the incoherent voice was not one that was at all familiar to her. The volume of the voice increased in her head, which scared her. She yelped, shuffled, and scrambled around the sand on her knees, trying to escape something she didn't know. It felt so close to her.

She tried running back toward the woods behind her, covering her ears as though trying to protect against a sound that would damage them and make her head burst. The uneven sand caused her to lose her balance and fall to her knees. She yelped again, and on instinct, she dropped to her side and curled into a fetal position. She felt a sharp throbbing all around her head until the voice seemingly broke through whatever barrier that made it impossible to decipher. *"Jessie..."* the voice said. It was a semi-deep sound with a velvety quality to it.

Almost immediately at that moment, the throbbing in Skylet's head stopped. She realized she heard the voice as clear as the morning sky she found herself looking upon. Skylet quickly sat up and looked around, sure of what she heard, but couldn't be certain if it was all in her head. Had merely ruminating on Jessie in connection with the cloak brought this on? She would not be allowed to follow the train of thought any further as she was interrupted again by a direction from somewhere deep in herself to look out into the ocean.

She saw nothing as the calm waters danced like fleeting whispers. Skylet scanned the ocean, her head turning left to right slowly more than a few times until she jumped back, shrieking at the sight of two large eyes, glowing like the moonlight with a hint of red, protruding from the surface of the water.

The creature maintained its position and kept eye contact with the girl.

Skylet froze, not wanting to make any sudden moves for fear of the sea-beast giving chase.

"I sense fear in you," a voice said, even more crisply than Skylet had heard before.

Now, she understood that the eyes of the creature looking back at her belonged to the owner of the voice. She released a breath of relief at knowing where the voice came from.

"You need not be troubled."

Skylet looked on, taken aback by how clearly the voice sounded in her head. She saw no mouth moving, seeing as the creature was still mostly submerged underwater. She wondered where the sea beast came from and what it was called.

Seeming to sense her thoughts, the creature granted her almost immediate responses to the questions she had. "I dwell in these waters. I was... called by someone I knew long ago." There was a brief break in the response until the voice added, "She does not seem to be here." The tone was one of disappointment as another thought entered its mind to express. "And yet... the cloak about you..."

Skylet had the thought of asking how the creature knew about Jessie, and once again, she received a response. "Jessie was a dear spirit to me," said the beast of the ocean. "I am called Sebastian."

Skylet began to get emotional. Tears formed in her eyes.

The creature slowly approached her and then rose from the water, looking down at her.

Skylet's eyes widened as she looked upon the grand size of the sea dragon, slightly bigger than Jessie was, but not by much. She marveled at his silvery light blue skin and his eyes, which she kept coming back to. "You knew Jessie?" she asked, her voice trembling.

"I..." Sebastian began, hesitating as he spoke, reaching a hand to touch his head. "I know her. I can somehow feel her here, or I did more strongly moments before. And so can you."

"How? How can you feel her?"

"I can sense energy secretions that come into the water. They create tremors that alert me, much like your land-dwelling spiders, when something enters their home of silk. When your cloak touched the water at some point, it must have triggered such a tremor. Tell me, where is

Jessie? I felt her so strongly for a moment. That is what led me here. To you."

Skylet looked down and shook her head, beginning to sob.

"My dear child," Sebastian said, his voice softening, his expression concerned. He crouched and came closer to her. "Why do you weep?"

Skylet looked up at him and tried to think of a way to answer his question. The word 'gone' was all her mind could muster.

Sebastian was silent. He heard the thought, wondering why it took so long for him to catch it before reasoning that somehow Jessie was not 'gone.' He, too, was confused by his own thoughts and feelings on the matter. "May I…" he paused, looking at Skylet mournfully.

Somehow, Skylet understood what he was beginning to ask in a way that surprised even her. It was not that she intuited his question. It was that she felt a doorway of communication that opened not only to her but from within her to him as well. It was wide open now. She didn't understand it fully but again suspected it had something to do with Jessie's energy and the events that led up to arriving at the beach at that moment in time, now communing with Sebastian, the sea dragon.

Reading the question he thought to ask from his mind, she put her hands out as if to receive an embrace.

Sebastian leaned his head into the space between her palms, and she leaned her head against his, feeling the warm dampness upon the surface of his skin, and then they shared a vision.

The sea dragon saw Jessie's last moments in the cell with Skylet. He felt the potency of the moment as if he were there. He also saw Jessie's thoughts at that time and the memories that the dragon brought to the forefront of Skylet's mind. He knew about and could see Arca and Séya. The fact that there were other dragon children made itself known to him.

Suddenly, Sebastian understood everything. His heart dropped inside himself. He even felt a pang of embarrassment over the altercation with Oros he had had moments earlier. He didn't know how to reconcile the feelings.

When the series of visions ended, he locked eyes with Skylet and said nothing at first. He took a deep breath and then looked off to his right. He noticed a bush far in the distance on the cliff of a hill that shook in a way that told him it wasn't the wind that resulted in the movement. Someone was watching them. They had been exposed for too long.

Sebastian shook his head slowly and lowered himself to Skylet's level more. "We have an audience," he said, his voice low. "Get on. We must disappear."

Skylet jumped up and took a step toward Sebastian.

"Slowly, dear," he said. "Whoever is there already has their view. Yet, they do not know that we are aware of them."

Skylet climbed onto Sebastian's back.

The dragon turned to face the ocean, took a few steps into the water, and extended his wings. He began flapping them, but one after another. Right, left, right, left, pushing large amounts of water away from himself before standing more upright. "Hold on tightly, dear."

Skylet wrapped her arms around as much as she could of the dragon's thick neck. Sebastian closed his eyes and held out his large hands as though preparing to stop something heavy moving toward him. Suddenly, he clapped them together once, resulting in a thunderous cracking sound. Then, with his hands in a grappling position, he extended them outward, fingers faced inward, and without warning, a mist appeared around them. It was faint at first, but lasted mere seconds before much of the area, going all the way up to the hills where the visitor was likely hiding, became covered in a proper fog surrounding them.

The haze was so thick Skylet could barely see whatever was directly in front of her. Squeezing Sebastian's neck tighter still, expecting them to fly, she was surprised that the dragon, instead, just went a little further into the water so that he could swim above the surface. "Where are we going?"

Sebastian looked up and turned his head to face Skylet partially. "To reconnect with your family."

21.

From across the lands outside and surrounding Mysteya, word traveled swiftly like the great winds preceding a storm. A sea monster had been sighted by a lone traveler. Of course, it would only be a matter of time before the Selnes forces were made aware of this.

A handful of soldiers arrived at a large campsite between towns as it was being dismantled in preparation to move forward with their search. The activity was lively; men and women grabbed their gear and armor while others brought down tents and packed up equipment strewn about.

One of the newly arrived soldiers approached two others who sat on a downed tree eating. "Where is the Principal?" he asked them.

Without looking up from his food, one of the men pointed toward the tent she was in.

"My thanks," the young man replied before turning away and heading toward the tent. He arrived, startled to see a spirited discussion taking place. Layona looked intensely serious as she listened to others around her leveling comments and opinions.

"Do we know that this sea monster is the same one from the attacks off the coast of Ondriten?" one of the soldiers asked.

"Who knows," one of the sentinels responded, tying her hair in a ponytail. "Let us assume it is. What does this mean for our search?"

"Principal," the young soldier who had just entered the tent interjected.

"Leave us, boy," a more hardened soldier shot at him.

Layona turned to face the young man and nodded. "What is it?"

Feeling the intensity from her expression almost transferred to him, it shook him enough to reach into his pouch and pull out a scarf quickly. He held it out to her as he began to speak. "We discovered this while scouring where the witch was spotted back in Mysteya." The scarf draped over his hand.

"Do you believe it belongs to the witch?" asked Layona.

"I am not sure, perhaps. I thought it warranted being brought directly to you."

"Foolish boy," the hardened soldier said. "What makes you think this scarf would be important to the Principal Sentinel? It could be from anywhere, belong to anyone."

"I understand you have some skill tracking," the young man told Layona.

"And what might you know of that?" she asked.

"Had you all not heard anything of the Principal being a tracker once?"

The tent was silent.

"The way I hear it back home, she was a good one."

Layona walked up to the young soldier and took the scarf from him. "Thank you for this information."

"Ma'am." the young soldier turned and left the tent.

"Is it true what the boy says?" asked Holera as she collected her belongings. "That scarf could lead us directly to the witch then."

"It might have been true once." Layona paused. "What of the woman seen with the sea monster?" She changed the subject.

"The woman was taken and killed by the monster, or so it was said," another soldier in the tent expressed. "The mist that appeared from nowhere made it hard to see where the monster went."

While the news traveled quickly, it didn't always travel as clearly. Apparently, there had been some embellishments somewhere along the way.

"What should we do?" one of the sentinels asked Layona.

"We continue to Hynlan Beach. From there, we separate. Some of us will move out to Ondriten to continue our search for the witch, the dragon, and the hunter."

"What of the sea monster?" the hardened soldier asked.

"There may be a link, but that is not our place. Besides, officials there under the king are likely investigating that. If need be, we collaborate with them."

"Eshen means, how will we handle a sea monster should we encounter it?" asked Holera, standing up to face Layona with a serious expression.

No one spoke to it, but it became clear rather quickly that the notion of such a threat was not at all what they were prepared for. Fighting against something like a dragon on land was one thing. A creature of the sea was another.

"We cannot afford any casualties. As we are simply searching and collecting, we must not engage with it."

22.

Oros walked along the beach deep in thought; his head hung down. After the scuffle with the sea dragon, he had gotten his mind back on tracking Skylet. It took some time, but he could locate her trail again, though it was even fainter than before.

Séya was quiet. They seemed at a loss for words on what to say about what they had seen.

Ulonae seemed the only one with much to say. The young one was excited, babbling away after seeing a big dragon for the first time.

After a few more steps, Séya finally spoke. "What happened, Oros?"

He did not respond.

"Where did that dragon come from?"

Oros stopped walking and turned to look out over the ocean. "There," he said. His voice was low.

"The water? Goodness me," the old woman replied. "I don't know if I've ever seen one quite like that."

There was a pause.

"What happened?"

Oros turned to face her. "I went to the water to refresh

myself, and it emerged to attack me."

Séya looked concerned.

Suddenly, a rich mist surrounded them almost in an instant. They looked around, and before long, they began losing sight of themselves and each other.

"I can't..." said Oros. "Séya!"

Séya knelt, and baby Ulonae made sounds suggesting that she, too, was nervous and no longer comfortable.

The old woman began waving her hands in a circular motion, using a spell to clear up the heavy mist. The water beyond them made splashing sounds; the waves became more active and vocal. Something was coming.

Oros grabbed his sword. "Séya! It has returned!"

The mist began clearing up, and through it, Séya saw the outline of a large creature approaching. "There!" she said, stepping back.

"Séya!" a familiar voice called out.

"Skylet," said Oros to himself.

"Girl! Is that you?" Séya kept moving her arms, the mist clearing up even more.

"Yes!" cried Skylet. "It's okay!"

"Do not be alarmed by me," Sebastian's voice was commanding yet warm. "I am a friend."

The large hand of the dragon landed on the beach with a pronouncement and a large indentation in the sand.

Oros and Séya jumped back further, and Ulonae squealed in excitement.

Sebastian bowed his head and crouched, allowing Skylet to slide off his back, landing on one knee.

"Are you all right?" Oros asked, startled. "We chased your trail here."

"I am fine," she said, looking down at first. Then she

looked at Oros. "Thank you." Still, she felt awkward. Even more so now as she thought of her shoving him just before she lost herself.

"What happened, child? Where were you?" Séya caught her breath.

"Further down that way," Skylet waved to her right.

There was a brief silence amidst the fog, which cleared just enough for each of them to see each other better.

"Jessie?" Séya asked, her voice lower.

"I can't fully tell," the girl began. "Yes, and I don't know. I am certain I felt her."

She turned to gesture toward the sea dragon. "This is Sebastian," said Skylet. "He felt Jessie too."

Séya looked up to Sebastian. "We thank you for returning her to us." Séya bowed deeply to express her gratitude.

"Dear woman, Séya of Mysteya," he said to her.

Séya looked up, surprised.

"You needn't thank me. It was Jessie's will."

"You know me?" the old woman asked.

"I do, and I know that which you carry in your heart."

Séya placed a hand on her chest, looking into the dragon's reddish moonlit eyes.

"But before we move any further, we must prepare to leave this place."

"Why?" Oros asked, uncertain of the dragon still. "Where must we go?"

Sebastian turned to Oros and moved closer to him. "My deepest apologies for my part in our earlier... misunderstanding." The sea creature outstretched his right hand, placing his palm firmly in the sand just before Oros, and bowed low enough that his nose nearly touched the ground.

The hunter allowed himself to take in the image of Sebastian before him and knelt to one knee. He placed a fist on the left side of his breast and bowed deeply in return. "You have my apology as well. My habits have not left me."

Sebastian rose. "I sensed as much. And great confusion as well, that now is more clear to me."

"Where will we go?" asked Skylet.

"To reconnect with your family." the dragon replied.

"What do you mean? We are all together now."

"You are searching for the others, are you not?" asked Sebastian.

Skylet blinked. "Yes," she responded quickly. "Do you know where they are?"

"We must travel to my home," the dragon replied. "I now understand more that was unclear to me before."

"We cannot all fly with you," Séya said.

"There will be no need," Sebastian looked at her. "Though I'm afraid you all will need some... assistance in order to accompany me there."

They all looked at one another.

"There isn't much time. We were spotted just before we arrived here," he said of himself and Skylet. "I can only keep the mist alive to continue hiding us for so long."

Without warning, Sebastian reached to his left forearm and used the talons from his other webbed hand to puncture himself. A rich purple blood began oozing from the wounds. Its color was even darker than any of them had seen in other dragons.

They all gasped in astonishment, except Ulonae, who suddenly wanted to get out of Séya's bag to examine the liquid.

Sebastian noticed, and half smiled at the youngling.

"What are you doing?!" Skylet asked.

"Do not fear," said the sea dragon. "Séya of Mysteya. I need your assistance with a special potion. Your sorcery."

The old woman tentatively took a step toward Sebastian.

"Potion? For what?" Skylet asked.

Sebastian turned to her. "How else are you all going to breathe in the water?"

23.

Sebastian generated and held an orb of sustained water in the space between his large hands. Oros, Skylet, and even Séya looked on in astonishment. Ulonae reached her tiny hands out, jumping up and down, waiting for the ball of water to be passed to her as it might be for a game. But this was no game. The dragon's expression was serious as he maintained the focus required to hold the ball of water and keep the mist active.

Oros noticed that the fog was yet clearer than it had been, which worried him that the benefit of being hidden was fast leaving them. He could see that the dragon was putting in considerable effort, and it occurred to him as he watched what was happening that while he had encountered dragons in the water and had stellar battles with them, he had never really met one that could seemingly manipulate the element. After learning of Jessie, some part of him thought it should surprise him less to acknowledge Sebastian's abilities. Yet, he was still astonished.

Oros went further into himself, thinking about what he knew of the creatures he once swore to hunt. While there was much he understood and had learned, there was more still he had no idea about when it came to the complexities of the creatures.

Sebastian momentarily shifted his attention to Séya, holding the still water orb. "Can you manipulate the blood into this ball?" he asked her. "Quickly, but carefully."

Séya took a moment to witness how the blood traveled over and around the silvery white scales of his forearm. She focused her attention on the wounds, which were now healed, but the blood traveled down, and before it could drip into the sand, Séya caught it with her sorcery and carefully brought it down Sebastian's forearm. She motioned her hands as though she were massaging his arm, but she was driving the blood in a particular way. She got it all into the water ball, which congealed into an orb within the center of the water sphere.

"Good, good," Sebastian said. "Come. I will guide you in the next step." He leaned in closer to Séya, bowing his head.

Séya stepped in and closed her eyes, her hands ready to continue working. Their heads touched, and a calm breeze surrounded them in a gentle cyclone.

Baby Ulonae escaped the bag and walked toward Séya, leaning against her leg. She wanted to be a part of the activity.

"No," Skylet said, quickly stepping in to pick up the youngling before moving away.

She could see Séya's fingers moving, working. A conversation transpired between the two.

Soon, Séya's hands were inside the water sphere. She touched the blood, moving it around.

After a moment, the two leaned back from each other and turned to face the group, both holding the water and blood ball together.

"Come," Séya began. "We must drink this. Now."

Oros and Skylet looked at each other.

"There is nothing to fear," said Sebastian, sensing their hesitation.

"I will go first," Séya said. She used her hands to guide some of the liquid to her face and then drank several gulps. "It is all right."

Oros looked at Skylet and then stepped forward to receive his serving. He gulped heartily.

Skylet looked at Séya as she stepped forward, holding the baby dragon in her arms, and received her serving.

"Hold her steady, dear," Séya said of Ulonae.

Skylet did so as Séya manipulated a small ball of the liquid over the youngling's head.

Ulonae squealed, her hands raised as if preparing to catch the ball.

"No, dear," Séya calmly said. "Open. *Ahhh.*"

The little one didn't quite follow the instructions correctly, but her mouth was agape in the excitement of a potential game.

Séya didn't waste any time. She quickly shot the ball into Ulonae's mouth, causing her to begin a coughing fit. "Pat her, girl," she told Skylet.

As she tapped the youngling's back, small bursts of fire shot out more than once, startling Skylet. The little dragon laughed.

"We are ready. We must go now," Sebastian said, looking around. The mist was nearly all gone. He bent down and allowed Séya and Skylet onto his back. He offered for Oros to join, but the hunter politely refused.

They all submerged themselves in the water, following Sebastian's lead.

24.

Henricks found himself sitting in the chair of his study, enjoying a warm drink in the afternoon. He sat near the window overlooking one of the many wonderful gardens on the grounds. Since joining the King's Court, the gardens were one thing that seemed to calm his overactive mind.

During less busy times, he devoted much of his leisure to studying many types of plants. His time as a Dragonhunter gave him a firm foundation of such things by utilizing herbs with healing and stamina-boosting properties. A hunter needed to know how to create such things from the world around them if they couldn't purchase them from a merchant. Aside from that, few markets ever had more nuanced items on hand. Dragonhunters had to be resourceful.

Now that his life was considerably less consumed by hunting and killing the fire-breathing creatures, there was more time to learn about subjects like conventional gardening for purposes that were less concerned with his own self-interest.

After finishing his drink, he decided to go down and appraise the garden below, noticing some of the castle staff, older women who had tended the gardens for many years. He happened to be fond of them and thought it a perfect opportunity to stop and engage them. He suddenly needed to distract himself from thoughts that crept in to disrupt his moment of rest.

Henricks stood up from his desk, glancing down at the small, still unwrapped bag on his desk. He shook his head and turned away to leave the room.

***

It was the afternoon, and Layona led the trek ahead. Two of her closest cohort members flanked her as they walked. A group of the Selnes army, including Holera and her comrades, followed along. They all mainly traveled in silence, with few exceptions of murmuring among different members of the group.

The Principal Sentinel busied her mind with the potential future of the search and the results it might yield. Or the failure of it. With Selnes forces, both peacekeeper and footmen alike, scattered still across various towns nearest them, all with the same goal, her mind wandered to the last place she wanted to stop for a visit: the island of Gyenola. Yet, the more she thought of it, even though it would take some time to travel there since they would need to wait for a ship to get to them, making the trip would be unavoidable at some point. Even if only a small number of the group from Selnes traveled there.

A nudge to her shoulder from a member of her company brought her back to herself in the present moment.

"Should you be any more lost in the thoughts of your own mind, not even I would be able to bring you back," said a deep voice to her right as they traversed through the wilderness.

Layona glanced over at Oberon, a seasoned sentinel from before the Great Destruction and one of her closest confidants. Graying at the temples, he was tall, not quite slender, and not quite stocky, yet his physical prowess made him a sure choice to join the search mission. But more than that, Layona appreciated his counsel and genuine care for her. In the most honest parts of herself, it was not a matter of choice. Wherever she went, Oberon was coming along.

They had been partnered since the beginning of her time with the Sentinels of Selnes. She impressed Oberon early on during the combat and the cerebral requirements it took to be a sentinel. Eventually, Oberon willingly gave up his position as Principal and, with the blessing of the council, Layona was to lead a local group of Sentinels. "It is time for new ways to be instituted," he once told her in a private conversation. "The shadow of the old days still dictate how some of us... more wizened members engage this work," he chuckled, touching her shoulder. "Now, it is your turn, dear. You will go further."

Yet, this mission was the first of her true tests beyond the boundaries of her home. And it weighed on her in a manner that might not have been visible to others in the company, but it was to Oberon. "What is it, girl?"

Looking ahead, Layona spoke in a low voice. "When your children come to you, full of worry and concern, what words do you share to comfort them?" Her face gave no indication of the feeling wrapped in the question.

"I tell them not to doubt themselves," he matched her tone. "To not doubt that they carry the feelings that will guide them to the highest truth within themselves."

They walked further in silence before Oberon broke it. "Is this satisfactory, girl?"

Layona looked at him before checking to ensure she didn't trip over a downed tree branch. "It is. Your children are fortunate. Thank you." She touched the center of his back firmly, patting it before letting her hand drop to her side.

Oberon put a hand on her shoulder, as he often did when she held such feelings of doubt. "No thanks required, girl, for we all could do with comforting words from time to time. Though, if we are being fair, I suppose it is one of my great gifts."

The two shared a chuckle.

Not much further behind them, Holera and her company of soldiers walked. She noticed the brief expression of affection and turned inward, thinking of Brawns and their shared connection. Even though there had been much time between when they last saw each other and his death, she cared for him deeply, having watched over him since they were children. She remembered a time when he was a kind and thoughtful child. Even then, he had moments of brashness and intensity.

Only a few years younger, he seemed wiser than she on occasion. That was who Holera wanted justice for. He did change once he joined the army in Selnes, with only glimpses of the boy she knew appearing as an adult. Still, she believed he deserved to be alive. Holera wanted to hug him, even though she knew he wouldn't fully allow himself to appreciate it. Either way, the apparent bond between Layona and Oberon made her envious. Holera kept walking along, her anger simmering just beneath the surface. Her comrades could feel it and silently joined her in that place as they walked in tighter formation around her, comforting her with a uniform emotion.

25.

They traveled with great speed in the water as though flying through the skies like birds might. They were mostly silent. Though they could breathe underwater, they could not speak in more than broken sentences, resorting to thought in order to communicate more fluidly. Something that took Oros some getting used to.

Sebastian pushed through the water without so much as a stroke, propelling himself, Séya, Skylet, and Ulonae with tremendous force. Remarkably, the dragon used his abilities to move Oros along with them. He was just to the right of the sea creature, allowing himself to be pulled as though by some magnetic force.

It amazed Oros to witness such a sight as Sebastian moving the way he did. Never before had he been exposed to such a treat.

They traversed through schools of fish and families of whales. Before long, they swiftly approached a curved wall in the distance. It glowed a subtle, low light. They were close enough to touch it within moments, but they didn't. Instead, they went straight through the veil of the wall and were astonished at what looked to be a grand colony of sea dragons. Creatures of many sizes and hues swam all around. Families gathered in various areas, and little dragons swam in circles, playing.

Some stopped to get a good look at the newcomers who had arrived. While others greeted Sebastian with a mixture of reverence for him and uncertainty about the company he kept.

They slowed to a deliberate progression through the colony and soon were approached by one member, dark brown skinned with a red-orange mane around its face that looked more serpent-like with its particularly long and slender body. Its limbs were more spaced apart than was typical of most dragons.

"Sebastian the Venerable," said the sea dragon formally, bowing. "Welcome home..." there was a pause as the creature looked on in confusion.

"And welcome you are always, Ulysus."

"Sebastian..."

"There is no cause for concern, dear Ulysus. The humans are friends."

Still, Ulysus gawked at them. "Forgive me," he paused. "They can exist in these waters?! How? I understood that humans could not reconcile breathing if not on land. If they are here, are we now threatened by others?"

"Be calm, Ulysus," said Sebastian reassuringly. "We are under no such threat."

Ulysus looked up at Sebastian's face with concern. "I am not sure I agree with this since humans do not seem to consider our best interests, but I trust you as I have in all my time here."

"It is much appreciated." Sebastian gave a slight bow. "Tell me, where are my sons?"

"Tending to a couple of injured younglings in the caves. Resulting from a scuffle, no doubt. They like to try and prove themselves often at this age, as you know."

Sebastian scoffed to himself. "Would you mind sending them to my keep? I would like our guests to meet them."

"Of course, wise one." Ulysus nodded, and without wasting a moment, he swam off in a most elegant fashion, bubbles pushed in his wake.

Skylet watched Ulysus, and in much the same way she once thought of Jessie and how the dragon moved, she saw a similar natural artistry to how the dragon commanded its body and the element around it. She was taken with this new kind of dragon and began wondering where he might have come from.

Sebastian responded by picking up on this more unique thought that stood out from either Séya's or Oros' musings. "Ulysus has been here for a very long time," he said. "He is even less trusting of humankind than so many of us here, who were mostly spared from the purge. His family, however, was not so fortunate. Taken long before the great near-extinction. At least, for the earthbound of dragon kind."

"What – happened?" Skylet asked.

"Betrayed by humans whom he befriended."

Skylet felt a wave of sadness come over her, which mixed with the grief in her heart about Jessie and Arca together.

Sebastian felt it, and it triggered his feelings of loss for Jessie. He hadn't had the room to let it sink in when Skylet shared the memory of it with him.

Suddenly, Séya felt a pressure surrounding her, as though the water would crush her. She didn't need to be told about the internal emotions crashing against the hearts and minds of Sebastian and Skylet like punishing tidal waves. She slid off Sebastian's back, floating in the water, her arms outstretched.

Ulonae seemed to enjoy not being bound to the ground, though she seemed equally confused.

Without warning, the old woman let out a guttural howl, *"Noooo!"* the sound of her voice sent shockwaves through the water. She lost control of her body and went limp.

Oros noticed and swam to help her.

Sebastian and Skylet turned to see what had happened.

Oros held Séya, noticing she was winded, as though the scream had exerted a great deal of energy from her. "Are you — all right?" he asked her.

"I am..." she began. "I am exhausted."

Oros looked up at Sebastian. "Please - is there - any-where - she might - rest?"

The dragon nodded once and manipulated the water to carry and push them as he swam up and through the col-ony. They swerved around jagged and aged earth, beaten by constant contact with water yet stubbornly refusing to be entirely destroyed. They approached and floated through an area of seaweed, dancing hypnotically in the current. At the end of the seaweed was an empty, mostly darkened chamber. There were uneven circles in the walls through which dim light from the sun reached and crept. Given how deep they were in the ocean, it was a wonder any light could be seen.

The floor was smooth, and there were small patches of growth on the edges. A few large boulders sat in different parts of the space.

They all entered, and as they did, they were greeted by two other dragons who came in behind them. "Father," one said in a tone that sounded so much like Sebastian in its calming and commanding qualities, yet it was lighter with youth. "You sent for us?" Aria swam close to the group, throwing curious glances at the humans present. He greeted Sebastian, who lowered his large head with a gentle brow graze.

"I did."

"Welcome, Father," the other dragon, Floren, greeted Sebastian the same way his brother did. Also noticeably confused by the presence of humans in their father's most personal dwelling.

Sensing the uncertainty of his sons, he spoke to set their concerns at ease. "These humans are friends. Do not fear."

They looked at each other and back at their father.

"How may we assist?" Aria asked.

"Tend to this woman, please," said Sebastian. "I sense a break within her. See to it that she is well cared for."

"Yes, Father," replied the first sea dragon son. He outstretched his hands and, using the water, much like Sebastian had before, lifted Séya out of Oros' arms.

The sensation was a gentle one to Oros. It was as though the water around him became a silk sheet, grazing his hands and arms, lifting the old woman away, placing her into a soft spot in the chamber.

Floren, the second son, floated to his brother and placed a large hand at Séya's head.

"Hello..." Séya sounded weak.

Surprised at this, the young dragon caressed her head. "Hello," he said. "I am going to search for what is ailing you. Keep calm."

"Oh — you needn't — worry – on that," she said.

Sebastian turned to Oros and Skylet, who held baby Ulonae. "My sons are skilled healers. Even more than I in some ways. She will be well in their capable hands."

Floren and Aria indeed seemed special. Twins, Aria was moments older. Thoughtful and practical when it came to healing. He was also quite the tactician and treated the work like the battle he saw it as, particularly when it came to working at helping many at once.

Floren could not seem to learn enough about the art of healing, yet he possessed great skill as a defender as well. He enjoyed attempting to prove himself in sparring sessions with his brother. Though in truth, now that they were older, Aria had quite caught up in skill and was more on level ground than Floren would ever admit. They shared a healthy competition and a deep love for each other and the colony they served.

Sebastian looked to his sons. "I shall return." He then directed his attention to Skylet. "Come with me, child. I nearly forgot in all the commotion here that there is one with whom you must reunite."

She looked confused. Skylet carried Ulonae as she floated onto Sebastian's back.

The dragon looked down at Oros. "Would you care to join us?"

Oros turned to face Séya being tended to by the sea dragons and then back at Sebastian. "My thanks to you," he said. "But, I will remain here with her."

"Very well," said Sebastian. "We will return."

Oros reached out to Skylet for the young dragon and held her close.

With that, Sebastian turned and pushed off, swimming through the area of dancing seaweed. Oros noticed again how they danced, but this time, the sparkling light in the water seemed to give them a magical quality. They invited him into a space that was all-encompassing and comforting. Something he thought was necessary for Séya as she was being cared for.

26.

Sebastian swam along while Skylet held onto his neck firmly. She noticed that below them were various domes made of earth, large enough to house several dragons of differing sizes. Some swam around, conversing with one another while their children played near them. Passing by at a neutral speed, Skylet caught a glimpse of at least two others, which she assumed to be a mother and daughter, through a hole in the ceiling of one of the domes. The mother seemed to be teaching her daughter how to cook food. Her massive hands held a large fish, at least to Skylet, if she were holding it. In the hands of a dragon, it looked to be the size of a much smaller one.

The mother released a controlled breath of intense heat, the waves of which took the shape of an uneven sphere that enveloped the fish. It surprised Skylet that she could see it at such a depth in the water. The younger dragon sat nearby, looking on intently. Naturally, this scene reminded Skylet of Jessie and Séya.

They kept going and reached a part of the colony developed within a vast, jagged wall that was part of a giant section of solid earth. Skylet noticed they were moving upward, swimming to the surface, which seemed closer to them than when they first entered the ocean. Initially confused, she pushed the idea aside as their heads popped through the surface. Skylet was surprised to find they had arrived in a cavern where the water didn't enter.

They swam and reached the cavern floor, getting out of the pool.

Younglings excitedly hurried over to Sebastian. "Sebastian! Sebastian!" one of them called out. This one had maroon skin and thorns protruding from the top of his head. He nudged his brow against Sebastian's lowered forearm as the old dragon caressed the youngling's face. "Hello there," said Sebastian.

Another dragon approached. She was older than the others but much younger than Sebastian. If Skylet had to guess, this one was an adolescent.

A deep green color, her yellow eyes glowed as she looked up to meet Sebastian's gaze. She outstretched her arms to receive a hug from Sebastian; other dragons did the same, and the old dragon opened his arms wide enough to embrace many of them.

"Hello, younglings," he said warmly to them. "Nayess," Sebastian looked at the deep green dragon. "Where is our new friend?"

"Back in the chamber." Nayess looked at Skylet upon his back.

Skylet noticed but didn't feel the same discomfort as when other dragons had seen her. Nayess seemed more curious than anything else that Skylet was there.

"Thank you, dear," said Sebastian. "Would you mind terribly informing him he has a new visitor?

Nayess nodded, nearly jumped over, and swerved around

some of the younglings in Sebastian's presence to do as he asked.

"Nayess has been learning the ways of the healing arts from my sons, which, as I am sure you know now, is very different than those of your humans." He lowered himself and allowed Skylet to slide off his back.

"These..." she began, her breath becoming labored and broken in a staccato form. She clutched her chest and dropped to one knee.

The other young dragons stepped closer, curious about the human before them.

"Stand clear, young ones," Sebastian's tone was one of firmness that did not read as fearsome, packaged in a comforting warmth. He sounded to Skylet like a parent containing a limitless well of patience, which felt more than necessary with a bunch of potentially rowdy and energetic young dragons.

"The breathing potion for our underwater travel is beginning to wear off," the dragon said. "Do not be alarmed. Merely inhale slowly to regain the natural rhythm of your breath."

"What about—?" she coughed.

"My sons will take care of them. They will not be without the air they need."

Sebastian placed a hand on Skylet's back comfortingly as she slowly began to regain her normal pace of breathing.

Skylet looked up at the dragons around them and then back up to Sebastian. "Who are we visiting?"

"I think it is best not to tell you here," he said quietly. "It is better that you see for yourself. Come." he put his large hand out for Skylet to grab to help her up.

The other dragons shuffled and sidestepped out of their path as Sebastian guided Skylet toward the chamber in the far reaches of the cavern.

Skylet looked around and could see other dragons of various ages lying in positions she recognized well enough to know that this back area that Sebastian was leading her through was an infirmary; these dragons were recovering from injuries. Just as they reached the end of the site, she noticed who she could only assume were the two young dragons mentioned when she first arrived at the colony. They were lighter in hue than some of the other dragons, pinkish red and brownish yellow, respectively. She could see parts of them wrapped in large groups of dimly glowing seaweed. Skylet assumed that some of the injuries were trickier and required such a remedy to aid the standard healing capabilities of dragons.

Sebastian nodded at the young male dragons, and they returned the gesture. As the old dragon and Skylet passed them by, they entered a small, darkened chamber illuminated by the flames of two torches made of earth and a glowing blue light coming from the floor. A wall blocked the view from the corner where the light came from, but Skylet could hear slight splashing.

Someone was there.

"I will go no further," said Sebastian, nodding her toward the blue light. "I will be just outside when you are ready."

Skylet turned and slowly made her way deeper into the cavern. When she reached the protruding wall, she peered around it to see a dragon lying on its back in a pond that seemed large enough to fit the massive creature.

It was looking up at the ceiling above, unaware that a

visitor had arrived. The dragon released a deep sigh.

"H-Hello," Skylet said tentatively.

The dragon whipped itself up, splashing around in the pond of glowing water. "Huh?" He looked at the girl standing by the wall to his left in the firelight from the torches. It took them no more than a moment to recognize each other, even in the poorly lit cavern.

"Skylet?" the dragon's voice trembled. "Are you really here?"

"Solly," she said, slowly stepping in closer to examine him. "It's me."

Solen gingerly got himself out of the pond and met Skylet. He bowed his head, and she did likewise, their brows touching. They wrapped their arms around each other, forming puddles of tears falling to the cavern floor.

27.

The early evening hours were chilly. Members of the large company sat together, huddled up near campfires. Others studied maps of the lands for their travel and, in rare moments during conversations, fantasized about going to faraway places in a different capacity than their current situation. These were mostly soldiers who spoke these wishes, at least from what Layona could hear in the distance as she stood with her back to the campsite, staring off into the woods.

Oberon approached her with a plate of fire-roasted fish and beans on the side. "Care to rest your mind for a moment and have a meal with me?"

Layona turned to face him, the aroma of the warm meal beginning to call to her. It was more than just the meal that brought her back to the present; it was how he prepared it. She could tell that Oberon had likely stashed away some special herbs and seasonings for the long trip, and it reminded her of the many evenings she spent with his family at their home for dinner.

Oberon enjoyed cooking. He enjoyed experimenting

with food even more. It was the possibility of discovering new flavors that intrigued him. No matter the risk of it failing or the protests of his children or wife, who sometimes cooked separate meals secretly as a precaution against his less successful offerings. He enjoyed the activity and reveled when he cooked for others, *and* they enjoyed his food. Some part of him felt like he had missed a calling to be a chef somewhere. Especially coming from Selnes, which was once a more prominent place to become a trained cook.

Layona couldn't say no to his offer if she wanted to. Yet, if she were being honest with herself, she wouldn't dare refuse anything he offered her. Most everything he made was more than satisfactory for her tastes. Besides, growing up with an estranged father, whose food she missed, and a mother who rarely had time to cook anything that tasted as wonderful as Oberon's food made her appreciate how something so minimal could still be a pleasant dining experience.

Layona took the tin plate and held it, feeling its warmth coating her palms. "Thank you," she said to him.

Oberon bowed slightly as he handed her a fork and began eating. "Please, dear," he said. "Have some before it becomes cold."

Layona cut into the fish with the side of her fork and scooped up some of the beans to combine the flavors as she consumed them.

"Come," Oberon said to her. "Let us sit here." He gestured to the ground, closer to the campfire.

They sat, and they ate quietly.

Oberon glanced at her occasionally, and like with one of his own daughters, he could almost see what she was thinking. He knew that even though it was nearing time for everyone to turn in for the night, Layona was far from ready to sleep. She was anxious to continue moving. "You think we are closing in on something," he said in a tone that left no room for questioning.

Layona looked up from the ground to see his eyes staring at her knowingly. Sometimes, she didn't like how he seemed to know everything while communicating almost nothing. Yet, at the same time, she appreciated how someone knew her in that way. There was something easy and safe about not having to exert the energy necessary to communicate a thought. And at times like tonight, times that seemed like energy needed to be conserved for something bigger ahead, the silence seemed a valuable gift.

Layona took a breath and leaned forward toward Oberon. "I can't be sure, but I do have a feeling." She ate some of the food on her plate.

"And what gives you this 'feeling'?"

"The scarf the young soldier brought to the meeting before we left the last camp. I caught a hint of something in how it smelled that was... familiar."

"Hm," said Oberon, chewing slowly, anticipating further explanation from her.

"I am thinking of leaving camp to search ahead."

"Of course," said Oberon. "And what is it about where we are that suddenly calls this forth in you?"

Layona paused, moving the beans around on her plate, draping them over some of the fish. "I think I caught traces of a similar smell around here."

Oberon nodded once, understanding ultimately what her line of thought would lead to. He scooped up one of his last bites and put it into his mouth, savoring the flavor of it before he began chewing. Once he swallowed that bite, he took a breath. "Well, I am sure to be awake when you decide to begin tracking."

She held his gaze, her brow furrowed. Layona nodded and went back to eating her meal. There was no way she would be leaving the camp on her own. Layona knew this. Oberon just would not have it.

***

It was later in the evening. Night creatures conversed in the distance. The fires were out, and long after most everyone had gone inside their tents, Layona sat with her back against a beech tree, pretending to sleep. Séya's scarf was wrapped around her face in a makeshift hood, so anyone who passed her on the way to relieve themselves couldn't tell that she might be awake.

She kept her position for a long while until suddenly, Layona heard footsteps well beyond her. She could tell someone was trying not to be noisy with their movements. Tilting her head upward slowly, she pulled back the scarf just enough so that her line of sight was clear, and as she did, she saw the outline of Oberon standing before her, his hand outstretched to help her up.

Without any conversation or acknowledgment of each other's presence, they immediately left the campsite. It was as though no time had passed from when they spoke over dinner to now.

Oberon took a moment to light a stick torch he took from his side with fire steel. When it was certain they were far enough out of earshot, Oberon broke the silence. "This scent you mentioned before. Can you detect it now?"

"Yes," Layona replied.

"Can you describe it?"

Layona turned her head to look at him for a moment. She breathed in the scent of the scarf, a part of her concerned that she would lose the trail of it. "There is something about it that almost smells the way fresh air would taste, for whatever that may mean to you." Layona's face contorted, trying to understand for herself what she had just said. "It's the last thing I thought I might have to describe."

"I don't mean to put you on display, my dear," Oberon tried to assure her. "A curiosity within led me to ask. Not unlike the dinners back home." He was referring to when he and his daughters would quiz her about what spices and seasonings were used in the food he made when she spent time at Oberon's home. Somehow, she knew without having tasted anything. Layona wasn't always right, but it was often surprising how developed her sense of smell could be.

Whenever she was asked, no clear answer was ever given about why that was. "I learned from my parents," she would say, and that was all anyone knew.

Layona paused as they reached a point on their hike where the earth went upward. Then she continued.

Oberon followed. They walked for what seemed like ages without a word between them.

Layona's mind raced. Breathing in the scent of the scarf, hoping that the breeze dancing past them in the woods wouldn't take away what was essentially the hook she remained latched on to. It was what gave her the direction to move in. She thought about how far they would move until they stopped to take stock of their journey and imagined what or whom they might find.

The two continued walking until the road ahead began to steepen downward. They held each other on the way forward so as not to lose their balance.

"Careful now," Oberon said.

Soon, they reached an area of flat and soft earth surrounded by tall spruce trees. It felt to Layona as if the very ground was so full of moisture that it would pour from the surface with just the right amount of pressure.

Just as they got their bearings, the soothing sound of waves pushing against the shores reached their ears. They stopped in their place.

"Do you hear that?" asked Oberon.

Layona nodded slowly, looking straight ahead. "The beach must not be far."

They walked along beyond the open space of marsh-like clay surface. The sounds of water meeting the shore increased, and the breeze slipping past them became more pronounced.

Soon, they reached the edge of the woods. They stood overlooking a sandy beach, which was barely noticeable by the light of the torch. It might not have mattered whether they could see it since the breeze was so present at that point that they would have recognized where they were, even if blindfolded.

Oberon raised the torch to determine how far over the cliff he could see. "What is it you think?" he asked. "I will continue to follow your lead as long as you are willing."

Layona was silent for a moment. She gathered two deep breaths through her nose to take in more of the scarf's smell.

The breeze from the water brought with it the scent

of salt and the hint of droppings from seagulls and similar creatures that frequented the area. Competing with what she could take in was also the trace of another familiar element. One she couldn't quite pinpoint. At least not until she suddenly remembered something from when she was a child.

"Down there," she said, moving without waiting for Oberon to carry the torch in her direction so that she could see where she was going.

"Oh, careful now," Oberon said.

Layona climbed down along the cliff edge, careful not to go too quickly in case Oberon lost his footing and needed to lean on her to keep himself up.

Not long into their descent, they needed to bend down and use their hands to keep themselves moving steadily.

Oberon was cautious not to lose the torch on the way down.

Layona's mind wandered as they climbed down to the beach. She remembered being taken by her father secretly to see an adolescent dragon up close one night. The creatures once fascinated her long before she became more indifferent to them as she grew older.

That night, she saw the dragon in a chamber chained by its neck and tail to a wall made of stone; a metal stake drove through its back extremity, connected to a chain so the beast couldn't use the extension of itself to attack.

In those days, Layona had been deep in the studying of dragons to become a scholar of them in a class of Firedrake Scribes; members of a group who witnessed from afar, taking notes on everything about the majestic beasts from the regions they frequented, to what they ate, breeding habits and the like. They were responsible for much of the knowledge anyone had about them.

Becoming accepted into the group of academics who spent their lives learning about the creatures was Layona's dream. Or at least that's what it was meant to look like to those questioning her interest in dragons.

That she enjoyed her studies was true and could not be denied. But she and her father worked toward another end.

Layona was to become a Dragon Scout. The Obscurians were a group of scouts created by her ambitious father, intended to be the foundation of training that would be taught to other groups of hunters beyond Selnes. Layona was the first member.

Because girls were not allowed among the ranks of hunters, she was trained without the guild's knowledge. The future of hunting dragons would begin with her. Scouts, while not instituted widely, were instrumental in locating dragons when hunters reached a block in their search.

During a combat training session, Layona misjudged her footing and moved too soon in an attempt to dodge an attack from the dark red-hued dragon. It swiped its clawed hand at the girl, leaving four gashes along the left side of her face and chest. She hit the floor of stone.

The gentle chill of the breeze surrounding her made her shiver slightly as she and Oberon reached the beach. It reminded her of the cold stone floor against her cheek as she lay on her stomach, suffering from her wounds. She could almost still feel the heat from the pain the talons visited upon her body.

Using all of its strength, the dragon broke free of the chains and, in an effort to finish the job, lunged at her while she lay on the floor defenseless. Before it could succeed, her father intervened, killing the beast.

Layona and Oberon walked along the beach, still not speaking, as the ocean waves hit the shore.

Oberon noticed that Layona's steps quickened as she went further and further beyond the range of light that the torch provided.

Soon, she stopped at a point only feet away from where the water began. Layona took in one breath and knelt, touching the smooth sand. "Can you bring the torch here?" she asked.

Oberon nodded and stepped over, kneeling near her. She never looked up to acknowledge him, and he didn't take offense, especially since he understood what it meant. Something made itself clearer to her.

Layona grabbed some of the sand just as the tide came crashing up against them. She wasn't at all shaken.

Oberon lifted the torch higher, ensuring the water wouldn't snuff out the flame. He gently touched her shoulder, signaling that he was preparing to stand. As he rose and stepped back to gain some distance from the tide as it came and went, she ground the handful of sand and watched as it poured through her fingers. Layona lowered Séya's scarf and caught the scent of the saltwater, the air, and the wet sand around her. And she knew for certain now. A dragon had been there, and not only that but so had Séya.

She stood, looked at the water beyond where they were, and began thinking. "It seems this is where the trail ends," she said, pulling the scarf back up to cover her mouth and nose.

"The trail," Oberon said. "What do you think we might

be onto now?" He could just make out her outline from beyond the torch's light.

She took a moment and turned to face him. "Dragons," she said.

A heavier silence visited itself upon them. Even though it had been a few months since the most recent encounter with one in Selnes, just speaking the name of the beasts carried something of a charge for both of them.

"Hmm," Oberon said. "So what next?"

Layona stepped closer to the light. "We head back to camp for now."

Oberon knew there was more. He stood and looked on expectantly.

"...We will alter our original plan of new towns to visit. Ondriten is the next place we'll need to see after."

"Ondriten?"

"That is the last place I wanted to visit," she said. "But my instincts tell me that if the dragon and witch had even been near there, at least one person would be helpful."

28.

Skylet held on to Solen's rough, scaly hands tightly, rubbing them as though she feared forgetting their texture, the memory of this moment of reuniting buried, lost in the abyss of her mind. She would not have it.

Skylet examined every inch of her brother, making sure he was real, and he did the same. She vowed to herself that no one would take him away this time. When she noticed small pointed stubs on his back that protruded from where the scars were, a new heat began growing in the depths of her belly. "Your wings..." she began, through sniffles, her voice trembling. Skylet's heart felt pierced to hear Solen explain how vicious men cut off his wings to prevent him from escaping when he and the others were first captured.

Solen turned his head slightly to look at his back. "They are returning now," he said, the timbre of his voice picked up slightly. He sounded hopeful for a moment, looking back at his sister, neither turning their gaze away from the other.

Skylet tilted her head slightly.

Solen noticed her face contort. "The pond," he said. "I

do not understand how it works fully, but I'm certain it is responsible."

Skylet looked down at her hands holding and caressing Solen's, and she began to understand how he got there. "And Sebastian?" it sounded like she was asking a question, but she was mostly trying to sort out how he figured into everything for herself.

"He brought me here," Solen said. "I hate to think where I would be if it wasn't for him and his family."

Skylet stepped in closer. "What happened, Solly?"

"Men chased me for two days," he said. "They eventually caught me, but I was knocked out."

Skylet looked on, waiting for more.

"I woke up here, being tended to by the sons of Sebastian."

"I can't tell you how glad I am that..." Skylet paused to take a breath. "I'm really glad you are okay." She squeezed his hands tighter.

"I never thought I would see you again." Solen released her hands and wrapped his arms around his sister again.

They held each other in silence for a moment before Skylet broke it. "Solly," she began, hesitating. She could already feel the weight of what she would say, and though she didn't want to say it, Solen was the only other person who could understand.

"Yes?"

"Did you see, Arca?" her voice trembled again as she spoke his name.

"I did..." Solen's voice suddenly sounded thick with grief. "It was many months after they captured us. I don't know how he found us, but you should have seen him fight."

The youngest of Jessie's adopted younglings, Solen looked up to Arca. Quieter and more introspective, he admired his brother's zest and impulsiveness, even though he saw how it sometimes got Arca into trouble.

Skylet and Solen allowed room to hold Arca's memory between them. The water outside the cavern and from the pond nearby, calmly swishing and splashing, added to the ambiance, but aside from that, they listened to their breathing, holding each other.

"We stopped at his gravesite," Skylet said. "Before we came here."

Solen sighed deeply. A moment followed, and Skylet felt the warm trail of Solen's tears trickling down the side of her cheek, her head nestled just under his chin.

It was then that it occurred to Skylet that Solen didn't know what fate had befallen his brother. Yet, he didn't seem surprised.

"I suppose I expected as much after more than a year passed, and he never came back."

"Oh..."

They held each other a little tighter. Enveloped in Solen's arms, Skylet was reminded of the last moment of closeness she shared with Arca the night he left to search for the others following his fight with Jessie.

"I'd like to one day visit his resting place, too," said Solen. "Tell him how he inspired me. Can we do that?"

Skylet looked up at his face; Solen met her gaze. "Of course we can, Solly," she said. "We'll all go. All of us."

"I wish I felt well enough already," he said. "I would go back for them now."

Skylet perked up and looked at him at the thought of their siblings. "Are they well?"

"I can only hope they are," he replied. "We were being moved to different cells when I escaped."

"Where, Solly? Where were you all held captive?"

"Somewhere with a king who governed the land."

Skylet took a breath. "Jessie," she began. "She showed me a place... a large dungeon. And another..." she paused. "Another dragon."

"Jessie," Solen said, remembering her. "How?"

"She has been communing with me," Skylet grabbed her cloak, drawing Solen's attention to it. "Solly, do you know of another dragon where they held you captive?"

"There were times when I thought I heard grumbling outside where they kept us," he said. "On nights when I wasn't sure I was asleep or awake, they sounded deep, like Jessie's were when we all slept in the mountain, but these grumbles were deeper and louder. But I never saw any other dragon."

Skylet thought back to the vision of large yellow eyes coming out of the earth and couldn't shake the feeling that there was more to what she saw.

***

Oros watched the sea dragons as they cared for Séya. They had ensured the potion that allowed Oros and Séya to breathe underwater was restored well before they struggled for air during their stay. He noticed how they worked fluidly and with a magic he couldn't begin to understand. As the twins swirled and worked their webbed hands around, he was reminded of times during training as a hunter with his uncle. Oros spent so much time studying movements, trying to emulate the spirit of the creatures.

The idea that some dragons were not only skilled fighters but also healers surprised him. He wondered what his Uncle Servalan would say about that, figuring that the great hunter's respect for dragons might only increase. He looked down at Ulonae in his arms, sitting quietly, watching the dragons as awestruck as Oros was.

The twins stopped moving around Séya and placed their hands on her head and chest, respectively. The two brothers leaned forward toward each other, their brows touching. They breathed deeply three times in unison as one being. When they exhaled the final time, water permeated from them with a force that pushed Oros back, causing Ulonae to stir and flail around, nearly floating away from him before Oros grabbed her and held her close again.

"What – happened?" he asked the twin dragons.

Floren caressed Séya's head as she lay on the seaweed bed, having seemingly dozed off since they had arrived at the colony. "She is overcome," he said.

Oros stood and approached. "I – am not – sure I follow – your meaning."

"Her heart is burdened," Aria said.

Oros didn't need to be told anything else. He knelt next to Séya and sat Ulonae near to her. Taking the old woman's hand, he held it as though it were something precious, like a pearl found in deep waters. And Séya was precious, struggling in her personal deep ocean.

"Aria and I will now leave you all alone," said Floren. "I'm afraid all there is for her to do now is rest."

Oros nodded silently, not looking away from Séya.

"Do not hesitate to call upon us should you need it," Aria added.

Floren made eye contact with his brother, and then they swam off.

Oros looked at Séya's face, breathing like she was having a pleasant rest. He noticed her wavy hair swaying with the flow of the water around them and almost in unison with the seaweed beneath her. How strange it was, at least for him, to witness the sight of her inhaling and exhaling underwater as deep as they were.

Oros looked at Ulonae, who sat still near the old woman's face. The young dragon seemed to understand that Séya wasn't well because she made sounds that reminded Oros of the times he heard injured animals in the wilderness as a young boy. "I cannot imagine," he began. Oros rubbed her hand between his as if trying to keep it warm. "The depth of pain you feel is beyond my comprehension. I will likely never connect with one as long as you have with Jessie." His eyes looked at the center of Séya's face as though attempting to will her awake. "You must rest now, and I will step away and allow you that. I ask only one thing of you at this time." He paused, looking back at the young dragon next to him. "Please, do not stray so far, become so lost, that we cannot find you. There is space yet for you."

Oros rested one of his hands on Ulonae's back between her tiny wings. "Selfishly," his voice dropped lower as if to share a secret, "I think an extra and more experienced pair of hands will be greatly needed to assist in caring for a little one like this. They might as well be yours."

He lifted the back of her hand, leaning his brow against it for a moment before collecting Ulonae and standing to give Séya space to rest alone. He sat just outside the resting chamber within earshot. Waiting.

29.

The soldiers and the sentinels landed on the island of Gyenola just before the afternoon. Layona took her time getting herself ready to leave the boat while Oberon had already exited and waited for her on the beach, fielding questions from everyone about their next order of business. "Just a moment," Oberon said to a soldier approaching him. "We will be moving soon."

Layona emerged from the ship and set foot on the beach. She called everyone to attention and began laying out her plan. "Our time here should be brief," she said. "Captain Holera and I will take a member or two with us as we head to Ondriten. As a town is nearby, it seems sensible to continue questioning to see what details come of it. As before, you'll all split up and begin. Take whatever time you need to prepare; the Captain and I will return as soon as possible, eager to hear your reports."

Holera nodded at Layona and grabbed a spear, which leaned against the vessel's side before heading for the group of soldiers nearby, which included Gonden and Delsce. "You two," she said to them. "You'll join me."

They nodded silently.

Holera turned and stared back at Layona and the sentinels, addressing the men closest to her, "We leave at once."

***

In a large courtyard, many men wearing padded training plates with purple and white under-suits stood, lined in columns and rows at attention, awaiting instructions.

A rough-looking man with a scraggly beard and deep lines along his face surveyed his pupils. "Begin!" He exclaimed. His voice was not as gruff as he looked, but it was clear. Sharp. Free of the weight of his experience.

Knowing what to do, the men before him scattered about, looking like mice trapped in a box trying to find a way out. But from where Henricks stood just beyond the edge of the courtyard at the top of a platform of stone steps, it was clear their movements were much more intentional to him. He watched intently as the men set themselves in a triangle formation and held it momentarily. Then, they formed into the shape of a large dragon and held their positions.

Henricks looked on, noticing the men shaped like the head of the creature. His eyes wandered along the group, recognizing the structure of the wings. Henricks' dark eyes scanned back to the tail, and his face suddenly became more serious. He looked down, beginning to wrestle with his feelings about the creatures. After a moment, he held his head up, brushed his wavy hair in the rare moment where he hadn't tied it back, took a breath, and turned to leave the area. He stood, his back to the men, closed his eyes, and listened as the instructor spoke.

"To locate one, you must become one," the man said,

projecting his voice. "To catch one, you must become one. You must be that and more." He let the words move through the courtyard, and the men remained silent to collect them.

"Remember this form. Call upon it any way you know how. In your mind, in your heart, your spirit, your very essence. You must be like a shadow."

Henricks began walking away from the training area. His mind wandered to a time during his first few years in Ondriten when he established and trained the first groups of Dragon Scouts there. The Shadow Drake arm, as they were quietly known in the land, had been a particularly devastating force that aided soldiers and hunters alike in finding and capturing dragons. It was a major contribution that got him appointed as a general on King Rondal's personal security force before becoming a member of the court.

"There you are, Roman!" King Rondal had emerged from seemingly nowhere to interrupt Henricks' thoughts. He held two expertly crafted wooden tankards full of ale. "Here, please," the king said, handing Henricks his drink before he had time to refuse.

"Ah – thank you, Your Grace."

"Would you care to join me for a dish? I'm sure you've yet to eat."

"You would be correct."

"Well, come—"

Before he could complete his thought, the king was interrupted by the commotion caused by two castle guards holding up a seriously injured man as he staggered toward Henricks and the king, breathing heavily.

"Your... Highness..."

"Goodness! Meran?!" Henricks cried, his calm demeanor instantly replaced by the concern of a parent coming upon an injured child. He quickly placed his drink on the stone floor as he rushed to help hold him up along with the soldiers. Looking at the man he once helped train, Henricks noticed that Meran had cuts and burns along his face. His uniform was tattered and charred. Henricks caught the unmistakable and thick scent of dragon fire upon the scout.

"What is the meaning of this?" King Rondal asked, surprised.

"It was urgent he see you, Your Majesty," said one of the guards.

"What happened, Meran?" Henricks asked.

"We stopped... the prisoner..." Meran replied, pausing to take deliberate breaths. "Then... something came...."

"From where?" asked the monarch. "Eastern sky? Western?"

There was silence in the conversation. At the same time, the training cries traveled through the stone archways under which they all stood.

"I suspect that Dorenata City might be at fault," said the king. "We have something in store for them if they wish for a fight."

Henricks scoffed at the king's words and turned to face him. "With due respect, Your Highness, any of the closest cities to Ondriten would be foolish to engage. They no doubt know they stand little chance against our forces, even if they do possess dragons." Henricks paused, turning his attention back to Meran. "This, I fear, is something else."

"The... Wa...ter," said Meran.

King Rondal looked perplexed at Meran's response. "Would you settle for ale instead?" asked the King, holding out his tankard.

"The monster... came from the water..."

"A sea monster?" asked one of the guards holding Meran up.

"A sea dragon," Henricks said almost to himself, surprised. He hadn't considered the creature had come from the water.

Meran was in such pain he could barely stand. His body began to shake.

"It is a miracle you returned to us, Meran," Henricks said. "Now you must rest and have those injuries tended to."

Meran nodded and breathed deeply, struggling to hold himself together.

"Please," Henricks said to the guards. "Take him to the infirmary."

30.

King Rondal and Henricks watched as the guards led Meran away. Henricks remembered his drink and returned to pick it up from the floor.

"You know dragons like no one here, Roman," said the king. "I want you to take some men back where they traced our prisoner."

Henricks turned to face the king. "My King—"

"I know you didn't want to approach the dragon directly. But this is a sea dragon. How often are they seen? Surely you understand the potential value."

"You would risk the destruction of this kingdom?"

"With you, it is a risk I am willing to take."

Henricks took a breath before responding. "I do not do that anymore, my liege."

"Of course," replied the king in a tone that Henricks didn't like. King Rondal took a drink from his tankard, looking across at the man who once saved his life. He did so as if appraising a tool, an object.

Henricks returned his gaze and sighed, allowing a moment to pass before he finally took a drink from his own tankard.

"You know, we've never discussed why you gave up the hunter's life, the path," said the king.

Henricks remained silent.

"One day, we might have to, just you and me."

"Perhaps we will."

The king took another drink, looking intently at Henricks.

"Let your will be done," Henricks said, taking a slight bow. "Your Highness." He turned and walked away from King Rondal, letting out a disapproving huff just loud enough for only himself to recognize.

***

Oros leaned against the far wall of the rocky dome, holding a napping Ulonae in his arms. He looked at the little one, watching her body expand and contract with each breath. His eyes made their way to Séya, who was still resting. Soon, she began to stir.

Oros jolted, noticing that the old woman was beginning to sit up. He collected himself and the baby dragon in his arms and made his way to Séya. He took care not to move too suddenly so as not to wake the young one. Reaching his free hand out, Oros gently touched Séya's shoulder, examining her profile.

Séya reached a hand over to place on top of Oros'.

"I am – all right," she said, turning to meet his gaze.

Oros didn't respond. He just looked at her, a concerned expression on his face.

"I am." Séya nodded, and Oros did the same in acknowledgment.

Séya patted his hand and proceeded to try standing.

Seeming to know this from somewhere far away, Aria and Floren swiftly entered the chamber to help Séya.

Oros stepped aside and watched, admiring their tremendous grace.

"You are finally among us again," said Floren.

"I am," said Séya, still not as lively as Oros had seen her before. "Thank you – for tending to – me."

"It is no trouble at all," Aria replied.

"Where is – Skylet?"

"With father. She is safe."

"Can you – take me – to her?" she asked, looking up at Floren.

Floren met her gaze and nodded once. He knelt, and Aria helped Séya up onto his brother's back.

Aria approached Oros, who climbed onto his back, cradling Ulonae.

The sea dragons took their passengers and swam out of the chamber.

31.

Skylet and Solen stood near the cavern's opening, look-ing out along the colony infirmary. She noticed the calm that seemed to permeate through the area as she saw the other dragons talking with each other, sharing laughs, or resting.

"This is a wonderful place," she said. "So many drag-ons here, living peacefully. I wish Jessie could see it."

Solen looked at her and put an arm on her shoulder, pulling her close.

"She has," said the distinct voice of Sebastian, who had just peered his head into the cavern.

Skylet and Solen looked up to acknowledge him.

"Forgive my interruption," he said. "I see you two are making up for lost time. That pleases me greatly." He smiled warmly at them.

"Sebastian –," Skylet stepped forward.

The dragon put a hand up to stop her. "Please, dear child," he said. "I need no thanks. Your brother was in need. It is that simple." He gave an approving look at Solen. "And how are you fairing, young Solen? Is the sensation return-ing to your wings?"

"Just barely," Solen replied. "I still can't move them yet."

"In time. Do not worry about that."

Skylet touched Solen's arm.

"You said Jessie saw this place before," said Skylet.

"Yes, a very long time ago," replied Sebastian. "She helped me bring many dragons here during the surface purge."

Skylet and Solen looked at each other and then back at Sebastian, who looked at the floor.

"There were many others that we could not save." Sebastian sighed deeply. "Jessie was particularly hurt by this."

Sebastian turned away to face the infirmary and looked around at Skylet and Solen. "She's...," he began. "I can feel her here, but the connection is faint. It is as though she is trying to break through something."

Skylet considered this and realized that it made sense to her. It was the very thing she had been feeling, yet she hadn't the words to describe it.

"You understand." Sebastian said to her, reading her thoughts.

Skylet looked into the eyes of Sebastian, clasping Jessie's claw that hung around her neck.

Something between the two of them was communicated at that moment. She suddenly felt a gentle warmth from the cloak draped over her shoulders. Skylet was compelled to walk toward Sebastian. The dragon closed his eyes and lowered his head to the girl's eye level.

She outstretched her hands and placed them against Sebastian's brow. The cloak reacted as if blown by a heavy wind.

Sebastian saw only darkness at first. "Jess?" he began

to tremble, anticipating what was to come. It would be only a moment before being greeted by a familiar warmth. It was as though he had been embraced by arms much larger than he was.

The dragon began hearing indecipherable whispers. They reached his mind like soft hands against thin drapes, trying to find an opening through.

"Jess," he said. Almost immediately, Sebastian heard a response. A voice so clear, it felt as if it came from him.

"*Ash,*" said the voice. Jessie's pet name for him. Sebastian sobbed. He wrapped his arms around himself as if shielding his heart from the cold. He felt compelled by some force to lift his head, and from within, he heard the voice again: "*Listen,*" it said.

Sebastian found himself suddenly surrounded by the colors and characters of the cosmos. He was not quite in a memory, nor was he in the future. Instead, Sebastian was in a space that contained all time and all memory. He reached his hand before him and was taken into a reverie depicting the last time he saw Jessie. In it, the two dragons shared a quiet moment at the shore of a beach. They sat close together, brow to brow, eyes closed, comforted by each other's soft, pained breath. Their tails wrapped around each other, and they held hands tightly, saying nothing.

Sebastian felt happiness and deep sadness all at once while sitting in the memory, watching it as though it were something completely separate from him. He could see himself and Jessie huddled close.

"We promised," said Jessie.

"We promised," repeated Sebastian. They spoke to each other as much as to themselves.

A space of silence crept between them before Jessie broke it. "We promised to protect them."

"We did. We promised to protect them all."

Jessie gingerly wrapped her arms around Sebastian, pulling him closer as if to merge with him. "My love to Aria and Floren," she said in the lowest tone of voice, as though sending her sentiment directly to his most personal space nestled in the very core of himself. "Every day. Remind them often."

Sebastian felt the weight of her words, and it stung his heart. He just nodded.

"And my love to you, Ash."

They squeezed each other tighter.

"My love to you," she repeated.

To Sebastian, her voice felt like it joined with the soothing breeze that traversed around them. "And my love is yours, Jessie," he said. "I love you."

A faint rumble came from the sky, and then silence once more. The two dragons released each other but still held hands, turning their attention in the direction the sound came from.

Sebastian lowered his gaze, knowing what that it meant. She was being called away.

Jessie looked at Sebastian, but he did not return her gaze. Instead, he let out a sigh that was as contained as he could make it once he became aware of himself.

The sky let out another loud rumble, accompanied by an echoing crash. It seemed like a thunderstorm would follow, but the sky was too clear for that.

The two dragons released each other's hands, and Jessie leaned in to kiss Sebastian's cheek. Then she stepped back and flew off toward the rumbling in the sky.

Still looking at the sand beneath him, he heard Jessie's voice in his head.

Safeguard our hatchlings, love.

He took a deep breath and replied before she got too far out of reach to receive it.

I will. Safeguard the hatchlings, Jess. To the end of this purge.

Yes. To the end of the purge.

Sebastian looked straight ahead of himself at the horizon, where the water met the sky, and then his eyes looked up, watching Jessie become smaller and smaller.

The memory faded, and he returned to the infirmary, where he opened his eyes to find Skylet looking at him. The two held each other's gaze, pregnant with emotion, tears trailing from their eyes.

32.

Skylet felt another world of depth to Jessie that she couldn't hold. As soon as she began attempting to grasp the memory, she dropped to her knees.

"Skylet!" Solen exclaimed as he rushed to hold her.

Sebastian also seemed as though he had the wind taken out of him. For a moment, he was not the regal and respected member of the colony all the dragons looked up to, seeming so much younger and lost. He calmed himself and slowly regained control of his breathing. "Jessie," Sebastian said under his breath. "I can still feel you."

Skylet took a moment to let herself settle into the new space between them. "Where did she go?" asked Skylet.

Sebastian looked at the girl, scanning her face. "She was being called to continue her service," he replied solemnly.

"Service?"

"Yes."

"What kind of..." she trailed off as her eyes shifted away from Sebastian to the cavern ceiling. Her brow furrowed in search of a thought.

The wise dragon tilted his head, watching Skylet. He

could tell when she retrieved the elusive thought because her face had changed. So did her question.

"What is Etherean?" Skylet asked.

"I sense Jessie has joined in this conversation," said Sebastian.

"She has been sending me messages from time to time."

The dragon nodded slowly and let out a sigh. "An Etherean is a special dragon," he said. "Jessie and I were among the small group selected who vowed to protect dragons during and following the purge."

Skylet and Solen sat together and intently looked at the dragon, waiting to hear more.

"With dragons under attack, we knew that most likely adult dragons would be fighting or captured, and it was paramount that any younglings left behind be cared for."

Sebastian took a breath. "Jessie was doing no real good staying here with us," he said. Then, sensing her surprise that Jessie had an extended stay at the colony, Sebastian responded. "Yes, dear Skylet. Jessie was here for a while."

She let the information sink in. "Aria and Floren were the first dragons she adopted then," said Skylet. "She was barren."

"She was," replied Sebastian. "Jessie was here when I birthed them. She stayed the whole time."

Both Solen and Skylet seemed confused but wouldn't dare question what they had just learned.

Sebastian felt their discomfort. "Only a small number of male dragons from the sea possess the ability to bring forth hatchlings in a generation. Sometimes it skips generations, and sometimes there are more carriers than usual."

"She helped raise your sons."

"She did," said Sebastian. "Yet, over the years, she clearly had more children." He nodded toward Skylet and Solen and continued.

"Looking at the two of you here, I can feel her love for you. Especially you, young Skylet. A human child among dragons; so different, and yet your spirit, just as rich, just as worthy as any youngling."

He paused, looked out into the infirmary, and allowed his eyes to rest upon the dragons. Scanning the area, he noticed his sons moving through the infirmary with Oros, Ulonae, and Séya on their backs. Nayess led the way.

Skylet and Solen turned to see them.

"Séya," Solen whispered.

Soon, they were all connected. The sons of Sebastian felt the conflicting thoughts and emotions present. There was a particular pain coming from their father, which they now shared in understanding how much of Jessie's presence was felt. They spoke nothing of it to each other or anyone else. Instead, they stood solemnly and comforted themselves with her memory.

Oros stood tentatively off to the side closest to Floren, holding Ulonae, who sat looking at Solen curiously as he reconnected with Séya.

Skylet stepped back and allowed them to embrace and cry in each other's arms. She glanced over at Oros, who met her gaze. Neither of them moved from their places during such an emotionally charged time.

Sebastion watched the reunion for a moment. He was reminded of a time during the purge when he and Jessie would bring dragons to the colony and watch families reconnect amid such destruction. While some families were together again, they were almost always never whole. They had lost members of their unit; the purge took away their homes and permanently altered their way of life. It always filled him with conflict as he tried to keep his calm and fluid nature. He felt similarly at this time.

Skylet took one step toward Oros and suddenly was overcome with a rush of emotion so intense she dropped to one knee.

"Skylet!" Oros called out.

She looked up at him approaching her, and then a red and orange light replaced her view of him. Like before, her eyes glowed brightly, and she began to levitate from the ground.

"Skylet!" Séya shouted, remembering how the earlier episode transpired.

"Be calm, dear Séya," Sebastian said; his tone was even, almost as if he were not fully present. As though he, too, were ascending somewhere.

He looked up and examined Skylet. Her eyes opened wide, glowing brilliantly. Her hands were fists at her sides, Sebastian noticed. He took a step toward her and reached out his hands to touch them. The dragon closed his eyes, and he was linked to a vision from Jessie.

Skylet and Sebastion could now see the large cell chamber where the other dragon siblings were kept. It was dark and cold, just like in the earlier vision she had. Before they could fully orient themselves, they saw a new image of the same hillside that Skylet had seen earlier. This time, it contracted and expanded just enough to be barely noticeable, as though it were breathing. The very pit of her stomach shook violently.

Do not fear. Sebastian's voice was soothing in her head. *I am here.*

"No, NO!" Skylet exclaimed, shaking her head.

We are here, child.

She heard Sebastian's voice again, but she felt Jessie's as well this time. They spoke in unison, a singular force.

Sebastian gently guided Skylet back down to the ground. Her eyes stopped glowing, and she collapsed in the dragon's arms.

"Who is it?" she asked through labored breathing. "Who is in the mountain?"

Sebastian took a moment. He felt he had done a well enough job shielding his thoughts from Skylet. But then again, her fear was too great to be open to anything else. He knew full well what lay beneath the mountain's surface, and he, too, felt a weight to look upon the sight. If he was honest with himself, he was afraid too.

"Someone I haven't seen for ages," Sebastian said solemnly.

"Who is it, Sebastian? Why am I so afraid?"

Sebastian didn't answer. He just cradled Skylet, stroking her head.

"We have to find the others," Skylet said through tears. "Jessie is telling us. We can't stay here any longer than we already have."

"Jessie is certainly sending a message," said Sebastian. "I agree. It is time."

Solen approached her and leaned his head against hers as Sebastian continued to hold her. "We are together now," he said. "Let's go and get them."

"Young Solen," Sebastian said to him. "You will have to lead us back to where you escaped."

Solen nodded.

"We must take special care. Your wings are not yet fully returned."

"I am not worried at all about my wings," said the young dragon. "I want to see my family again. Whatever I have to do to achieve that, wings or not, I will lead."

"We have to leave now," Skylet said.

"I recommend we wait until it is later in the day. Twilight," said Sebastian. "We'll need all the cover we can get. There'll be more people we must avoid, armies and whomever else. We cannot afford to be caught."

"Then that is what we must do," chimed in Oros. They all diverted their attention to him. "We'll be ready.

<h1 style="text-align:center">33.</h1>

Ondriten was a place Layona had read about in books as a child. She visited only once, never having any real reason to be there. Her life was so far removed from anything royal that it was the last thing on her mind. Yet, she found herself walking through the busy streets of the kingdom. Holera and her men followed just behind Layona, Oberon, and another sentinel.

They soon arrived at the Castle of Purple Flowers. The very site of which perked up Oberon. "Whatever your feelings on this place," he began. "The vibrancy of those roses is something to behold, isn't it?"

Layona said nothing. She only nodded.

"The way the scent meets one's nose well before getting as close as we are is lovely," said Oberon. "Elian would appreciate it." He allowed a smirk, thinking of his daughters. After a few more steps, he looked over at Layona, and like recently on their evening hike, he noticed her demeanor. "You seem heavier than when we landed this morning."

Layona continued walking. She pondered on how to respond.

"I don't want this visit to be a waste of our time," she sighed.

"Of course."

Soon enough, they reached the pathway that led directly to the castle doors. Layona noted two burly, bearded guards standing still on either side. A third, clean-shaven one with an angular jawline, paced from left to right at the bottom of the cobblestone stairs that led to the doors.

The sentinels and soldiers got closer. The guard noticed and immediately perked up, stopping his pacing. "Good morning to you." The castle guard was very serious and without a trace of warmth in his tone.

"And to you," Layona replied in kind.

A slight tilt of his head suggested the guard seemed surprised by this, expecting Oberon to be the one to speak. "State your business here at the castle," he said, looking at Oberon.

Oberon stared back, recognizing the dynamics at play. He decided he wouldn't entertain the guard with a response. Instead, he would see how long the lack of eye contact with Layona would last.

"We are officials from Greater Selnes," Layona began. "We must see the royal court's chief member."

"What for?"

"We are in search of fugitives who must be brought to justice."

"I'm afraid that's not possible," said the guard.

"Please," said Layona, pulling out the parchment with the necessary information. "Look at this."

The guard took the parchment in his hand and scanned it. "I see," he said. "Serious crimes indeed." He paused before speaking again. "How do you think the king's advisor can assist you? He is quite preoccupied."

He returned the parchment and glanced back at Layona, doing a double take. He now looked at her intently, appraising her features. His face contorted in confusion, not being able to place why.

Layona was unfazed by his newfound recognition of her presence. "Call it intuition," she said, not wanting to say any more than she had to.

"I'm afraid I cannot allow entrance solely on 'intuition,' Mistress."

"Principal Sentry, please." Layona raised a hand slightly, correcting him.

"Our commander is fallen," said Holera forcefully, interrupting the exchange. She stepped forward to stand near Layona. "From one soldier to another, can you please send for him? We must see justice done."

Holera's face was hard and seemed to communicate something only she and the guard understood. The two stared at one another with the same dark eyes and furrowed brows. The castle guard nodded, and Holera did likewise.

He turned around and made his way to the tall castle doors.

"Thank you," Layona said under her breath to Holera.

"I... want justice as much as you do."

Just before he could get to the gates, they began to open from the inside. A group of men exited the castle. Layona noticed they weren't standard-looking soldiers. These men wore light armor plates for maximum flexibility, which were double-lined with dragon skin. This was a precaution should they need to fight something beyond their comprehension.

Not only that, she knew with complete certainty that

these were Dragon Scouts. She recognized the format and placement of their garb, having worn early versions of it herself as a child. The brainchild of one man, there was no doubt he would be joining the outriders.

Soon enough, she saw him. Henricks. He followed behind two men as they went down the stairs.

The clean-shaven castle guard approached and stopped him. "Master Henricks, you have visitors," he said.

"I do not have time," replied Henricks irritably. "I am on assignment from His Majesty."

"Master Henricks," the guard said, trying to stop him.

It was no use. Once Henricks reached the bottom of the stairs, he found himself facing a stoic Layona. Henricks stood unsettlingly still as he met her gaze. "Oh... Nona," he said, flustered. "Quite the surprise."

"I am the Principal Sentinel," she said. "I am just here to ask you a few questions. Then I'll be on my way."

"Master Henricks," the castle guard caught up to him. He began to speak, but he was surprised by something oddly similar between Henricks and Layona and rethought saying anything. The guard now better understood his earlier confusion. With that, he took a step back and watched.

"Of course," said Henricks. "Principal Sentinel. How can I assist you?" He seemed stung with each word he spoke.

"We are in search of fugitives," she said to him.

"If I may," he began, gesturing a hand to step off to the side, away from the group. "Might we speak separately?"

She obliged, and the two stepped just out of earshot of everyone.

"What is this about?" Henricks asked.

Layona took out the parchment and handed it to him.

"We are in search of a dragon and a sorceress who must answer for their crimes."

Henricks calmly looked at the parchment and rolled it up, handing it back to her. "It seems a hunter is also among the group." He paused.

"Well?" she said expectantly. "Do you know anything about it? Might you have seen something?"

"Listen," he began. "I am aware of the ordeal that transpired in Selnes, but I have seen no dragon. Nor have I seen a sorceress, or hunter for that matter."

"I suppose not," she said testily.

"I would tell you if I had," he said.

"I'm sure you would," Layona rolled her eyes.

"Please," said Henricks. "I've no reason to mislead you."

"So, hunters still protect their own then, yes?"

Henricks blinked at her.

"We breathe by the hunt, breath of the blade made of moonlight, or burn by enemy's fire." Layona delivered the words of the oath of Dragonhunters with a quiet fervor that struck Henricks. She stood upright as though she were a giant in his presence. Henricks was slightly hunched across from her. It was a sight that few had seen of the king's right-hand man.

She looked at his face. Her expression was stone solid, and nothing Henricks did or said could seem to penetrate it.

He sighed and looked down from her at the ground. "Not anymore," he said. "But you already know this."

Layona looked over at Oberon, who was watching the exchange.

"Really? And what of these scouts," Layona gestured to the men standing off to the side, awaiting his instruction.

"You are undoubtedly leading them."

"I am on assignment from the king to investigate an attack."

"Obviously, a dragon attack, then."

"A sea dragon," he said. "Obviously."

"Well, I've taken enough of your time. We will let you carry out the king's orders." She nodded and immediately turned away.

"Wait," said Henricks.

Layona turned to face him.

"How is –?"

"She is well," Layona interjected sharply, waving him off. "I'll send your thoughts."

"Your gift came back," said Henricks.

"Good. Keep it. I do not want it."

Henricks sighed.

Layona turned and addressed her group.

"Let us head back now," she said, walking ahead of everyone.

Oberon and Henricks locked eyes and exchanged nods as they went their respective ways.

34.

The party from Selnes left the castle with little fanfare. Children ran around them, playing or gawking at them in awe.

Oberon kept pace with Layona, who walked faster than when they were on their way to the castle. He sensed her feelings but decided not to speak on them, knowing the trouble he might be in for.

Meanwhile, the Principal Sentinel seemed lost in her thoughts, huffing with every step and releasing more steam from her system.

The soldiers held their thoughts about what had transpired before them. "That was a waste of time," Gonden said, loud enough that only his comrades could hear.

"Humph," Delsce agreed. "What did we learn? Nothing. No one saw the witch or the dragon. All the distance we covered for what? To come across the splendor of the great kingdom."

"Have you forgotten to use your eyes?" Holera interjected.

"What do you mean?" asked Gonden.

"Did you not see the men coming from the castle?"

Neither of them responded.

"Their armor, lined with dragon skin." She paused, letting the words sink in. "Someone has seen a dragon somewhere."

The silence between them gave way to the sound of gravel and dead leaves crunching beneath their boots as they moved along the trail.

"What do we do, Captain?"

"We stay patient," she said. "Wait for the spark. Then we take action."

****

Henricks and his men traversed the forest of redwoods and birch trees in relative silence. He was deep in thought about the visit from Layona, which was the last thing he expected. He tried his best to regain focus on the task ahead, but that only made him angry at King Rondal and more furious at himself. As he traveled in a state that suggested he was not present, the overwhelming thought in his mind was Layona. Nona, he called her as a child. Or Nona Scout, a name he used during their training sessions together. Despite seeing her as an adult, she was still Nona to him.

Her arrival after so many years of distance was bittersweet. She was as beautiful as Henricks imagined she might be when she grew up, even more than that. She was both a reminder of something good, something once comfortable, and the physical embodiment of his past returning to haunt him. Then, of course, his past always haunted him. It was never too far from his mind. It was why he ended up in Ondriten.

With each step, his mind hurled him back to when Layona was a child. He was a harder man then. An intense life as a Dragonhunter left little room for tenderness, even for those closest to him. He remembered the nights he would secretly train the girl in all things dragon-related against her mother's wishes. He wanted to make sure she understood every element of her enemy. She would be the best student there ever was when it came to dragons. Henricks would ensure this.

He taught her everything from fighting techniques for different dragons to correctly ingesting dragon blood for more effective use. It had to be dried on parchment or old leaves to be burned and inhaled into the system rather than mixed in a drink. The effects were more potent that way.

Henricks held many moments of pride within himself, barely ever expressing to her when she excelled, which she often did. Then, when he wanted to share those feelings with her, he couldn't because she was gone.

On the night of the Great Slaughter of Selnes, Henricks decided he would be the one to stop it. He did start it, after all.

Not expecting his wife to be home when he brought Layona back with an injury from a training session with dragons, Henricks and his wife argued. As a town council member of Selnes, she sometimes attended late meetings. That night, the meeting finished early, and she came home to the mortifying sight of her daughter lying on a cot in the main room with a few bandages over the side of her face, running down her neck and to the top of her chest. Her training garb ripped.

Naiyera's tall frame stood in the open doorway. She

exhaled when she saw Henricks sitting over their child near a small fire, a hand on the girl's brow. "What happened to her?" asked Naiyera through breaths as she quickly approached her daughter on the cot. She knelt to get a closer look.

"Hello, Mother," young Layona said.

Naiyera removed her gloves and placed a smooth hand on the side of the girl's face that was not bandaged. Her eyes examined Layona, stroking her long hair. "Are you all right, dear?"

"I am fine, Mother," said Layona, touching Naiyera's comforting arm.

"You must think I'm some fool, Henricks." Naiyera scolded, still looking at her daughter on the cot.

"She is fine," he replied. He turned away and looked into the fire.

The room fell silent except for the crackling flames and the breathing of the three of them huddled close together. The force of Naiyera's breath made it clear to Henricks that she had more to say. He took in a quiet, deep inhale of his own and braced himself.

Naiyera set her gloves aside and stood up. She walked away from the cot and calmly unclipped her thick and long dark cape, which draped over her shoulder, placing it on one of the wooden chairs in the dining area. "This is exactly what I was worried about," she said tersely.

Henricks was silent.

"I've kept quiet about you training her. I've known about it for some time and said nothing to you or the fellowship about it."

"And why would you? Aren't you proud of her?" Henricks asked. "You should see her."

Layona shifted herself on the cot and stared at the ceiling of their home. She wished she had enough energy to leave the room.

"Of course, I am proud of her. I'm aware of her gifts. But as a member of the council, this is a violation of the rules for hunters, which don't allow girls to be trained."

"I know the *rules*," Henricks hissed, annoyed. "The council should have no say in our affairs. They couldn't possibly understand what it is we do."

Naiyera was silent.

"Besides, I happen to be a pretty good hunter," said Henricks. "I think I know the violations well enough."

"This isn't about your ego, Henricks! This is about our child!" Her voice was higher in tone now.

"Our child is great!" He turned away from the fire to face Naiyera, meeting her timbre. "She just made a small miscalculation. What better lesson is there? She'll be even better now!"

"How could you allow this?!"

"She isn't a princess, Naiyera," Henricks shot back.

"She shouldn't have to be for you to care about her safety!"

Henricks gave her a pained look. How could she say such a thing? "I do care about her safety," he said, lowering his voice. "Look. The scratches are healing."

He knelt and gingerly peeled off some of Layona's bandages. The dragon blood he had applied following the accident was from one that had not yet reached its prime, so the blood was not as potent and was less instantaneous in how it healed injuries.

"No more, Henricks." Naiyera was firm and clear. There was no mistaking. She meant those words.

Henricks scoffed and turned away from her.

"Don't look away from me. Do you understand? Nona is finished with dragons."

Henricks turned his attention to the fire. "She wanted to do it in the first place," he said quietly. "I did not force her. Perhaps I pushed too hard tonight. But —"

"NO MORE!" Naiyera interjected, her arms folded.

The room was quiet.

"Mother," Layona began. "I will be all right. May I just—"

"I don't want you dead, girl. The answer is no."

"Mother."

"Layona, No!"

The conversation was over. There was nothing else to express. The fire burned on, and they all kept whatever thoughts they had to themselves.

Naiyera released a deep breath and walked to the cot. She knelt and took her daughter's hand. "Listen, girl," she began. She started to continue her thought until she heard something in the distance outside that sounded like a scream.

Naiyera turned to face the small window opening beyond the cot. One scream became a few more, but they were still distant. They all looked at each other and then out of the window. Soon after, rumblings and tremors came from the ground. They were faint at first but quickly became strong and visceral. The whole home shook.

It seemed every sound faded away, and Henricks heard one word rising amongst all the growing screams and rumblings.

"*Dragon!! Dragon!!*"

Someone shouted the warning. The unmistakable sound of a bellowing roar followed it.

"You went on a hunt this evening," Naiyera told Henricks, helping Layona get up from the cot. "Go and grab your bag, girl."

With a Dragonhunter in the family, they had planned for the likely possibility of moving quickly. Layona collected her things as fast as she could.

"Did you take her with you?" she asked, grabbing her cloak, some rolled-up parchments, and a few important family heirlooms.

"I did not..." Henricks replied, who stopped to get a glimpse of what was happening through the window space. Fire burned in the town square nearby. The dragon was destroying everything, screaming as if in pain.

"Come, Layona!" Naiyera shouted. "Why is it here? Dragons do not attack unprovoked, right?"

Layona arrived back and stood next to her mother.

Henricks looked away from the window and began muttering something to himself as he went to collect his sword and other gear.

"Babies," he said as if realizing some deep truth. "It was the babies." He hadn't known that Naiyera understood what he thought he mumbled.

"What have you done, Henricks? What happened tonight?"

"Get far away from here, do you understand? The other hunters and I will address this at once."

"Father," Layona said. "Come with us."

"That dragon must be stopped, Nona. With Servalan away, the remaining hunters must engage it."

He grabbed his daughter's hand and nudged his wife toward the door. "Go, now!" he said.

Naiyera gave Henricks a knowing and disapproving

look before turning to open the door.

"If you can get to town's edge near the start of the forest—"

A loud crash hit just outside the house, and terrible rumblings from the ground followed while screams and fires burned all around. Suddenly, something large crashed through the ceiling of the home, reducing it to rubble.

When Henricks came back to himself, he realized he was buried under a pile of wood and stone debris. He dug himself out as quickly as he could among the chaos that surrounded him.

"Nona!" he cried, looking frantically around himself. "Naiyera!"

The muffled shout of a child told him she was near.

"Father!"

Henricks frantically dug to reach Layona, her hand protruding through the rubble. He pulled her out and quickly looked her over to see how badly she was hurt.

"I am all right, Father," Layona said. "Mother!"

Henricks and Layona went straight into the rubble and continued digging for Naiyera, who they soon found. Her eyes were closed, and she was unresponsive.

Henricks placed his palm on her smooth and tanned face, which surprisingly only had a few minor scrapes.

"Naiyera," he said forcefully.

She didn't respond.

"Mother!" Layona cried.

Naiyera grumbled and moaned before raising her voice in pain.

"Can you move, dear?" asked Henricks.

"My leg..." Naiyera said, through grunts, wincing in pain.

Henricks looked up and saw the giant dragon just beyond a great fire and rubble. It looked like a huge dog frolicking around playfully. But this wasn't a game of fetch. Its large tail swiped and thrashed about, destroying homes and crushing families as they tried to escape. The fire it breathed seemed never-ending; walls of flame were so high Henricks couldn't see the night sky from where he was. Now, all he saw was rage. He needed to put an end to it.

"Take this," he said to Layona, pulling out a flask of dragon blood and handing it to her. "Put this on whatever wounds you find on her."

Layona took the flask and wasted no time.

Henricks looked around the debris and found his sheathed sword. He quickly jumped off of the pile of rubble, walking in the direction of the dragon.

"Father!"

"Stay with your mother!"

"Henricks!" exclaimed Naiyera.

"I will return," he said before running off.

"Henricks! HENRICKS!"

Her screams were drowned out by the crashing, rumbling, and cries of the townspeople.

"He has gone, Mother," Layona said in a low tone.

"I cannot... I cannot see you, girl," Naiyera said.

Layona looked down to see her mother's eyes open. Nothing looked out of place as far as she could tell. "What?"

"I cannot see," Naiyera's breath quickening.

"Mother!"

"Darkness. Everything is dark."

Just then, other neighbors stopped as they ran by. "Naiyera! Layona!" one exclaimed.

"Help! Help here!" Layona cried.

A group of men and women came to help them and

get them away from the desolation. Henricks, meanwhile, moved with quiet confidence. While everyone ran away from the destruction, he jogged toward it. He was driven by anger at the dragon. But if he was honest, he was angrier at himself. How could he not anticipate this? No matter now, he thought. Time to rectify his mistake.

He stepped through crowds of townspeople and dodged falling and fiery debris to reach the heart of the chaos. There, he saw, up close, the dragon of a dark blue, nearly black hue. The fires around it lit its giant body in all of its grand splendor as it stomped and raged, slamming into buildings and breathing fire everywhere.

Henricks quickly scanned his surroundings, searching for a point of attack, when he noticed the broken and burned bodies of men who had unsuccessfully attempted to engage the dragon. He wasted no more time, rushing in through a wall of flame and began slashing at the dragon with his sword before moving out of the way of a swift tail movement, slamming into the ground.

The dragon turned and looked down at Henricks as he zipped around. He managed to lock eyes with the monster and felt something stir within himself that was more than a recognition of his enemy. He had come face to face now with the direct consequence of his choices as a Dragonhunter. In that, he recognized, there was no method or tactic to how his opponent attacked the town. Every bit of its energy was poured into the destruction. It was clear to Henricks that this dragon was not planning on surviving the night.

They battled with an intensity unlike anything Henricks had experienced, even at his advanced skill stage. There was no room for the more formal aspects of fighting an enemy of respect between the two. This was a brawl. Whatever it took to end it was what was going to happen.

Henricks dodged attacks with great skill, intent on shaping the battle to his liking, but the erratic nature of the dragon was too much for him to manage. He tried to anticipate an attack with its oversized hands or tail, and he would be lucky and guess correctly at times. Other times, he would narrowly miss as he slashed and cut away at the dragon, drawing blood with each strike.

At the height of the battle, when its speed was at its quickest, there seemed to be that elusive moment in a fight for some hunters, but not all of them. That moment was almost one of great calm, a kind of state where the act of fighting didn't feel like a chore but rather like walking or breathing. Each strike and movement was as easy as could be.

It lasted only a moment, and just as Henricks was getting comfortable in it, he shook himself out of it, and as he did, a devastating swipe of the dragon's tail came at him. It connected, knocking him into a tree and dislocating his left shoulder. Seeing that Henricks was down and in pain, the dragon wasted no time as it rushed through a wall of fire, nearly drooling at the prospect of killing him.

Henricks had only seconds to force himself up with the help of his sword and fall out of the way of the swiping attack of the dragon's large hand. He wasn't wholly unscathed; the sharp talons ripped along his left leg, blood immediately pouring from the gashes.

The dragon turned and saw Henricks lying on his back, struggling to get up. This was the time to finish it. The monster rushed Henricks, and as it was preparing to slam the total weight of itself on top of him, Henricks saw fire building within the creature's open mouth. He pulled out a small pouch that he slammed on the ground with his good hand. It popped, and a burst of bright light emitted from it, blinding them both and hurting his hand.

The light only lasted a second, long enough for Henricks to roll himself out of the way and grab his sword. Neither of them could fully see yet, but Henricks felt his way to the dragon and began delivering slash after devastating slash with his good arm. The dragon flailed around desperately, tripping Henricks up where he landed on his back again. His sight was returning, and so was the dragon's. In one move, Henricks was able to get to one knee, and the dragon rushed and went in for a swipe with sharp talons, narrowly missing Henricks' face. He saw a vulnerable point just underneath the dragon's arm, and Henricks knew the battle was over. He gave a mighty thrust of his sword in the heart of the pocket of the dragon's underarm and twisted it, finishing the move with a swipe, leaving a deep gash in the dragon's arm where blood poured from the wound, covering Henricks' blade and running down to his hand.

The dragon fell away from him, landing on its back, howling in pain.

As quickly as he could, Henricks spread the copious amounts of dragon blood from the sword over his wounded leg and crawled to the back end of the dragon, where he was sure to be out of reach of its hands. He weaved around to one of the exposed hind legs and slashed a vulnerable point there to ensure movement would be difficult. The dragon kicked and howled. Henricks twisted out of the way from an oncoming slip of its tail, falling back on one knee. He thought to stab at it but decided not to.

When Henricks reached a far enough point from the dragon, he stood, looking over the immense, fallen beast as it writhed and cried out, breathing fire into the sky. He thought he noticed tears coming from the creature, which struck something within him. He had never seen or even thought dragons could cry.

Turning away, he limped off from the battle site; the wounded screams of the dragon penetrated his core as he left the creature to be claimed by whomever and be dealt with accordingly.

Now, almost twenty years later, on a mission from the king to potentially battle a sea monster, he could still hear the cries of the great dragon Ulonae. Henricks understood what he had taken away from her, and that was only the beginning of his punishment.

35.

Layona and the group were in the thick of the woods now. Soon, they would reach a small town just south of the border that separated the castle town of Ondriten from the rest of the island.

Holera broke from her men and went up the few feet to Layona. "So, do you believe him?" she asked.

"What?" replied Layona, returning from her thoughts to the present moment.

Oberon slowed himself down slightly to allow the two ladies space to speak. He held his hand out to the other sentinel in their party to signify that he should do the same.

"Do you believe what he said about not seeing a dragon?"

"It doesn't matter what I believe."

"I see," Holera said, turning to steal a glance at her men.

They were watching her.

Oberon caught the exchange but thought nothing of it. Holera turned back to look ahead of herself, keeping pace with Layona.

"I'll share what I think," she said. "I think that someone knows something."

Layona didn't respond.

"Why do you think the men we saw were in dragon-skinned armor?"

"I don't really care, Captain." Layona was slightly irritated. "For whatever it might be worth to you, they are going to investigate a dragon that frequents the area near the ocean.

"Do you mean to say that this dragon is from the sea?"

"I don't believe we are searching for the same creature, Captain."

"Hmm," Holera said, almost to herself.

They continued walking in silence for a moment or two more before Holera took a breath. "Well, Principal," she began. "I think I would like to see for myself."

Layona just scoffed, still looking ahead of herself.

Holera let out a breath and, in a blindingly fast action, tripped Layona with a foot sweep. In a literal blink of an eye, The Principal Sentinel found herself against the earth's surface, her face in the dirt.

Holera jumped on Layona's back and pressed down on her opponent's head with one hand while holding a knife to the back of her neck with the other. "Don't," she said with a calm sternness to Layona. The captain turned to look behind herself.

Holera's men knew what to do.

Oberon could barely draw his weapon to help before he was overtaken and tackled from behind by Delsce.

The third sentinel never saw what hit him in the back of the head. He, too, was on the ground holding the back of his head, screaming in pain, while Gonden had a knee in the center of his back.

Holera waited until it looked like the sentinels were subdued enough before she leaned close to the side of Layona's head to speak. "Forgive me," she began. "I no longer care to waste any further time, moving from town to town, questioning people, yielding no results."

"You will answer to the council for this," Layona managed to get out through heavy breaths.

"And who..." she paused to take a breath. "Who will answer for Brawns?"

"What?" Layona grunted.

"He was like a brother to me."

Layona was surprised. This was the first bit of real emotion coming from Holera.

"I will see justice done if I have to do it myself."

"That... that was not our task, Captain."

"You are a sentinel, Principal. That was never *your* task."

There was a pause.

"But it was always mine. I am a soldier first. And as a soldier, I do not have the patience for a trial."

"Captain..."

"You will tell your men not to pursue us. We are separating ourselves from this company."

Layona was silent.

Holera pressed the knife into Layona's neck. "You need to say it."

"Sentinels, stand aside... the soldiers will not continue with us."

Holera turned, looked at her men, and nodded. They released Oberon and the other sentinel but kept their respective weapons trained on them.

"And what will you do?"

Holera didn't respond. She jumped off Layona, keeping the knife pointed ahead of herself should Layona get up.

"After me," Holera called to her men as she backed away from Layona.

When they were at a satisfactory distance from the group, Holera, and the soldiers turned away and disappeared back the way they came into the forest.

36.

Skylet leaned against a jagged wall of earth, looking out over the many dragons in the infirmary cavern. She thought of Beresay, Tithla, and Eagan, her remaining siblings. Reconnecting with Solen was further food for the fire burning within her. And then there was Jessie, whose energy was so present in the colony.

Skylet's mind wandered back to all the times they shared and returned to the feeling of surprise at how much she still hadn't known of Jessie. Only having been around her a mere blip in the space of existence that was the dragon's long life, she wanted to learn more. She had many questions for Sebastian but was anxious about what lay ahead. Though it wasn't quite dusk, it was later in the day, and Skylet began feeling useless.

Solen wasn't too far behind. He approached her and looked out over the infirmary with her. "I can see you are holding a great deal of weight on you," he said. "I was just thinking a moment ago how much smaller you were the last time I saw you. And now, you are a mature one."

Skylet turned to her left and stroked the side of his face. "Jessie is showing me things," she said. "Lots of things,

Solly. And I don't know how to hold it all."

"Listen. Listen to me, Skylet." Solen turned to face her and put his large hands on her shoulders. "Look around you. Look at all of us."

They both turned to see Sebastian conversing with his sons, standing over Séya and Oros as they doted on Ulonae. The youngling seemed to be enjoying herself in the place of many dragons.

"We will share the burden with you."

Skylet took a deep breath, and tears formed in her eyes. Before a drop could fall, Solen put the back of a large finger to her face to wipe it, careful not to scrape her with his talon.

She found herself surprised at how smooth his scaled hand was. Perhaps all the time he spent in the healing waters had something to do with that.

"I need to tell you something," she said.

"Anything," he replied, placing a hand on her face.

"I have a feeling," she paused.

"What is it, Skylet?" Solen's face was concerned.

"I think another dragon is guarding the others."

"What? What do you mean?"

"I mean, I've seen something through my communion with Jessie. Something big. And alive. And... waiting."

Solen said nothing. He just nodded slowly while maintaining eye contact with her.

Skylet looked over at the group again, and her eyes made their way to Sebastian. "I think Sebastian knows, too," she said.

"Really? How?"

"He didn't answer my question when I asked about it." She paused and then turned to face Solen again. "I think it's personal for him, that dragon."

Solen looked over at the group.

"Keep this between us, please," she pleaded. "I'm scared."

Solen turned and looked back at her, pulling her in for a hug. "Of course."

At the far end of the infirmary, Ulysus entered. He took his time passing by all of the dragons recovering from their injuries. In a manner that they all respected Sebastian, so too did they also appreciate Ulysus. The dragons greeted him as he passed by, and he returned the sentiment warmly, yet it was clear that Ulysus had something on his mind. He made a beeline straight for the back of the infirmary, where Sebastian and everyone gathered. Just before he reached them, Aria noticed and greeted the elder dragon. "Great Ulysus," he said.

"Young Aria," Ulysus nodded.

"Ulysus," said Sebastian. "Is all well?"

"It is," Ulysus bowed slightly.

"Oh? And what is it that brings you here?"

"This one," said Ulysus, pointing at Skylet.

Solen and Skylet looked at each other and back at the group before turning their attention to Ulysus, confused.

"I see," Sebastian exhaled deeply, yet his tone remained calm. "Ulysus, please. Everyone here--"

"I just would like a word with her," said the elder dragon. "If I may, wise one."

Sebastian tilted his head. Then he nodded. "Be kind, Ulysus."

"Of course," the serpent-like dragon entered the space where everyone was and kept his eyes on Skylet, a furrowed expression on his face. He swerved his long body deeper into the area and moved in close, coiling himself around so all of him could fit into the rest area.

Solen held her firmly as if to affirm the girl's safety with him.

Ulysus noticed this. "You may calm yourself, young one," said Ulysus to him. "I have no intention of harming this child you seem to care so much for."

Solen stood firm, meeting Ulysus' stern gaze with his own.

The mature dragon pointed a clawed index finger at Skylet's cloak. "Wherever did you get such a beautifully hued garment?" he asked. "I must say in all my many years, I cannot say I've ever come across one of my kind with as lovely a color."

There was a pause between them.

Skylet took a breath as Ulysus waited expectantly for a response.

She looked up at Solen, whose eyes were on her, and released him. Skylet stepped closer to Ulysus and stood straight, meeting the elder dragon's gaze. "I was raised by a dragon," she said. "This cloak is one of the last gifts I received from her."

Ulysus' face softened. Skylet's did not. She remained stoic, staring through Ulysus.

"Dear child," he began. "Forgive me."

Skylet exhaled.

"I have not met very many of your kind who are, shall we say, genuine."

"I understand," Skylet replied. "Outside of them," she gestured to Séya and Oros. "Neither have I."

"Then it seems we have something in common," said Ulysus with a slight smile.

"It does look that way."

Skylet looked away from Ulysus' face and noticed old scars down his neck and some further down on his forearms and hands. She recognized the type. They were strikingly similar to the ones she had seen on Jessie once before. Moonbeam Metal scars.

Skylet looked around at everyone watching the conversation, the tension slowly dissipating with every passing moment. She noticed them beginning to have other discussions.

Turning back to face Ulysus, she said, "Men took my family away too. That is why I am here."

Ulysus said nothing. He just looked at her knowingly.

Skylet stepped closer to him and spoke low enough that she was sure only he could hear. "My brother and I will be leaving here to go find them and bring them home."

Ulysus nodded slowly, the two not breaking eye contact. He understood exactly what she wasn't saying. "And you will not be hindered," he said, giving Skylet a wink.

Skylet nodded and then turned to face Solen, who met her gaze. Then he turned away to look out over the busy infirmary.

37.

Henricks and his men kept a consistent pace, carefully avoiding entering the neighboring towns closest to the kingdom. He didn't want anyone sparking any premature concern if they could help it. As ideal as that might have been, avoiding all townspeople was not entirely possible. The occasional forest explorer or someone out hunting for food would cross paths with the men on their journey. Not too many words were exchanged. No matter how much someone might have wanted to engage in a pleasant conversation, Henricks made it clear he and his men had no time.

Henricks was known widely beyond the walls of the kingdom, and when he was seen, it was rarely for social events. Almost always, some investigation was happening, and this time was no different.

Soon, they could hear the water from the ocean not far away, but he could sense, by how some of their steps dropped, that the men could use a rest. They had been traveling for a long while on foot, and it would not be long before the sun began setting. Henricks didn't want to take any chances should they find themselves in a skirmish, especially when there was less light. He wanted the men not to be exhausted. "This is a good place for us to rest a while," he said, stopping to turn and face them.

They sat and shared small bags of nuts and fruit. Talking among themselves in hushed tones, Henricks turned his back to them and looked ahead, thinking about his plan once they reached the beach. He hadn't the slightest idea. The men would do anything he ordered, but he wouldn't send them to their deaths should they come across the enemy they were sent to engage.

He thought momentarily before hearing rustling from different points in the woods beyond them.

Taking a knife from a sheath at his side, Henricks tapped it twice against the metal underside of a brace he wore on his left forearm.

The men knew what that sound meant. They all silenced themselves and got into position should they need to defend themselves from a wild animal or something else.

Henricks' eyes narrowed as he scanned the area beyond him. He was as still as a statue. So were the other scouts in his company. A gentle breeze rustled through the trees as the calming sound merged with that of birds chirping in the distance.

Henricks pointed the knife to the right, signaling to the men that they would no longer be traveling straight ahead. While he wasn't sure he and the other scouts were being watched, he wouldn't risk not preparing.

Quickly and stealthily, Henricks and his men made their way in the new direction like a breeze traversing through the area. They were as quiet as the smallest creatures of the woods. So much so that by the time Holera and her fellow soldiers peeked from behind the trees sheltering them, she couldn't tell whether the scouts were still there. The soldiers would have to track and follow them again.

***

Layona and the sentinels traveled in silence until they stopped at the foot of a large birch tree. The young man who had been hit over the head by one of Holera's men had a lump and was bleeding. Layona sat him down to check his injury and decided it was time to change his bandages. She gingerly unraveled the coverings around his head as he winced and groaned to himself.

Oberon stepped in close. "May I assist," he asked.

"Can you take these, please?" Layona asked, handing the old bandages to him. "Thank you."

"Of course," Oberon rolled them up carefully as though they would turn to dust and blow away in his hands. Then he put them into a pocket of his long overcoat. He reached into a different one, pulled out a thick fabric handkerchief, and handed it to Layona.

Without missing a step or even making eye contact with Oberon, she reached out and took it. She carefully wiped the blood from the areas where it ran to. When she finished, Layona pulled out a new small roll of cloth bandages from a pouch at her waist and carefully wrapped the young sentinel's head.

His shoulders jolted up for the first two wraps.

"Hold still," she said. "I am being as gentle as I can."

"Yes, Principal."

Layona let out a heavy sigh as she finished off wrapping the bandage. Her mind went back to the ordeal with

Holera and her men. Her brow furrowed, and Oberon noticed. He stepped closer to put a hand on her shoulder. "Allow me," he said, removing a small knife from a sheath at his waist and using it to cut the end of the bandages off so that Layona could tie them behind the young sentinel's neck.

"Thank you," she said.

Oberon nodded and stepped back to allow her to finish.

Layona touched the young man's head as though appraising a work of art she had just created. Once she saw that everything looked neat enough, she let a hand softly glide to his shoulder and patted it twice as an indicator that he was free to stand up and continue the journey with them.

"Thank you," the young man said.

"Sentinel," Layona said, nodding, helping him to his feet.

Soon, they were on their way again. No one said a word for the first several steps away from the birch tree and deeper into a new section of the woods.

Oberon broke the silence. "So, what—"

"No," Layona said, cutting him off.

He calmly continued. "As the Principal Sentinel, you have to make decisions that are, to put it mildly, challenging."

"Oberon, please."

"Sometimes, those decisions can challenge the very core of your beliefs. I know."

"Well, maybe you'd like the position back," Layona shot back.

"That is not exactly what I mean to say."

Layona exhaled audibly. "I know," she said. "I am very

sorry. I just... I'd rather not discuss what to do next about the soldiers."

The young sentinel deliberately slowed his pace down, allowing himself to fall just behind the two of them, sensing that this was a conversation he felt best not to be in the way of.

They hiked for a while longer before Layona spoke again. "The truth is, I don't know what to do about them."

"I understand."

"I don't think I want to be Principal anything anymore."

"How can you say that?"

"What about our report to the council? How can I explain what happened?"

"We both will be there," Oberon gestured to the younger sentinel hiking with them. "We will report the occurrence. Plain and simple. Beyond that, let the council do what they will."

Layona shook her head.

"You would forfeit my faith in you?"

"What?"

"If you were to forfeit your role, you would forfeit not only my faith but all those who believe in you. The challenges come with this job," he said. "This does not mean we stop pressing."

The sounds of their footsteps snapping twigs and crunching dried leaves broke the silence for a moment before Oberon continued. "Besides, the girls adore you."

Layona looked at him as he spoke now. She loved his daughters, who weren't that much younger than she. Feeling like she let Oberon down was one thing. But it was something else and much deeper to consider disappointing them.

"You give them hope," Oberon said. "You've shown them an example of what they can strive for and achieve in whatever they deem worthy of their time."

"But I have failed—" she said.

"And you will fail again," replied Oberon. "And so have I."

He stopped talking for a moment as they came upon an area of higher rock formations. He climbed over them and extended a hand out to Layona to help her climb over it. He did the same for the other young sentinel. Once they had overcome the obstacle and began walking again, Oberon continued, "You are perfectly capable of holding the post, Principal. You have come this far."

Layona looked down, and then she looked ahead of herself as they kept going.

"And if I have anything to say about it, you will go further still."

That was the end of it.

They both looked ahead and kept pace on the hike. Soon, they could hear the water of the ocean in the distance. For Layona, they couldn't get there fast enough. She couldn't wait to board the ship and begin putting everything about this trip to Ondriten behind her. Henricks and the dragons; Holera and the soldiers, everything. She wanted it all over with so she could return to her life beyond this mission. Her imagination ran wild at the thought.

38.

It was very near time to leave the colony. Skylet and Solen huddled together, going over the plan in hushed tones while everyone else paid them no attention. They would slip away unnoticed and make their way to the surface. There was only one problem they needed to sort out: air. Getting out beyond the infirmary without it would be impossible, let alone getting out of the colony and to the surface. Somehow, they would have to solve that problem, but who would help?

Skylet remembered that Sebastian and Séya combined their power to make it possible for everyone to breathe underwater as they journeyed to the colony. If they were to leave without anyone's knowledge, someone else besides Ulysus would need to be included.

Skylet and Solen stopped talking for a moment to have space to think more about achieving their goal. Unfortunately for them, they would not finish the conversation. Séya, Oros, and Ulonae were approaching.

"She seemed excited to join you here," Séya said of Ulonae. "After all, she has never seen other dragons before today."

Oros put the youngling down and let her go over to Solen.

The dragon collected her in his arms. "She is a darling," he said.

"Her name is Ulonae," said Séya.

"What a beautiful name." Solen gently stroked her head.

Séya smiled as she watched the two dragons.

Oros noticed it was the first time in a while that she looked so lively.

Solen was such a natural; it was as though he had held younglings all along. Dragons of the woods, like Solen, had an innate ability to nurture. They were viewed by those who revered them as cultivators and protectors of all things within the vast woods of the world. Woodland dragons also had a knack for gardening, a fact that Séya reveled in when she used to engage in the activity with the young Solen.

So few dragons of the wood were known to have survived following the purge after hunters and others burned down much of the forests they occupied, but thankfully, the blessings of the wood live on through Solen.

He rocked young Ulonae gently in his arm while the others looked on, quietly smiling.

Oros watched them bonding, and though it pleased him, he couldn't help but feel a tinge of sadness that Ulonae seemed to take a quick liking to Solen now. He understood, of course, but the little one had nestled her way into some part of him. Oros pondered on this for a while before his thoughts went back to Skylet. He watched as she and the two dragons huddled close to each other.

Séya leaned in and stood over them. She placed her

hands on their shoulders. "You've grown so much since I saw you last, Solen."

The dragon looked up and smiled at the old woman.

"Jessie would be so proud of you," Séya shook her head. "She *is* proud of you. Wouldn't you say, girl?" She turned her attention to Skylet, her hand still resting on the girl's shoulder.

"What?"

"Jessie," said Séya. "She is proud of Solen, isn't she?"

An intense warmth suddenly emanated from the cloak draped over Skylet's shoulders. She closed her eyes, and the cape performed a subtle flap and brushed against Séya's arm.

The old woman smiled warmly and kept her eyes trained on Skylet.

The girl opened her eyes, meeting Séya's gaze. "She is," Skylet said. "Jessie is proud... and happy..."

Séya let out a deep sigh as her eyes welled up with tears. "I'm sorry, girl."

Skylet looked down at baby Ulonae and then turned her attention to the other dragons resting in the infirmary.

"I apologize for my lack of openness when you told me about Jessie's messages."

Skylet turned back to face the old woman and stood up, looking at the brown eyes she found so familiar.

"I'm..." Séya began. "I just miss her."

"Me too," replied Skylet. "But, she is here... She isn't clear, but... I feel her."

Séya nodded slowly, looking slightly pained.

Skylet stepped in and embraced Séya, who held her tightly. "Are you feeling better, Séya?"

"I am improving, thank you."

They released each other.

"Any new messages from her about the others?"

Skylet hesitated.

Overhearing, Solen interrupted the conversation. "Séya," he said, just loud enough that she could hear but not so loud that Ulonae was disturbed from her comfortable space in Solen's arms.

"Yes?" she turned to face him.

"Did she take to eating fruits as quickly as some of us did when we were younglings?" He chuckled to emphasize the sentiment.

"Honestly, she seemed so excited by a new environment and new faces that looked nothing like hers. She had to be reminded there was food in front of her to eat." Séya snickered.

"So much stimulation for you, little one," Solen turned his attention to Ulonae, who cooed quietly.

"She is overly excited about everything and is learning all the time," said Séya.

There was a brief pause, during which time Oros contorted his face as he observed the exchange. Something didn't feel right about it to him. He came back to himself and noticed that Solen was looking at him.

Not shying away, Oros met his gaze. Both of them bore serious, skeptical expressions on their faces.

Séya and Skylet looked at each other and back to the two, exchanging shared stares at one another.

"Oh, you two haven't truly been introduced," Séya began tentatively. "Oros, this is Solen. One of the dragons Jessie and I cared for when he was a little one."

Oros nodded and bowed as a sign of respect to the dragon.

"Solen, this is—" Séya was cut off.

"I know who he is," said the dragon, whose tone wasn't so much sharp as it felt almost dismissive. "A long lost sibling and the man responsible for my brother's death. Welcome to the family."

The air between them all was now thick with tension.

"Solly," Skylet began as she touched his free forearm.

"Skylet told me everything."

Oros was silent.

"It is more complex than you realize, Solly," Séya interjected.

"After being held captive for several years, you'll forgive me if I am mistrustful of a man wearing a cloak so obviously meant to be a prize for his efforts." He sounded more aloof than angry. Yet, not warm toward Oros.

"Tell me, hunter," said the dragon. "Why are you here?"

"I am here to see the journey through and help retrieve the lost dragons."

"Well, you may have earned their trust," Solen replied before turning his head away from Oros slightly but still keeping in him his peripheral view, "but in my experience, men like you have never been worthy of trust."

Oros remained silent.

Solen turned back to face the man he called a hunter. "And I will not be easy to win over," he said.

Oros nodded slowly, not breaking his eye contact with the dragon. "I am pleased to make your acquaintance, Master Solen."

"No, the pleasure is mine, hunter."

"Solly," Séya began. "He is no longer a Dragonhunter."

"Of course, Séya," Solen was not convinced, and his

tone reflected as much. He looked down at Ulonae with a smile. "A hunter never stops hunting," he said under his breath. "They do not change. Only the targets do."

39.

Ulysus went down the aisles of the infirmary. He took his time, having genuine conversations with the young patients. Some of the really young ones he stopped to play games with or tell funny stories to.

Soon, he came upon a young female drake lying on her side in the makeshift cot, staring off somewhere. She seemed to be resting, but her eyes were not closed. Her pinkish-white hue made her almost sparkle in the light of the torch fires along the walls.

She's perfect, thought Ulysus as he approached her and curled a part of himself near the cot. "Hello, child," he said.

"Hello, Master Ulysus," she replied. "Are you in need of something?"

"Not at all, dear. I am merely here to see how your injuries are healing."

"I still do not have full use of my leg, but every day, more and more feeling is returning."

"Well, thank the skies for that," the old serpent dragon smiled warmly.

The pinkish-white drake returned a smile to him, seeming to perk up more. She sat up on her cot.

"I wonder," Ulysus turned his head away from the young one, looking in both directions as though he were expecting someone to arrive. "Do you have a favorite treat, child?"

She tilted her head, raising an eyebrow. "Master?"

Ulysus chuckled.

"I mean from the surface, dear," he replied. "If you could have one thing from the surface that you long for, what would you have?"

She looked down with sadness, remembering her life before the purge made its way to her home. "There was one thing," she began, looking away from Ulysus as though she could see the memory off somewhere. "Something called a Nutberry Tart."

Ulysus smiled, watching as she allowed the memory to overtake her.

"My aunt used to make it for my siblings and me whenever we saw her. She used berries and nuts found in the trees and bushes where she lived. It was so tasty."

"That sounds like a wonderful treat and a beautiful time," said Ulysus.

"It was," she said.

"Listen, child. I wonder, what would you say to enjoying something like that tart soon?"

"Wherever would you get the ingredients to make it?"

"Well, I cannot promise to get you the tart. However, what if we could bring back some of the berries and nuts you remember?"

The young dragon smiled. "I think that sounds wonderful."

"Wonderful," Ulysus replied.

Almost as soon as he spoke, he noticed her expression

change to a somber one.

"What is the matter, dear?"

"Master Ulysus, it is dangerous on the surface. You may not return."

Ulysus leaned in and placed a hand on the edge of her cot. Smirking, he nodded. "It is dangerous, but I think I will not be alone."

He winked and touched her forehead before turning away and uncoiling himself to leave the area.

Ulysus had originally intended to come up with a decent excuse to get to the surface. Something that wasn't so intimate. Yet, he found this was a much better excuse than anything else to get back to the surface, which he hadn't seen in quite a while.

He walked, noticed Sebastian and everyone still conversing just out over the infirmary, and made a beeline for Floren. "Young Floren," said Ulysus.

He turned to greet the elder serpentine dragon. "Master Ulysus, yes?"

"I have a favor to ask of you?"

"Of course."

"Let us talk this way," Ulysus gestured away from the group.

Sebastian and Aria glanced over, as did Séya and Oros, but thought little of it.

Meanwhile, Skylet and Solen quietly watched.

"I must go to the surface," Ulysus said. "I am bringing a couple of our distinguished guests with us."

Floren was confused. "If I may ask, why? Aren't you the least bit concerned about the dangers above?"

"Well, of course I am, young one. But, you see, I have made a promise to one of our dear children here that I would bring something special back for her."

"Oh, I see. And what is it you require from me, sir?"

"Well, I will need help generating the necessary air for them to travel."

"Oh! Father can—"

"No, young Floren," said Ulysus. "It must be you. Your father has enough on his plate, after all. Managing the remainder of our guests and making them feel more at home. You understand."

Floren looked down at the floor. He wasn't sure why, but something felt off about the request. "I cannot produce anything that lasts as long as what Father can."

Ulysus looked down and let out a breath.

"I'll need Aria's help."

Ulysus looked toward Floren, who met his gaze, anticipating the next thing the elder dragon might say.

"So be it," Ulysus replied. "And if your father asks to know what we're up to, just send him my way."

Floren nodded. "When do you need this request fulfilled?"

"As quickly as you can would be ideal."

Floren bowed and casually made his way over to his brother, who was standing near Sebastian. Ulysus stayed where he was and glanced at Skylet and Solen, who acknowledged him. Then, they all turned their attention to the sea dragons and watched.

Floren touched his brother's shoulder gently, and Aria immediately sensed conflict. "What is it?" he asked.

"I need your help," Floren replied.

Sebastian then turned his attention to his sons. "Is everything all right?"

"Yes, Father," Floren said.

Sebastian furrowed his brow. "You both know that I can read your thoughts."

They stopped in their tracks.

"I do not believe there is nothing is amiss. But I remember our previous discussion about reading your thoughts so, I will refrain from that now."

"We just want to surprise someone special here in the infirmary."

"Ah, I see," replied Sebastian. "You might have just expressed that." He smirked at them and then gave a slight nod, which they understood was their cue to go about their business.

Sebastian watched as Floren and Aria huddled close to Ulysus and began talking. He then went over to where Skylet and the group were and addressed them. "Well," he began. "I must say what a joy it is to see you all connected and conversing with one another. It is one of the few things that comfort me amidst the heaviness on our minds this day."

"Yes," Séya said, turning to meet Sebastian's gaze.

No one else responded; they all silently agreed.

"I will retreat to my chamber until we must leave, which will not be too much longer."

"Leave?" Séya asked.

Oros also perked up at hearing this, looking at Sebastian.

"We intend to journey to the castle in Ondriten to retrieve the missing family members."

"I see," Séya said. "Well, I'm sure we'll all be ready."

Oros turned to her and started to question whether or not Séya was even ready to make such a trip to a castle that was likely on edge. But he thought better of that. He shook his head and turned his attention back to Séya and the group.

Sebastian also thought to question Séya's response. Except he did not. "Of course, dear Séya. Rest awhile here with everyone." He bowed at the group and turned to leave, making his way down through the infirmary.

Skylet stood up and stepped toward Séya. She touched her shoulder. "Are you well enough to travel, Séya?"

Oros thought that Skylet was bold to ask such a question. But then again, the rapport was there between them, he reasoned.

"I want to see them too," Séya said, her voice low with a hint of irritation. "Whoever kept them in captivity all this time will answer to us, girl."

Skylet nodded and looked down, her hand now touching Séya's forearm. She held it there, rubbing her thumb over the old woman's arm.

40.

Ulysus, Floren, and Aria watched as Sebastian made his way through and out of the infirmary.

"All right," Ulysus began. "To the healing chamber."

The elder dragon led the way beyond where Skylet and the group were to the chamber where Solen had been recovering. They went all the way to the very back, where the room curved into a deep crevasse. It was only so big, so all three of the large dragons of different shapes would not fit in. It didn't matter as much anyway. They just needed a place to work.

"Now, what is the best way for our guests to breathe in the water," Ulysus asked.

"Father can—"

Floren touched his brother's shoulder. "There are several ways," Floren said. Then he turned to Aria. "I was considering the spheres."

"What? How many?"

"We will need enough for the trip to the surface and back. And Solen will be accompanying us."

Aria looked down and nodded. He stepped into a position and held out his palms. "Let us commence."

Floren held out his hands and closed his eyes.

Ulysus stood by and watched.

***

Henricks allowed his men to move ahead of him as he fell behind to discreetly scan for anyone who didn't belong following the group. Though he saw no one, he couldn't shake the suspicion.

He and the scouts had gone far off their path to disrupt the scent of any potential followers, but at this point, they were beginning to loop around and return to the correct way towards their destination. Now, the temperature in the air was changing, the breeze blowing toward them was cooler, and they could hear the water in the distance, as alive as ever and always.

It was then that Henricks slowed himself to a stop and let his men move ahead. They knew where they were meant to end up. The last scout in the group turned to address Henricks. "Master Henricks," he said.

Henricks turned to face him and shook his head.

The scout nodded once and took his leave.

Henricks looked on as the scouts were nearly beyond his line of sight, and then, he turned around, watched, and listened. Surrounded by the overgrowth and the richness of the deep forest, he allowed himself to embrace the calmness of the area.

He took some deep breaths, centered himself, and allowed his body to relax, which he realized he hadn't really done in a while. He found himself in a rare moment of peace, something he tried to get to now and again, but he often gave up because the weight of his past mistakes always seemed too heavy. Right then, however, everything fell away from him. The rift between him and his family, the dragon unit he was responsible for shattering, the guilt, and the emotional turmoil were not with him then. What he was left with was himself and the forest, and the gentle breeze that whisked through the area.

A rustling in the distance, slightly louder than the sounds that resulted from the breeze, confirmed his suspicions that he was not alone. The untrained ear would not have registered such a subtle change in the volume of the swishing. But his ear was not untrained due to his years of learning to hunt dragons. Those same skills translated to hunting anything.

Henricks closed his eyes and smirked slightly before becoming serious again and addressing the silence of the woods. He opened his eyes. "I am not alone," he said, his voice firm and clear. "Reveal yourself so that we may speak calmly."

Henricks stood and waited.

There was no response or movement.

Henricks took another breath and sat cross-legged in the middle of the soft earth, making himself comfortable.

Still, there was no response.

He sat a while longer, looking up at the trees and the sky visible beyond them, before removing some of his gear and placing his sword and knife beside him. He continued waiting.

Just as he began thinking about changing his seating arrangement, someone stepped out from behind a large oak tree. It was Captain Holera. She held her spear upright and stood, looking stern and serious, yet something was unsure about how she began approaching. She seemed to

Henricks almost like a nervous child.

His eyes met her as she moved closer. "Hello," he said.

Holera nodded at him.

"Did I see you at the castle earlier? You seem familiar."

"You might have," said Holera cagily.

"I notice that the Principal Sentinel is not with you."

"You could say we parted ways."

"I see," Henricks said calmly, pausing to take in what he had heard. He didn't like how it sounded coming from Holera, worrying that something may have happened to Layona at the hands of the soldiers, but he did very well hiding his concern from the captain. He gently began fixing his outer robes, looking down at his crossed legs. "And is she... safe?"

"I suppose she is."

Henricks nodded slowly.

"Who is she to you?"

"Someone I hadn't seen in years before today."

There was a brief silence between the two as Holera digested what she heard. Her mind began to unpack Henricks' words until he brought her back to the conversation. "I would ask if your family in arms would care to join us, but I'm afraid I do not have enough snacks for everyone."

Holera frowned at the remark.

Recognizing her confusion, Henricks pulled a small brown bag from the belt at his waist and untied the string at the top of it. He dumped some of the nuts into his hand and showed her. "Would you care for some?"

Holera stuck the back of her spear into the soft earth and took a seat across from Henricks. She, too, crossed her legs and got herself comfortable. "What I would care for is answers," she said. "The dragon you are looking for. I want to know about it."

"What is it you would like to know?"

"Have you seen it before?"

"I have not," said Henricks. "But I have seen its work."

"What do you mean?"

"A party of men encountered the beast," he paused for effect and to have a few nuts. "Only one returned. Just barely."

"So they sent you to investigate."

"It is slightly more involved than that, but precisely."

A silence crept into the conversation again. The leaves on the trees rustled as the breath of wind blew through. The muted sound of Henricks crunching the nuts periodically became an interesting additional instrument to the music of the wild that surrounded them.

"Why you?"

"You could say that I have a unique... history regarding the creatures."

"You a hunter?"

"I used to be," said Henricks, carefully putting a few nuts into his mouth as though he were beginning to allow his mind to wander. "I was quite good as well; I made it all the way to Stage 3." Allowing a bit of hubris to show, he sounded both proud and pained, sharing that last bit.

"Where from?"

"Selnes. That was my home for many years."

Holera's eyes widened slightly upon hearing that bit of information. "So you saw the destruction."

Henricks nodded. "I stopped it."

Holera looked on expectantly.

"I also effectively started it all," he said.

"How do you mean?" she asked.

"How long have you been a soldier of the Selnes army, if I may ask?" Henricks deflected.

Holera made a face that showed she didn't particularly care for the abrupt shift in conversation. "Seven years," she said.

"Ah, well, after the destruction." He put a few more nuts into his mouth, and before chewing, he spoke again. "But, you remember it, do you not?"

"I am familiar. My family and I came to Selnes afterward by about two years."

"I see."

"What of it?" she asked. "How did you cause the destruction?"

"I killed the dragon's children before they even hatched."

Holera blinked. She said nothing.

"No one, not even the king, knows this." Henricks considered this for a moment and then shook his head.

"Well, I suppose that isn't entirely true. One person knew." He stopped short of saying anything more.

The captain immediately understood, nodding. She looked down at the earth before her and waited for him to continue.

"In response, the dragon laid waste to Selnes. What a terrible night," said Henricks, his mind returning to the aftermath of the destruction.

"So many soldiers, so many families, gone."

Holera thought about the words she had just heard. Tensions between the sentinels and soldiers were understood more deeply by her. Somehow, it made the divide that much clearer sitting across from someone who was there the night the great town of Selnes was destroyed.

"Something tells me you know about that," said Henricks, bringing her back to the moment.

"What?"

"Loss, young soldier. Is it not what is driving you?"

"I want justice."

"A compromise, a middle ground offered to us by the fates, no?"

Holera looked away from him and off to the trees around them.

"Since we can never recover what is now lost to us, sentiments like 'peace' and 'vengeance' or 'justice,' anything we can grasp, become the consolation prize."

"You sound as though you know something about that."

"I may," said Henricks, beginning to tie the bag of nuts up to place back onto his belt.

"So, what is your prize for what you've lost?"

"It is less a prize for me than it is punishment."

Holera looked on expectantly.

"My past," he said. "The weight of the ultimate of my transgressions. The pain I've caused for which there is nothing to alleviate it. It is just."

"In times of war, those of us called to fight must do whatever is necessary to survive," Holera said, taking a breath. "I understand that hunters and dragons have been at odds for a long while... You did what you had to." Her attempt to make Henricks feel better was ultimately unsuccessful.

"Did I?" asked Henricks rhetorically. "Snuffing out defenseless, unborn dragons was a necessary sacrifice?"

He saw in his mind's eye the memory of the great dragon's tears as she screamed in her pain and defeat.

"If we are to survive, yes."

Henricks looked down and released a deep breath; he seemed almost sad for her. "No, dear soldier," said Henricks. "There is no prize for me at the end of all this. With any luck, my carrying this weight will soon be finished."

"Well, before that," began Holera, "my men and I wish to accompany you to see this dragon for ourselves."

"I will not stop you should you care to be present," said Henricks. "But I caution you only this once. If the dragon appears, stay as far away as you can. Whatever you do, do not engage."

Holera nodded slowly. "You sound like the Principal Sentinel," she said, remembering Layona's briefing to the group before they made the trek to Ondriten. "Or rather, she sounds like you."

Henricks chuckled. "Then she has learned well."

"She is your daughter."

"A fact I believe she would wish untrue these days."

Henricks nodded and stood himself up. He reached a hand out to help Holera, and without a thought, she took it.

41.

Skylet and Solen found their way to the edge of the infirmary just around the corner before the pool of water began. It took nearly all the energy they could muster to separate from the group. With Séya and Oros preoccupied with baby Ulonae, it seemed the best time to get away.

They stood together and waited. Every so often, Skylet would look around the corner to see if anyone had followed them. Once, Nayess stopped by to see what was going on. She seemed suspicious and asked them what they were doing, hiding out around the corner. They expressed that they were waiting for Ulysus, which seemed enough for her not to ask any further questions. She walked off and threw a glance at them that said that she still thought it was strange that they were there.

After a few moments more of silence between them, they heard steps approaching. When they looked, they saw Ulysus holding a translucent bag that seemed to be made of water. In it were several small orbs the size of a ball that a child might play with.

"Here," he said quietly, handing the bag to Skylet. "Each of you takes one now."

They reached into the bag, and each pulled out a small orb. Skylet noticed that it felt spongy, as though if she squeezed it, it would release water.

"What are we supposed to do with it?" Solen asked.

"We're supposed to eat it," Skylet replied.

"Really? How will it work for me? I'm much bigger than you are."

"Not to worry, young Solen," Ulysus assured. "The brothers have concocted something that should sustain even you for at least as long as we need for the journey. That said, you will have to use two to Skylet's single one."

"Do we have enough?" asked Skylet.

"We should be fine."

With that, they popped a spongy orb into their mouths and chewed. A burst of gel permeated the inside. As Skylet expected, it had an almost gummy consistency, like some of the candy treats Séya would bring back from her trips. At first, the taste was quite horrid. Skylet thought it was akin to what a kind of sludge from the bottom of the ocean floor would taste like. However, midway through the chewing, a subtle sweetness came through the terrible earthy flavor, and she began to appreciate it.

Solen didn't seem to mind either way how it tasted. His mind was purely focused on the function.

"Now, let us not waste time," said Ulysus. "Jump in as soon as I do. I will generate a force by which you can travel alongside me. Do not move too much in either direction, young Solen, lest you become thrown outside of the current I create."

He took a moment to look around and see whether or not anyone was too close. Skylet and Solen did the same. When they were satisfied, Ulysus nodded and jumped into the pool. Skylet and Solen quickly followed. Then, they were off to traverse through the colony.

They hadn't counted on Oros watching them from behind a rock at a distance. The cooing of baby Ulonae stepping up to him brought his attention to her. He knelt and picked her up, looking back at the area where Skylet, Solen, and Ulysus had disappeared.

***

Layona and her group were yards away from the ship when something stopped them. The tide slowly lifted the vessel, subtly shifting it to the left. Layona saw the boat move and wondered how far off it might float, hoping the anchor would keep it from going too far.

Oberon tripped over a large rock, catching himself, which took her attention away from the ship to help him up. That was when the young sentinel startled them. "Look out there!" he cried.

Layona and Oberon whipped around to see what he was talking about. The water rose in a dome shape, as though a large bubble would form from it or a massive chunk of the earth would grow from beneath it.

They all kept a sharp eye on it as it subsided. No one moved for a moment. When nothing happened, they started walking again, and that is when Layona saw it. Something shifted around on the surface of the water. From their distance, they were all still too far away to make anything out with any clarity.

The closer they got, Layona could see the water splashing violently. She put her hands out to gesture to her company to tread slowly, keeping her eyes on the ocean. She wondered whether it was a sea turtle or some other such creature until she saw the large head of a golden brown dragon pop up from the surface, with a person holding tightly to its neck.

Her eyes widened, and she wasted no time. Layona dived sideways onto the earth. "Down!" She whispered sharply to the sentinels, who followed her lead without question and jumped to the ground.

"What is that?" The young sentinel whispered in fear.

"Shh!" Layona meant that. It was enough for him to keep quiet.

Meanwhile, Ulysus, Solen, and Skylet made their way to land, checking to make sure no one spotted them. They quickly scurried into the thick of the woods. As far as they knew, they were alone, though it troubled Skylet to see the ship nearby. She worried about who saw them and what they might do but then pushed the thought from her mind, resigning herself to the fact that, at this point, it didn't matter who saw them. She was going to find her siblings. She knew the risk was high moving before dusk, but there was a fire in her gut from Jesse's last vision. Risk or not, they were going to the castle.

Skylet almost hoped they would run into someone wishing to stop them. She was ready to defend the group if necessary.

"Does this area look familiar to you," Ulysus asked Solen once they were inland enough to feel they had a moment to speak.

"It does," Solen replied as he looked around the area quickly. "It was dark, but I am certain the scouts chased me somewhere near here."

"Then my job is done here," said Ulysus.

"How do you mean?" Solen faced the elder serpentine dragon.

"You needed to get out of the colony discreetly. You have done that. I must now leave you."

"Where are you going, Ulysus?" Skylet asked.

"I made a promise to a young one in the infirmary..." he trailed off.

Skylet stepped toward him and outstretched her arms. The two embraced each other, and Skylet pecked his cheek.

When they separated, Solen took the elder dragon's hand, pulling him in for a hug.

"Take special care, young one," said Ulysus.

"And you."

Just as they were going their separate ways, Ulysus turned around to address them once more. "One other thing," he said. "Nuts and berries, young Solen."

Solen's head tilted.

"Have you the slightest idea where I might find them?"

42.

Layona stayed pressed to the earth. It was as though if she tried hard enough, she could sink herself beneath the surface so deep that if one were to walk over where her body was buried, they wouldn't be able to tell she was there. She, Oberon, and the other young sentinel waited for what felt to her like a very long time. Having trained to scout dragons, she was familiar with spending long periods in one position not to arouse a potential target. Being on the earth there at that moment, having seen a dragon for the first time since she was a child, opened the door to a feeling within her that took her back to the place of being a scout-in-training and trying to remain inconspicuous.

Once she felt it was safe to take a look, she slowly got up on one knee.

"Principal," the young sentinel whispered.

She did not respond. Layona just put a hand out to touch his leg and then gestured her palm downward twice as if to say, 'keep your voice down.' She looked up above some of the brush and bushes toward the coast and saw no sign of them. The dragons and the person were gone. "The two of you, get back to the ship," she said in a voice low enough to surprise Oberon, whose eyebrows raised at the sound. He couldn't remember if he had ever heard her pitch reach that depth.

"What are you thinking?" he asked her.

"I don't know yet."

"You cannot move on something you do not know," he replied. "They all could be a real threat, and you do not know whether they mean good or ill." Oberon knew her well. She was going to track them.

"I have a feeling," Layona said.

"A feeling? Principal, please," the young sentinel chimed in.

"Listen," she said. "I am not suggesting you both return to the ship." Layona paused to let the words sink in. She didn't need to say anything further. This was an order.

Oberon released a deep breath.

"Part of being a Principal is being trusted," he said. "I am trusting you. We are trusting you to return to the ship." Oberon clenched his fists tightly. Having gone through versions of the very same conversations with his daughters, he knew Layona was going anyway, whether he liked it or not. He had to let her. "Return so that we may go back to Selnes."

"I will."

The two stared at each other, but it didn't last long. Layona nodded once and turned away from them.

In the same movement, Oberon started to step toward her, his hand partially outstretched. She turned away so quickly that she missed the gesture.

In a few seconds, she disappeared from them like a mist back into the depths of the forest. He watched as the brush and leaves from the bushes rustled in her wake and then released a breath. "Come along, young man," Oberon said to his companion, patting his back as they headed toward the ship.

***

Oros was back sitting above the infirmary. Ulonae rolled and frolicked near him, running between him and Séya. He took a good moment to look at all the injured dragons. Though his mind was on Skylet and Solen, wondering where they went and why, he couldn't help but grapple with the sight before him. In the deepest part of himself, some piece of him felt somehow responsible for the pain and misery these unfortunate souls were experiencing.

True, he wasn't directly responsible for each and every one of the dragons here in the infirmary, but his history was. He was part of an order whose job it was to hunt dragons. He didn't kill every dragon he faced. For all he knew, one of several of his injured or maimed victims could be recovering right there before him. There were so many there was no real way to tell.

"I imagine all of this must be quite the challenge for you," said Séya, breaking through Oros' thoughts.

"What?" Oros turned around to face her.

"Being around all of these dragons, which you don't have to engage in a fight with." She chuckled.

Oros wasn't amused. Nor was he disappointed. Rather, it was as though he were coming out of some trance-like state and needed some time to catch on to Séya's comment. "It is... difficult, quite frankly."

Séya nodded understandingly.

"I'm afraid I no longer know what I am to do. I feel as

though I have nothing." He sighed. Then he looked down at the ground, seeming to consider his words more deeply. "Well, nothing except to do right by Skylet."

Séya smiled warmly at him. "You do have that," she said. "I feel so badly that the two of you haven't really been able to speak since the burial site."

"She needs her space. I understand that."

"You have a pure heart, sweet Oros," Séya said. "I wish your parents could see you now."

Oros just nodded in silence, and the conversation ceased. Then Séya seemed to have a revelation about something. "Oh! I wonder what is taking them so long?"

Skylet and Solen made up some excuse about needing to leave the infirmary for another area of the colony because Ulysus wanted to show them something important about the history of the water colony and how Jessie helped preserve it. While there seemed to be at least some shred of truth in that story, Oros didn't trust it, having seen Skylet and Solen move away from the group to chat with Ulysus and leave the area with Sebastian's sons. This was another skill he learned from Uncle Servalan, who was rarely trusting of people as he always seemed to know when things were off.

Now Oros noticed. Yet he had been so deep in thought when he returned after having followed them to the exit of the infirmary he hadn't realized how much time had passed since they had gone. He had a feeling they had left the colony but didn't want to worry Séya by sharing that.

A thought entered his mind, and without sitting with it to explore it, he stood up and walked away from Séya and Ulonae. It was as though he was all by himself.

"Whatever is the matter?" Séya asked.

Oros turned to address her. "I don't know yet," he said.

This was not the whole truth. He knew he had seen Aria, Floren, and Ulysus enter the healing chamber. Still, only Ulysus came out with something that looked like a bag attached to the back of his leg, which suggested to Oros that it was something that Ulysus didn't want to have displayed in the open for anyone to ask questions about. Whatever it was, he had noticed Skylet and Solen taking something out of that bag. He reasoned that it was important enough to get them to follow Ulysus into and through the colony once more.

Air, he thought to himself. *That is what he gave them.* He was confident that the twins had something to do with what he saw as Ulysus, Skylet, and Solen left the infirmary.

What was going on with Aria and Floren? Why hadn't they come out of the healing chamber? Oros was going to find out.

He made his way there, letting his eyes adjust to the darkness and the dim light coming from the small pool of healing water where Solen had been recuperating.

He cautiously went deeper into the chamber, giving himself more time to adjust to the increasing darkness. When he got close to what felt like the very back, he reached his hands out in front of him to touch the cool and jagged earth. His instincts told him to move to his left, and he did so slowly while feeling his hands across the wall. He kept going until a sound stopped him. Something in the depth of the chamber was breathing. He noticed suddenly that his nose detected the strong smell of a dragon, which he had smelled more times than he could count. Yet, the difference was that this dragon smelled like the sea.

The twins, or at least one of them, were near. Oros

kept feeling his way along the wall as it curved to the left and opened into another chamber. He stopped and looked around the darkness and was surprised to see the two brothers holding each other's hands, their heads bowed toward one another, touching. Their bodies emitted a dim blue light, which flashed slowly, like a beacon of some kind.

Their eyes were closed. They breathed in unison. Oros couldn't be sure, but he assumed the two were engaged in some ritual or prayer. He wanted to respect their activity, but then his mind wandered quickly to Skylet, and he realized that she was the reason he entered the cavern in the first place.

Oros stepped up to them and gently placed his hands on top of the dragons' hands. His hands were, of course, much smaller than theirs, but even the feeling from his hands registered with the dragons.

They slowly came out of their trance-like state and looked down at Oros. Almost immediately after recognizing who was before them, they recoiled backward and lowered themselves to the ground as though they were weakened.

"Are you all right?" Oros asked them.

"Your thoughts..." Aria began.

"They are powerful," Floren added. "They overwhelm us in our current state."

"Current state? What has happened to you both?"

"You wish to know about Skylet," Aria stated slowly.

"We used substantial energy to generate the means for her and the other dragon to travel through the water."

"And where is Ulysus taking them?" asked Oros. "Do you know?"

"Ulysus has other tasks to complete," said Floren. "He

made a promise to someone here in the infirmary."

"I must make sure she does not get into trouble," Oros said.

"What you are asking?" Floren began. "Our energy is significantly depleted."

Oros let out a sigh. "Please, can you help me find her?" he said to the twin dragons. "You've no idea how long it has been since—" Oros stopped himself, realizing they probably did have an idea since they could feel his very thoughts.

He looked down at the floor and dropped to his knees, looking back and forth between both dragons.

Aria and Floren exchanged tired glances at each other, and then, after another moment, they gingerly grabbed and held each other's hands and helped one another to stand up. At the same time, Oros sat on his legs, watching the dragons as they steeled themselves for how much further they would have to push internally to help Oros.

43.

Layona traveled stealthily like an animal of the wild. She traversed the woods with urgency, yet allowed room to be still and not move for long periods. In those moments, her mind wandered to when she began to enjoy the work of a dragon scout, which sometimes included the hunt. One memory hit her as she sat crouched behind many large bushes. As a child, she had snuck out of the house to track Henricks to a meeting of the guild of Dragonhunters.

During a crucial gathering, she hid behind a curtain just beyond the podium where old, unused weapons and shields were stored. She had been sneaking out to these meetings for some time and thought she was doing well enough because she was never spotted. Or, at least, she was never made aware that she was spotted. Until that night.

Near the end of the meeting, as she peeked through the ever so slight opening of the curtains, she saw a couple of the men stand from their seats in the circular arrangement and approach the podium. She quickly dashed away from the opening like a cat, not wanting to be seen. Young Layona held her breath and sat curled up with her shoddy piece of parchment against her chest, thinking that in case someone discovered her, she could have it so close to herself that it would absorb into her, and no one would ever know the secrets and knowledge she possessed about the art of hunting dragons.

She heard the footsteps get closer and closer. Two men stood just beyond the curtain, enjoying drinks and hearty conversation. *It must be a break in the meeting*, Layona thought to herself. After a few moments, she became impatient, hoping the men would hurry up their boring chatter about the day they spent with their families, the dinners their wives cooked, or some other such nonsense and get back to the important things like hunting and killing dragons.

Soon enough, the footsteps began moving further away from the podium area, and Layona relaxed. But suddenly, a new set of footsteps joined the rhythm, which threw off her ear as she listened for when it was safe to return to her comfortable place. She thought about making a break for it through the hole she snuck into that led to an opening from the inside of the large room where all the men met. But she reasoned that the information she was getting was too valuable to leave.

Suddenly, the curtain whooshed open with the force of fierce winds. Layona froze, looking up at an imposing figure she recognized as Master Servalan, one of the most incredible Dragonhunters whose reputation preceded him. They locked eyes, neither of them speaking. Servalan's face was expressionless as he looked at the child, who seemed startled, but she wasn't afraid.

Servalan reached down near the girl, causing Layona to jump back. He grabbed an old shield near her. But before he collected it, he said to her in a tone low enough that only she could hear, "You've done well sneaking into several of these meetings."

Layona's breath quickened. She couldn't believe she had ever been seen.

"If it were my choice to make, you would be allowed here," he said. "However, the rules are what they have been, and it is not up to me to change them."

She could still hear his voice as if he were right beside her. The memory of Servalan's imposing figure was still with her all these years later. She remembered all the whispers about him growing up in town, tales of his exploits and conquests. Through it all, one thing remained. Though his exterior was tough and he seemed impenetrable as a man, the single aspect about him Layona remembered most was the last words he said to her before leaving her to decide whether to stay for the remainder of the meeting or go to avoid being caught by another, less kind hunter.

"If you don't want to be discovered, remember, your intentions are your north star."

When she looked confused, he clarified his statement. "Your every step must be intentional. Deliberate."

There was silence between the two. Servalan raised his eyebrows slightly, silently asking her whether she understood him.

She quickly nodded.

He nodded in return and closed the curtain, leaving her in the darkness. "Here it is, Yestep," he said to another hunter nearby. Layona was sure he didn't need to do that but decided that it was necessary for him to sell the fact that he was looking for the old shield he grabbed. He also made sure to leave a slight crack between the two curtains in case she decided to stay, which she noticed.

A squirrel scurrying across a nearby tree brought her back to her adult self as she watched her targets well ahead. She remembered Servalan's words. "Your every step must be deliberate."

This bit of sage advice made much more sense to her now as an adult. She held those words deep within herself from everyone. Even from Henricks, who she knew admired Servalan greatly. To have received a direct note was a gift she continued to find useful, especially now. It helped make her so good at picking up training with Henricks growing up. Whenever there was any mistake she may have made during the process, she attributed that to the fact, at least in her mind, that she was not being intentional enough. Maybe her mind would wander in the middle of a training fight with a dragon, and a step was missed, which would be costly. Or she would get too into her thoughts about a particular technique regarding some of the memory tests Henricks would give her on terms and tactics.

Now, as she looked on and watched Skylet and Solen move along, she slowly pushed herself. Parts of her body were becoming numb, yet she couldn't move so quickly lest she arouse their suspicion. She carefully brought her body back to life, crawling with the precision and skill of a cat, moving when necessary, and immediately staying herself like a statue when she felt the moment called for it.

Meanwhile, further ahead, Skylet kept pace with Solen as he led the way. She noticed that occasionally, he would slightly shake his head. "What's wrong, Solly?"

"Ah, just," he began. "Nothing."

It took her a moment to realize that he remembered

being chased while escaping Ondriten. She reached out her hand and gently placed it against the side of his large arm as they continued to walk together.

They spoke no more words for a long while.

44.

The water at the shore was calm, and the sun was setting. Soon, it would be dark. Suddenly, the relaxed water thrashed around, and Oros burst through, coughing and gasping for breath, willing his tired body to the shore. He was lucky. The air from the orb Aria and Floren made for him to reach the surface had run out. It took everything in his being to make it out.

All the gear weighed heavy on his body as Oros came out of the water, crawling until he was completely ashore. Then he turned and plopped on his back to catch his breath. It wasn't until his breathing returned to normal that Oros turned himself over and attempted to stand up. It took some time, but he managed. Oros looked into the vast woods ahead and took a deep breath, preparing to use his skills to track his sister. He had been here before. It would just take a while along his journey for the smell of saltwater on his body to fall away so he could catch the scents most helpful in his search.

He was certain that Skylet and Solen had been nearby at one point or another before he had arrived. There were notes of Solen the dragon and Skylet's cloak in the air ahead of him.

He nodded to himself once and began to take one labored step after the next into the woods, figuring it would be dark when he found himself in the thick of the forest. He resigned to the thought that it should be just enough time for him to feel like he was making some headway.

Finding Skylet consumed his thoughts, yet he also thought about Séya and Sebastian and the group at the colony. He felt terrible about leaving without telling Séya his plans, especially knowing how involved she wished to be. Then, of course, there was the matter of baby Ulonae. Something about her tugged at the insides of his chest. As he stepped deeper into the woods, he saw flashes of the different moments shared with the young dragon. He remembered the first time Séya helped him hold her or when he was trying to distance himself, when Ulonae made it a point to be close to him. He sighed deeply and continued his mission, moving past Henricks' men hiding nearby, successfully camouflaging themselves in the woods.

***

Henricks and Holera walked silently, her men close, keeping pace with them. They could hear the ocean's water gently kissing the shore more clearly now. It was dark, but thanks to the sound, they were clear on the way to go. Just as Holera turned to speak to one of the men to her left, there was a rustling in the bushes. It was distant but a rustling nonetheless. They all immediately stopped in their tracks.

Henricks took a quick breath in from his nose and knew immediately. A dragon was near. "Down!" he whispered sharply before kneeling.

Holera was the quickest of her group to drop. Almost as soon as they saw her fall, they followed suit.

Henricks put a finger to his mouth to tell them to stay silent. He wasn't sure if they could see him, being that it was effectively dark, but he hoped that his outline was visible enough.

Then, he heard it—a grumble. Like the rustling, it was not close by, but it was recognizable. His insides shook as he felt the faint rumbling of the earth beneath him. Though he hadn't seen a dragon in nearly twenty years, there was no mistaking that sound came from one.

Then he heard something surprising. A voice. He couldn't make out what it was saying clearly enough, but it was a person.

As quietly as he could, Henricks reached into a pouch on his belt and took out a small flint steel fire starter with a patch of brush inside it. When he struck the two sides of the flint steel together, a fire caught in the center of the brush holder, and he held it up to his face, calmly gesturing to the group which direction he would be going toward the sounds he heard.

Henricks walked, still keeping low while shuffling bushes and low-dipping branches out of his way to get a better look at what was ahead.

Holera stayed still at first, watching the light in Henricks' hand get smaller and smaller.

"Captain," one of her men said in a whisper that sounded as if it were trembling.

Holera turned to face him and then put a hand on his shoulder, patting it twice. "Follow me," she said, her voice low, just outside the range of a whisper. "Stay low, stay close."

They continued onward.

Henricks got as close as he could before he saw a distant light of a fire held by a young woman. His eyes barely registered her, for at her right was the shadowy outline of a large dragon. His eyes widened at the sight as he watched them move in the direction of Ondriten.

***

Sebastian had arrived back in the infirmary and made a point to return to where Séya sat, holding a napping baby Ulonae. "Dear Séya," he said. "Why are you here by your lonesome? Wherever has everyone gone to?"

Séya looked up from the young dragon, a look of surprise on her face. "What do you mean, Sebastian?" she asked. "Didn't Oros relay the message from the twins?"

Sebastian looked closely at her, realizing she was genuinely caught off guard. "I know nothing of any message," he said. "Have you seen them?"

"Oros apparently spoke to them inside the healing chamber there."

Sebastian's brow furrowed as he started to make his way over to the chamber entrance when he stopped and turned to address Séya. "Would you care to accompany me?" he asked as he stepped over to her with a hand out to help her up.

She nodded, sensing a deep concern from Sebastian. She took his hand, and they went to the healing chamber.

Sebastian was much bigger than his sons or many of the dragons in the colony, so for him to fit inside and move forward, he had to crouch and hunch his body significantly to move even marginally comfortably in the cavern. Séya's breathing became quicker the deeper they went and the darker it got inside. She was still tired, having not moved as much since before arriving at the colony. Séya tried to disguise it by seeming more able than she was since she had not fully recovered from when she had passed out earlier. She held Ulonae just a little closer to herself.

Sensing Séya's energy, Sebastian put his large hand around her back comfortingly and spoke telepathically to avoid disturbing Ulonae. *Dear Séya, please hold on to me.*

The dragon stopped so Séya could place her free hand against his large, scaled, muscular arm. They stepped deliberately deeper into the cavern until they reached the jagged wall at the very back.

Stay here, Sebastian transmitted to her.

The dragon peered around the corner of the wall and glanced into the cavern where Floren and Aria were lying on the floor as though they were sleeping. They were positioned in the opposite direction of one another, one brother's head facing the tail end of the other. Their bodies glowed dimly but brightly enough that Sebastian could see them as clearly as anything else. He looked intently at each of them, scanning them for signs of life, noticing them breathing in sync. Sebastian watched as their bodies expanded and contracted, reaching his hands into the cavern to touch each of them. *My sons*, he thought, as he released a sigh.

"Sebastian," Séya whispered. "Are they all right? What's happened?"

The dragon didn't respond immediately. Instead, he took in that question from Séya as though it were a new question he was considering for the first time. Sebastian went further into the cave where his sons were and bowed, placing his head firmly into the cavern floor, his hands still touching them.

He closed his eyes and saw flashes of light. Even though they were down, recovering from the massive amount of energy they had used earlier, Sebastian could still comb through their thoughts, though it would be a challenge.

He set to work, and soon, he began to see quick visions from the perspective of both sons. He saw Ulysus talking to Floren, and they worked together to create air orbs. A transparent bag was being handed to Ulysus before that image quickly faded, and then he saw Oros pleading with the brothers for their help.

Then all was dark.

"Rest, my sons," he said in a low tone of voice. "Come find me when you are able."

Sebastian got himself out of the cavern and reached Séya. "Come," he said. "We must leave the colony at once."

45.

Layona trailed Skylet and Solen, keeping a safe distance from them. She used the light from Skylet's torch to retain sight of them. Layona noticed that though they stopped occasionally, they were moving consistently. They knew exactly where they were going and were on a mission to get there.

A distant rustling in the brush came not far from where Skylet and Solen were; Layona saw them stop abruptly. Skylet quickly put out the torch, and they crouched down. Layona did the same, but just enough to see over the layer of bushes. Her eyes adjusted well enough to the darkness to see the shadows. She had the edge over most in the dark, though. As a child, during her training with Henricks, she had ingested dried dragon's blood burned into a mist to inhale.

There was plenty of debate in the dragon hunting community about the best way to consume it. Was it in liquid form or a mist form? The benefit of ingesting it in liquid form is that even though reflexes seem sharper, one tires much faster and then has to consume the blood more often, which in the long run is a setback for hunters in a fight with a dragon.

Ingesting it as a mist typically meant doing so much less often, say once every few months or more. Prolonged exposure, though, and at such a young age as in Layona's case, it seems, is near permanent and can be called upon when needed. This had allowed her to see better than anyone else might in the darkness like dragons can. Since many live in dark spaces like caves, their eyes are well suited for life in places with little to no light.

Now, Layona felt more of her inner dragon come alive with the hunt. She could tell that what made the rustling noise beyond where Skylet and Solen were was not a threat from what she could now see. It was just another night creature of the woods trying to make its way around. She relaxed for a moment until she heard a faint and consistent pattering coming from behind her. Footsteps. Multiple sets. But they weren't heavy, like an army. They were nimble.

Who could be coming into the woods now? she thought as she rolled to her left slowly. If she stayed put long enough, her question would be answered. Layona worried she was losing her targets but figured she knew where they were going. She was going to have to trust that her hunch was correct. For now, she didn't want to risk being spotted alone.

After what was becoming a long time, someone sped past like a swift shadow. Layona could hear the jangling of items on this person. She got to one knee and saw that the figure wore a cloak and carried a sword. Registering those images in her mind, she widened her eyes, returning to her original position on the ground. *Could it be?* she thought to herself. *The hunter from the Selnes incident...*

She set the musing aside as there came the multiple

pattering sounds again. In moments, the area near her was occupied with people moving swiftly, with a rhythm among each other. She didn't have to look up to know with absolute certainty that these were at least some of the scouts she had seen leaving the castle earlier, which meant that Henricks was nearby. Had he ordered his men back?

Layona also realized that Captain Holera and her men might also be close. She suddenly felt regretful that she sent away Oberon and the other young sentinel on her detail. The feeling soon left her when she realized how close she felt to something that had an almost electric pull. Something called to her, but she wasn't sure what it was. She just knew that she was compelled to follow it.

After the scouts traveled well beyond her, where she could no longer hear their graceful movements, she decided it was time for her to continue. With the men traversing the way they were, something was about to happen, and she didn't want to miss the action.

***

Oros was making further headway deeper in the woods now. He had lost sight of Skylet and Solen, but his sense of smell, growing less and less faint, was intact, and the smell of dragon was still near enough to him. His pace was consistent, and his energy had mostly returned to him, yet Oros still wished to conserve himself should he need to call upon his abilities to keep safe.

A sudden breeze swept through the forest, brushing leaves and twigs around. That was all the time it took for the Dragon Scouts to surround and close in on Oros.

The sound of the wind blowing through the area was

the opportunity they needed to mask their subtle movements. Oros turned around at the last moment, realizing he was not alone.

"You there," one of the scouts said sharply. "What is your business here?"

"Please," Oros began. "I am after my sister. I want no trouble with you."

"Have you seen a dragon, sir?" another scout asked. "Or should I call you 'hunter'?"

"I hunt dragons no more," Oros replied. "If there is nothing else, I will be on my way."

He turned to walk away, and as he did, he noticed two shadows zip by him like two lines in the process of making an 'x' to prevent him from continuing. Oros stopped momentarily to get his bearings before moving ahead. He saw two men quickly approach him when they saw he wasn't stopping. "Halt, sir," another one of the scouts said, placing a firm hand on Oros' left breast while the other man grabbed his shoulder and forearm with the other hand.

"And what is the meaning of this?"

"We have been notified of a dragon who killed one of our members," said one of the men.

"I know nothing of this."

"Well, judging by your attire and gear, you seem quite prepared to face a dragon."

"Again, my sister has traveled this way, and I must find her."

"We have orders to make contact with a dragon of the sea," the scout said. "Do you know how we found you?"

Oros didn't respond.

"We saw you come ashore. Now, you either encountered the sea dragon and barely escaped with your life, or something else is afoot that is not apparent to us yet."

Oros suddenly felt as though his predicament was very familiar to him. His mind briefly wandered back to when he had Skylet in a similar position. A wave of guilt hit him deep in his gut, and then the fire to reach her replaced that guilt. He was ready to leave this conversation.

"I know nothing about that," said Oros. "But what I do know for certain is that a dragon of the sea is nothing to be toyed with. If you value your lives, I suggest you return to whoever gave you the order to make contact with such a dangerous creature and relay that message."

There was a silence that came over the group as the quiet breeze whipped around them all.

"Kindly excuse me," he continued. "My young sister is among these woods. Enough of my time has been given here."

"Who is your sister?" another scout asked.

"That is not your concern," Oros shot back as he kept walking.

"Should she be entering the kingdom, on dragon business no less, it is our concern."

"Aren't you all far from the castle walls?" asked a voice deep within the woods behind them.

All the men, including Oros, stopped and turned around to face the direction where the voice came from. They seemed surprised that it was the commanding voice of a woman.

"Who is there?" one scout shouted. "Show yourself!"

"Yet, no one here is a knight," said Layona, keeping herself hidden behind a thick oak tree. "Nor is anyone a castle guard; those have the task of dealing with matters concerning the kingdom."

"What is your business, woman?"

"You have no dealings with the hunter," she said. "Leave him be."

"Why should we consider the word of a coward, hiding away in the shadows like a common street cat?"

"Is not Master Henricks leading your company?" she asked, sidestepping the scout's remark.

No one responded for a moment as they took in her question.

"Who are you, and how do you know of Master Henricks?"

"Never you mind about that," she said. "Where is he?"

Oros couldn't tell, but it seemed as though the stranger was stalling for him. Whether she was or not, Oros did not waste another moment. He untied a pouch that hung on his belt, letting it fall to the earth. He noticed the outline of the scout who stood to his right, looking downward to see what fell from the hunter's waistband.

In the split second it took for the scout to kneel to collect the fallen item, Oros stepped his heel heartily on the pouch he dropped. It exploded into a puff of smoke, which permeated the area in seconds. Oros took his leave and dashed ahead.

The scouts were audibly confused, but they kept their quiet composure as they zipped around the area to get clear of the thick smoke, which had them coughing.

"Find the woman!" one of the men called out.

It wasn't long before some of the others in the group realized that Layona was gone. She disappeared among the fog like the cool breeze that ran through the woods.

46.

Oros jogged for a while through the dark woods. He noticed traces of silvery moonlight pouring through the trees, lighting his way. He picked up speed, moving straight ahead once he felt clear from the scouts he had left behind.

He saw no trace of Skylet or Solen but figured if he kept on his path, he would find clues about where they had been. No sooner than he had that thought did he come across several large footprints along the damp earth. Next to them were human footprints. He stopped to kneel and get a good look at the prints. There was no question that he was on the right path. Oros stood and began jogging again.

His mind jumped back briefly to the woman's voice he had heard earlier. Who was she? Why did she speak on his behalf? Were it not for her, Oros might have still been held there by the scouts. She seemed to be an ally, but he didn't have time to ponder the circumstances. He needed to make sure he could catch up with Skylet so that she wouldn't be hurt by any forces attempting to stop her, with Jessie's cloak around her or not. If it came to doing whatever he could to protect Skylet, he was going to do it. No matter what.

Oros kept going until he reached an area of the forest that was open and surrounded by tall pine trees. The earth beneath him was uneven and led into an incline through another vast area of thick cypress trees. He jogged straight into it until a voice made him stop at the top of the slope.

"Hunter of Selnes," it called. The voice sounded winded and reverberated through the woods.

Oros recognized it immediately. The woman who called off the Dragon Scouts. Had she chased after him? She must have, the former hunter thought to himself. Oros almost unconsciously allowed himself a slight smirk, impressed that she found him. He slowly turned around, calming himself to catch his breath. His eyes gradually shifted from left to right; there was no one he could see in the empty grass surrounded by trees. The moonlight was bright and clear enough to see anything that happened to scurry about.

"As I told the men before," he began between catching his breath. "I must find my sister."

A moment went by without a response.

"I'm afraid I must leave you," he said, turning around to move forward. However, just before he fully turned toward the deep woods ahead, he caught movement from the corner of his eye at the far end of the open area behind him. He whipped his head around to see what it was.

The silhouette of a woman appeared from the dark forest behind her and stepped into the moonlight, revealing herself.

Oros was stunned. Had she appeared there? Did she possess a kind of sorcery like Séya? Or was it something else? She seemed almost supernatural to him. He noticed how the moonlight made the edges of her dark hair shine.

She was composed and self-assured. He felt her commanding presence and was surprised at how unafraid she was to be in the woods alone with a stranger. All of this captured his attention, and then she spoke once more. "Would you oblige me?" Layona asked as she caught her breath. "Step into the moonlight, please."

Oros was unprepared for such a polite request. He started to deny her and mention trying to find Skylet again, but now he felt compelled to do as she so kindly asked. Slowly, he stepped beyond the shadows of the woods behind him and out onto the top of the slope, leaning the weight of his left side against his leg that kept him balanced on the hill as he looked slightly down at her.

Layona stared, awed by how nearly mythic he looked, as his cloak rustled with the slight breeze. Her eyes looked him up and down and back again, and she felt something familiar, grounded, and, at the same time, empty. She saw how firmly he stood, how calm he seemed. His shoulders relaxed, arms and hands casually at his side. She felt his intense dark eyes meeting hers; she could make out the details of his face in the moonlight. Her brow furrowed. She felt as though the face across from her was not new. Yet, she had no idea where she might have seen it.

"Do you know who I am?" she asked.

Oros took a moment to study her some more. His eyes went from her boots to her robes to the gear she had upon her person, including a belt that displayed a sheath with a large knife and a few other standard weapons. "You are a sentinel," he said. "And quite an important one."

Layona nodded. "I have been searching for you."

Oros scoffed. "I am aware of that. I expected you to find me sooner."

Layona pulled out a rolled-up parchment from the pouch that sat around the back of her waist. "Then you know about the attack on the primary encampment in Selnes several months ago," she said, holding out the parchment to Oros.

He hesitated to move for a moment. Oros just looked at her, holding the parchment out to him. Then his eyes made their way to it, and Oros slowly walked closer to her and took the parchment from her hand. He was surprised at how much taller she was up close. Oros could barely see across the top of her head.

He opened the parchment, angling it toward the moonlight. He skimmed the first few lines, but his eyes then jumped to the near bottom of the page, where he saw sketches loosely resembling him, Jessie, and Séya. A wave of heat rushed through his belly, and he was careful not to let on that what he saw affected him.

He also noticed a mention of another person in a hooded cloak, which he presumed to be Skylet, but apparently, she hadn't been seen well enough because there was no sketch of her.

Oros calmly rolled the parchment up and handed it back to her.

"Is it clear to you why I have been searching for you?"

"It is," Oros replied. "You mean to arrest me."

"I have been tasked with bringing you and the witch back to Selnes," Layona said. "You must stand trial for your crimes."

"I see," Oros turned his back to her, looking up to the sky and over at the moon.

Layona caught sight of his sword, noticing how the part of the blade just beyond the hilt was visible at the top of his sheath. It sparkled slightly in the light of the moon.

Almost immediately, her mind returned to the night she was found by Servalan hiding beyond the podium at the meeting for Dragonhunters. When he turned to leave her behind the curtains, she noticed the sword in the strap on his waist that night, particularly the hilt. She realized it looked the same. *It couldn't be the same sword*, she thought. *Could it?*

"I cannot be arrested," said Oros, bringing Layona back to the moment.

"Oh? And why is that, 'hunter'?"

"Please," he began. "I am no longer a hunter of dragons." Layona blinked. She seemed genuinely stunned by this response.

"I made a promise to my sister…" Oros paused, turning to face her.

"Yes?"

"I made a promise to my sister to help her find the other dragons."

"Other dragons?" Layona was surprised.

"Yes, listen to this," said Oros. "If I am to stand trial, then so be it. But I cannot come with you until my promise is fulfilled."

Layona said nothing. She just looked at him as if to consider his words more deeply.

"Would that be a suitable bargain?"

"It isn't much of a bargain if you should end up dead with whatever it is you are about to get yourself into behind your sister."

Layona folded her arms for a moment and pointed a foot into the earth, rotating it in a circular motion. "If you are planning to keep your word to her, I have no reason to believe you would not keep your word to me. After all, I am fairly positive that you were once an honorable Dragonhunter. And you are still honorable, it seems."

She paused and unfolded her arms, letting them hang to her sides. "We have a bargain."

47.

Skylet and Solen traversed the woods for what felt like ages. They came upon a darkened section of the forest, at the end of which was an opening lit by the moon.

"Climb on," Solen said, lowering himself so Skylet could get on his back. "Hold tightly."

Skylet held on to him with all her strength as he dashed through the dark tunnel of low branches and foliage. When they reached the end, he stopped when he came upon a mound of earth. They were still on the outskirts of town, so there weren't any people around who would have certainly created a problem for them.

"There," he said. "The castle. Somewhere in there is where we were held. I hope the others are okay."

Solen hung his head and let out a deep and heavy breath.

Skylet slid off of his back and walked around to face him. She looked up at him and saw his expression contorted into a scowl as he looked beyond her at the castle in the distance.

"Solly," she began.

He looked down at her, his golden yellow eyes glowing in the dark.

Skylet reached up and held his face. "We are going to find them, yes?"

She could feel the slight trembling of Solen.

"Yes," he said. "We are going to bring them home."

They met each other's gaze and stood until Skylet nodded slowly and turned to face the castle. "We obviously can't go straight in through the entrance," she said. "Can you show me which way you escaped from?"

"Yes. The soldiers were moving us at the time I broke free. So," he shrugged his bulky shoulders. "I don't know where they were taken if they are still alive."

"Let's not worry about that right now," said Skylet. "Just get us to where you escaped from and stay hidden as best you can."

"Why? What are you thinking?"

"I think I might have an idea on how to find them, but we need to get to where you escaped."

"Of course," Solen said. "We must stay along the very outskirts to avoid being spotted."

***

"Where do you suppose they are going?" Holera asked.

"They are going to the castle or somewhere near there," replied Henricks. They were a little more than halfway back to the castle walls. Gonden and Delsce flanked them as ordered by Holera, should they come across any resistance.

"Why ever would they be going back there?"

"It seems to me that they are after something," said Henricks, stopping short of saying too much. He figured that it wouldn't matter either way if the soldiers knew

258

about the other dragons, but still, he thought it best to err on the side of caution and withhold any information about that, especially since they had just seen one dragon, likely for the first time in their lives. He didn't want to introduce any further potential panic into the group.

Holera looked down as she took steps ahead. A moment later, she noticed fog merely feet from them.

"Do you—"

"I see it," Henricks replied.

They all stopped to examine what was in front of them properly. The smoke was clearing.

"Do you think someone set a fire?"

Before Henricks could answer, Holera heard distant voices, rustling, and stumbling sounds.

"Where do you think they went?" one of the voices asked.

"I don't know, but we'd probably better get back to the beach and wait for Master Henricks."

Henricks recognized the men's voices as his scouts and called out to them. His tone was clear and loud enough that they could find their way to him. "There is no need to return to the beach," he said. "I am here."

"Master Henricks!" one of the men called out, stumbling through the fog to their far right, coughing. He landed on his hands and knees.

Henricks stepped over and helped him up. "Taziel, what happened here?"

"We followed a Dragonhunter from the beach back through here," he said. "He claimed to be looking for his sister."

"Where was he going?" Henricks asked.

"He didn't say. We stopped him and attempted to

question him until a woman distracted us. Soon, we were engulfed by smoke, and they were gone."

"I see," said Henricks, pondering Taziel's tale. "Well, it seems we must all head back to the castle. I will report the events to the king myself."

"Won't the king be displeased, sir?" Taziel asked. "We haven't captured the sea dragon."

"Please, do not concern yourself with that," Henricks replied. "Leave the king to me."

48.

Back at the ship, the mood was neutral. Soldiers and sentinels found ways to entertain themselves amidst the boredom. Some played games, and others sat quietly, pondering on things only they could grapple with. Oberon held two plates of a simple meal of greens, beets, and seasoned fish from the water. He placed one plate across from the young sentinel, staring into a wall torch near him. Brow furrowed, he seemed preoccupied with something.

Oberon placed his dish on the table and sat across from the young man. "Tonight's dinner looks especially pleasant, wouldn't you say?" Oberon's voice was low with a hint of gruffness that the young sentinel hadn't heard before. To him, Oberon was a warm and grounding presence among the group, and his voice usually reflected that. Tonight, though, something was different.

The young man turned his attention from the torch and toward Oberon, a look of both surprise and confusion on his face. He watched as the elder sentinel bowed slightly and began enjoying his meal, though he, too, seemed almost immediately wrapped up in a pressing thought.

"No," the young sentinel said. "I wouldn't say."

"Oh? And why not?" Oberon casually asked in between bites.

"Sir, I am still worried about the Principal Sentinel. I have been thinking, and I wonder if we shouldn't just dash the orders and go back for her."

Oberon did not look up from his plate. Instead, he jabbed a fork into the greens and beets and deliberately lifted the utensil to his mouth, taking in the food. Chewing slowly, Oberon allowed the bitter flavor of the greens and the earthy tang of the beets to blanket the inside of his mouth. Then he separated a piece of the nearly perfectly prepared fish with his fork and welcomed the savory bite, grateful for how it cut through the bitterness of the salad before marrying with the opposing flavors.

He seemed to escape into the food experience to not deal with the young sentinel's feelings and, if he were honest with himself, his own feelings about Layona's decision to separate from them.

When he swallowed the serving, he spoke to the young man across from him, who waited patiently for a response. "Young sentinel," began Oberon. "You must be patient."

"With respect, sir, patience? It feels as though we are just waiting to respond to something dreadful. Are you not worried?"

"Of course I am."

"Then should we not leave? I cannot be at rest with the knowledge that our leader could be lost to us."

"Allow me to ask you something, young sir," Oberon looked up slowly from his food and met the young man's gaze. He could see that the young man seemed desperate for comfort. "Have you ever had to let go of something you deeply cared for?"

"I'm not sure I follow you, sir." The young man looked

down at his plate, almost defeated.

"When you reach my stage in life, you will hopefully have had enough experiences that teach you, at times, you must put your trust in something. You must relinquish your hold on it and give yourself to faith."

"Faith, sir?"

"Yes, faith. Faith that the best course of action is the one before us."

The young sentinel let out a deep sigh.

"I have faith in the Principal Sentinel," said Oberon. "She is capable. Do you not have faith in her?"

"I..." the young sentinel hesitated. "I am not certain, sir. This is my first assignment so far away from home."

"It is, is it?"

The young sentinel nodded.

"Well, have faith in me then. Can you do that?"

"I will do my best. However, I must say that I do not like this sitting and waiting at all. Not one bit."

"Nor do I," Oberon replied. "But, I like the Principal Sentinel very much. Don't you?"

"I can say for certain that although I am new to her methods, I do, sir," the young sentinel smirked a bit.

It warmed Oberon inside to see the young man lighten up, even if it was for a brief moment. He even let slip a half smile of his own. "And despite my concerns," the elder sentinel continued as he scooped another bite of the food into his mouth. "I like the odds that she has everything well under her control."

The mood between them became serious again as Oberon reached a hand across the table and placed it over the young sentinel's, gripping it. "She will return to us," he said. "She will."

The young man nodded despite still not feeling sure

about it all. He then looked down at his full plate of food.

"Now, try and eat something," Oberon said. "Any sentinel traveling with me must keep his strength up."

49.

Just outside the ship, the water was calm and brightly lit by the moon nearing its highest point. The nighttime breeze was gentle, and all was quiet except for the crickets, owls, and other night creatures doing their business.

A rumble in the water several yards from the ship alerted everyone. Within moments, a large section of the sea exploded upward in a tidal wave. Something massive shot out and went straight into the air like a spear.

Two men had been patrolling the upper deck and the shore, respectively. They heard the uproar in the water, turned their attention to the noise, and saw a wall of water crashing down.

The soldier raced to the doorway on the ship, leading to the lower deck, and yelled with his whole being. "Brace! TIDAL WAVE! BRACE!!"

Those in the lower deck swiftly braced themselves. Oberon and the young sentinel looked at each other, immediately jumped from their seats, and positioned their bodies as best they could to protect against the force of the oncoming wave.

The water hit with tremendous force, and a wave

rushed toward the ship. It pushed the vessel so hard that it was forced to the shore, nearly toppling over on its side.

The crashing water forced the sentinel, who had been keeping watch up the beach, and then pulled him back toward the tipped ship, slamming him into it. He tried to stand up, looking toward the sky. His eyes looked up to the large moon, where he saw the silhouette of a giant creature with its wings fully spread out in the center of the bright sphere. "Goodness," he said under his breath. He quickly tried getting up but slipped in the wet sand, landing on his back. "Monster!" he cried. "MONSTER!!"

"Where?!" The soldier knocked over on the ship's upper deck looked around the shore.

"Up there!!" The sentinel pointed to the sky, but at that time, whatever he saw was so small in the moonlight; it was a dot and could have been a bird for all anyone knew. "It must have come from the water!"

The soldier looked up and back at the sentinel lying on his back. "Have someone assist you," he said. "You must have hit your head."

***

High above the water, Sebastian flew with Séya and baby Ulonae in tow. Straight upward, higher and higher, he climbed until he reached a height so great the air was thin, and the breeze was biting cold.

Séya held the youngling tightly into her bosom since the young one was not accustomed to such temperatures. But as soon as she did that, she immediately began to feel a sudden and intense warmth. It took her a moment to realize that Sebastian was somehow manipulating the moisture in the air around him, and maybe the water within himself, to make warmth at such a high altitude. She was grateful, leaning her head against the back of his neck to create more insulation for Ulonae, keeping her between Séya's chest and Sebastian's body. *Thank you,* Séya transmitted in thought to Sebastian.

Of course, dear Séya.

They cut through the air in silence before Séya had another thought. *How are we to find the castle? Solen was supposed to lead us.*

Sebastian grumbled to himself and let out a deep breath. *I'm afraid I must open a door that terrifies me.*

Séya's heart sank for him. *Whatever do you mean?*

I must seek out an old... Sebastian's thoughts trailed off as he tried to search for a good word that captured what he felt. *Well, you might say an old friend, but the connection is more profound than that.*

Séya was silent in her thoughts. She looked down at Ulonae, whose eyes were staring up at the old woman as they flew onward.

50.

Layona and Oros had come through the last vestiges of the woods and approached the edges of Ondriten. At some point, the trail of the dragon smell wasn't strong enough to follow precisely. Instead, Layona led the way, having just been there earlier in the day.

The castle stood looming in the distance, overlooking the city streets. They could hear activity even from how far away they were; the town before them was alive. It would be impossible to sneak around unnoticed.

"Are you familiar with this place?" asked Oros.

"Not well enough to be a guide, my apologies," Layona replied. "I know what path to take to arrive at the castle, but something tells me that isn't the path you want."

"Quite right."

They stood together in silence when a waft of something caught Oros' attention. He didn't react outwardly to it at all. Instead, he turned away from the town ahead and looked to his left.

Layona had caught the same smell. And like Oros, she did nothing to let on that she had. "And yet," the Principal Sentinel began. "New pathways reveal themselves from time to time. There may be a different way in."

Oros turned to her, a curious expression on his face.

Layona met his gaze.

"She is near," Oros said.

"Then go find her and fulfill your promise," Layona replied.

Oros turned away to follow the trail of the scent. He took two steps, and the Principal Sentinel spoke. "I will be waiting here, out of sight, when you are finished. Come find me, and I will take you back to my ship."

Oros nodded and turned away swiftly to go after Skylet while Layona stepped back into the shadows of the woods to make herself scarce. She had a feeling that Henricks and the scouts would soon figure out that they were near the castle and would be heading back, and she didn't want to be seen.

***

Sebastian had landed on the slanted side of a mountain and lowered himself enough so Séya could slide off his back. "If you wouldn't mind waiting a moment, Séya, while I sit and attempt to locate where we must go."

"Of course," she said, trying to soothe Ulonae. She bounced slightly with the youngling in her arms as the little one became restless.

Sebastian wasted no more time. He sat and closed his eyes, bowing his head. Three long, deep breaths later, Sebastian stared into the void of darkness before him. As he began his next breath, fuzzy images greeted him. They were like gentle hands brushing against him. He saw a sunny day along a lush countryside and then a flock of

269

birds flying in the skies in coordinated patterns.

Soon, his visions became more specific. Mountainous terrain appeared as though he were flying alongside it, going upward. Then, the image was like the memories he had seen earlier when sharing his thoughts with Skylet. It crashed into his meditation, shaking him. Jessie's face appeared, but it wasn't clear to him. The lines around her head were hazy, yet it warmed his heart all the same to see her. *Ash*, Jessie's voice echoed in his mind.

Sebastian reached out as if to hold her face, and suddenly her face changed. It became the face of another dragon. This one was clearer, sharper, and edgier, complete with scars. The dark violet hue of Jessie's face became brown with darker tones. The eyes turned from Jessie's yellow-orange into a golden color.

The following image Sebastian saw went back to the side of the mountain that expanded and contracted. The castle in Ondriten next flashed by his vision quickly, and the destination they needed to travel to became clear to him.

A large golden eye opened, and a fire reflected in it. And that was when Sebastian heard a familiar, heavy, dark, and gruff voice. *Hello, old friend...*

It shook Sebastian out of his meditation. He grumbled heartily and needed to catch his breath.

Séya was there, her hand on one of his large, trembling hands.

"Are you all right, Sebastian? What did you see?" she asked.

The sea dragon hung his head, then turned and looked at Séya, who met his gaze. "I know where we must go now," he said. "Allow me room to compose myself, and we will be off."

51.

Solen led Skylet on a faint trail that went upward. After hiking uphill for a long while, they passed a large, wide ditch to their right.

"Down there is where we were taken from," he said, motioning toward the ditch.

Skylet turned and looked as she kept pace with him.

"The guards had us all chained together by the neck, and they led us in a line one after another up this hill."

"How did you break free? There must have been a lot of guards with Moonbeam Metal weapons."

"There were some, of course," Solen said. "But they counted on us being weak, having been in the dungeons all those years, in our own sick and waste."

Skylet kept silent, waiting for more.

"Somehow, there weren't enough of the Moonbeam Metal collars and chains to use on me, so they just gave me two collars with double the chains."

They approached a part of the pathway on the hike that curved to the right. Beyond the path ahead, they needed to make a right upward and continue. "It was right near here where I mustered enough strength to break free of my chains and neckbrace to escape."

"What about the others?" asked Skylet.

"I turned back only once and saw Beresay barrel over one of the guards who tried to throw a spear to stop me. She gave me time to gain distance between them and me. And then..." he paused. He didn't want to tell her that he heard some of his siblings howling in pain, and that he was too afraid to look back and see them suffering.

"And then I just kept running as far and as fast as I could." He scoffed, remembering how slippery the earth beneath him was. "It was just beyond this turn here that I left them."

They stopped, and Skylet stepped beyond him, looking ahead up the pathway. She gasped, realizing that the area suddenly felt familiar.

"What is it?" Solen asked her.

"I think," she began. "I think I know where the others might be. I've seen this place or some part of it. Jessie showed it to me."

Solen looked more intently at his sister and noticed her clutching the talon necklace at her chest.

"What is the matter, Skylet?"

"I'm terrified to continue, Solly."

He gently placed a large hand on her back to comfort her. "Is this where the other dragon is?" he asked.

Skylet shook her head. "He will be close by. Something tells me that is where our family is. They are being guarded."

Solen looked up toward where they needed to be, "Then let's go and find them, all right?" He looked her in the eyes. "We'll go together."

Skylet felt her chest warm up like when she visited

Arca's grave. Her hands also tingled with intense warmth. She couldn't place why, but she felt it nonetheless.

Together, she and Solen began their ascent up the hill, the outline of mountainous terrain looming in the distance.

52.

Henricks and the scouts, along with Holera and her soldiers, made their way to the outskirts of Ondriten.

Layona stayed hidden amongst the brush and behind large trees, watching them all go beyond her. She overheard a brief exchange between Henricks and Holera about entering the kingdom.

"Listen," said Henricks. "It'll probably be best if you and your men wait in the courtyard while I report to the king. He might be almost as interested in the dragon we came across as the sea dragon."

"A compromise then," said Holera.

"Precisely."

"We can wait in the courtyard, but once you find the other dragon, we're coming with you."

"I will not stop you."

They kept walking straight ahead. Henricks drew a deep breath through his nose, exhaled, and nodded once. He turned his head to his left side but never looked behind himself. He was sure that Layona was close by. Henricks suddenly remembered when he learned of Layona secretly attending the Dragonhunter meetings, swelling with pride whenever she used her newfound knowledge during her training sessions with him.

He made no indication that he knew she was close and kept moving, holding the hope within himself that she would be safe from anything that might happen before the night's events came to a close. Then his thoughts brought him to the new dragon he saw and how the king might react to the news of one being so close, possibly already within the kingdom walls. He had an idea, but after their last exchange, he wasn't so sure.

***

Oros trotted along at a consistent pace, occasionally stopping to kneel and examine the partial footprints left behind by Solen and Skylet in the dirt pathway before him. Up the hill he went until he reached a curve to the right. Without a second thought, he turned into the next part of the ascent. His heart pounded harder; he could almost feel how close he was to them. Oros suddenly became more worried about Skylet's safety with every step he took.

***

Back at the ship, the soldiers and sentinels tried to sort themselves following the surprise wave that crashed into them earlier. Groups of men and women lined up on the tipped side in an attempt to push it back from the shore, but it was no use. So they stood around complaining or worrying about the next wave.

Inside the ship, below deck, Oberon sat up, surveying the dining area. "Is everyone all right?" he called out.

"A couple of bumps over here, but so far, mostly all right," one of the female sentinels shouted back while checking on a couple of downed soldiers, who begrudgingly allowed her to look at them and their injuries briefly.

Even though the two groups had been traveling with each other for some time, tensions between sentinels and soldiers remained.

Oberon turned over to the young sentinel near him. "What about you?" he asked. "Any bumps that need looking after?"

The young sentinel shook his head. "No, sir. I am fine... but what do you think was the cause?"

"I haven't the slightest idea," said Oberon as he attempted to stand, holding out a hand to help the junior sentinel up.

The two stepped around knocked-over tables and people recovering from the episode. Passing the upper deck, they stepped onto the tilted main deck.

Oberon leaned over the edge of the boat and saw the line of soldiers and sentinels working together to try and push the ship away from the shore. He shook his head at the futile attempt and then climbed down from the boat and walked around to the front of it, coming across a sentinel on his knees looking out on the moonlit water.

The older sentinel knelt near him and put a hand on his shoulder. "Are you all right, young man? What happened?"

"Oberon, sir. You would never believe me."

"I have been a sentinel for a very long time," he said. "You would be surprised at what I would believe."

The shaken sentinel turned his attention to Oberon, who looked upon him with kind and understanding eyes, which even in the moonlight could be felt. The young man blinked once and turned to look back out on the water. "I saw a monster emerge from the ocean," he said. "It was large and had wings. That is what caused this damage."

Oberon did not react. He just listened calmly. "Did you see which way it was headed?"

"It just went straight up," he said. "It looked as though it were flying toward the moon, sir."

The elder then turned his attention away from the young man, looked back upon the water, and thought back to Layona, Henricks, and the scouts, and he began to suspect a connection, though he didn't share this with the junior sentinel next to him. "I do not for one moment doubt that what you witnessed was true," he said. "You should get to your quarters and get something dry on, young sir. Here."

Oberon stood and helped the sentinel up, who nodded at him and prepared to step away. "Keep vigilant," said Oberon to the young man.

"Yes, sir."

<h1 style="text-align:center">53.</h1>

Solen and Skylet had been moving for a long while, and it seemed the longer they hiked, the warmer Skylet felt. She sat on Solen's back and hunched forward. Her eyes narrowed as though she were searching for a target to defend herself against. They were getting closer to something. She didn't know what, but she was sure of that much.

Soon, it became clear that the pathway was beginning to level out. They kept moving until they heard voices speaking in hushed tones.

Solen stopped immediately and crouched. "Do you hear that?" he asked, his voice low.

"Yes."

Skylet spotted large boulders nearby. She slipped off Solen's back and quickly ran to the boulder across from them. She put her hands out, palms facing Solen as if to say, 'Stay there.'

Skylet peeked from around the boulder and saw the outline of a group of men in the distance, but she noticed them clearly, in a way that she hadn't before. Her vision seemed sharper than she recognized, and she could see the stark and clear outlines of the men, who looked like they were wearing armor. Remembering her experience in Selnes just months before, she quickly concluded that they were soldiers of the kingdom.

Why were they there? What were they talking about? She pondered those questions, among others, until she heard one word that shook her to her core: "Dragons."

She missed the full context of the conversation. Still, she figured, given where they were, relatively out of the way, so high in the hills at the lower end of a mountain and in shadow in the middle of the night no less, that this was not a pleasant conversation about dragons. Suddenly, the heat she felt in her hands and chest extended to her whole body. Skylet could nearly feel everything inside herself brimming to the surface, packaged in anger. The other dragon siblings were close. She could now sense it so strongly there was no convincing her otherwise.

Without thinking, she drew her hood over her head and stepped from beyond the boulder, moving straight toward where the soldiers convened, talking amongst themselves.

"*Skylet!*" Solen hissed in a sharp whisper. "*Skylet!*"

But it was no use. She calmly kept a consistent pace toward them.

One of the soldiers noticed a shadowy figure approaching. Not recognizing the body shape and the walking style, he took only a moment before calmly reaching to his side to draw a broadsword. "Make yourself known to us... At once!"

"I am kin to the dragons I heard mention of," Skylet said. "You will tell me where they are."

One of the other soldiers scoffed as he turned to face her. "You must be sure of yourself, for one so small," he said.

Without warning, Skylet brought her hand across as though she were slapping the air. The cloak, once draped over her shoulders, mimicked her hand gesture by stretching itself out and sweeping across, knocking over the soldiers.

Solen just arrived, bearing witness as Skylet made short work of the men. "Skylet..." he said, marveling at her cape moving as it was.

She twisted around and grasped at the air. The cloak came back around and swooped in to wrap itself around the first soldier, picking him up from the ground and holding him in the air. "Where are the dragons?" Skylet asked calmly.

"The dragons are under my care," said a voice that sounded like it was made of silk, speaking from beyond where Skylet stood as she held up the struggling soldier.

She leaned her head beyond the wrapped man to see King Rondal standing feet away, looking every bit the part of royalty the likes of which Skylet had never seen.

54.

The monarch of Ondriten stood poised as though preparing to deliver a rousing speech to his army before a battle. He was backlit by the moonlight; his royal garb and crown looked as though they were emitting a silvery aura.

Skylet scanned the figure up and down and back again, barely able to make out his face and the stubble at the base of his well-defined jawline. "Forgive my men here," said the king. "As I'm sure you suspected, they are merely charged with serving this kingdom."

The king glanced beyond Skylet and noticed the shadowy outline of Solen behind her, his eyes glowing in the darkness. He was not relaxed, looking as though he was ready to protect her should he need to.

"I see you've come with an escaped prisoner," said King Rondal.

"Prisoner," Skylet spat.

"That dragon is missing wings," he said. "Or it was. It appears they are now growing back. Hm. I hadn't realized that this was an ability dragons possessed."

The king took a few pacing steps and turned to face Skylet and Solen again. "Hm. Interesting indeed."

"He is not your prisoner," Skylet said. "This is my brother. We are here for the others. Take us to them now, and we will leave with no trouble."

King Rondal stared into Skylet's face.

Not afraid, she met his stern gaze with one of her own.

The king scoffed. "Before that, let us introduce ourselves," he said, almost playfully, which Skylet didn't like. "My name is King Rondal, the ruler of the great kingdom of Ondriten. And who might you be?"

"As I told this man," Skylet shook the soldier in the wrapped cloak to emphasize who she was referring to. "I am kin to the dragons you have *under your care*. Take us to them now."

"I see," said the king, turning his back to her while he took in a breath. "I'm afraid I cannot take you to your family unless you kindly release him. The poor man has been struggling to free himself this whole time."

"Fine," Skylet spat, unwrapping the cloak from around the soldier, who dropped to the ground.

Solen kept a stern eye on him and the other two downed soldiers recovering from being swept off their feet.

"Thank you, young one," said the king. "Please follow me."

Skylet didn't move at first. She simply watched as the king took a few more steps until he stopped and turned to face her.

"Well, come now. Do you not wish to see your family?"

Skylet slowly stepped toward the king, who turned and continued ahead. "It is just down this way."

The king led Solen and Skylet beyond two tall landmasses and in a straight direction toward another, more towering mountain.

Skylet recognized the shape of the mountain from her visions, and she jumped back for a moment.

Solen, trailing behind her, gently put his large hands over her shoulders and guided her ahead. "Be on guard, girl," he whispered low in her ear. "I do not trust him."

"Me either," she said.

"If I may say so," called back the king, "That is quite the cloak about you. Where ever did you get it?"

Skylet didn't respond.

"Ah, a secret. I understand. I am not sure I would reveal the secrets of such power either," the king chuckled.

They traveled by the moon's bright light, guiding their way ahead.

"Around the corner of that mountain will be our destination," said the king.

They continued reaching high rock formations that towered over the path they walked.

Skylet and Solen looked up and around themselves, checking for threats.

"I'm afraid you must forgive me now," the king said as he stopped just ahead of them, turning to face Skylet.

"What for?" she asked. "Holding my family captive?"

"Well," he paused. "You see, I'm afraid I cannot let you leave with them. There is just so much value they have brought to this kingdom in so many ways."

"You will take me to them, NOW!"

The king stood unaffected by Skylet raising her voice.

Skylet immediately reached her hands out toward the king, and the cape responded. The edges of it zipped toward the monarch, who did not fight it. He didn't even attempt to escape as it grabbed his hands and feet, lifting him horizontally like an animal on a spit about to be prepared over the fire.

Skylet raised her hands in a grappling position. "I will tear you in half," she said. "Tell me where my family is."

The king let out a loud and piercing whistle. In the blink of an eye, an archer appeared from the top of one of the high rock formations to the right and released an arrow at Skylet and Solen.

Skylet released the king's feet with the cloak and quickly tried to bat away the projectile, but it was too late. Solen was struck in his back, just near where his new wings were growing.

He roared in pain and reached back to try and pull the arrow out.

The sound of a newly released arrow came from the left, and Skylet, trying to catch it, just managed to throw it off course slightly, and instead of hitting Solen in the center of his back, the arrow struck the top of his tail and the base of his back.

The dragon dropped and rolled over, reaching back to grab the other arrow. He instinctually breathed fire up along the earth formation to the right, but the fire barely made it halfway because he still hadn't fully recovered his strength.

That same archer had now grabbed a crossbow from the group of weapons behind his back and prepared to fire when suddenly, a large boulder fell from the top of the mountain just beyond the king. The impact shook the ground beneath everyone from where Skylet was to where the archers were.

One fired a shot from the crossbow, and the tremor made him miss his mark.

In seconds, a giant arm reached out from the boulder and then another. Soon, it became clear that the boulder was not what it appeared. Large pieces of earth lay fallen off of what Skylet understood to be a dragon as large as Sebastian and Jessie.

It was not just any dragon. It was the very same one she saw in the visions. His dark golden eyes slowly opened. They glowed like the moonlight, and everything inside Skylet sank to the very bottom of her stomach.

55.

Skylet quickly dropped the king and stepped back. She could feel her body overheating, yet she froze with fear.

"Eaon," said the king. "Would you expel them, please? Oh, and be sure to bring me the cloak when you kill the girl."

The dark brown dragon spoke no words, and the king stepped back toward the foot of the mountain behind him.

Eaon wasted no time. He just charged at Skylet head first, grunting with each step of his run.

Like open wings, the cloak spread itself outward behind Skylet, and she put her palm out to Eaon's face as he ran to her. His expression was contorted as if he was experiencing some kind of internal pain. Skylet's hand was emitting a heat wave so powerful she felt vibrations moving down her arm and through her hand. She didn't question it, comfortable knowing her thoughts and feelings were linked to how the cape behaved. And then there was Jessie, the other half of the equation.

The force of the heat, while ultimately ineffective against a fireproof dragon, still knocked Eaon against a rock formation nearby. He was close enough to try and take a swipe at Skylet. He took his chance, and one of the cape edges parried that swipe away. A hint of something familiar became apparent to Skylet at that instant. It was beyond simply recognizing him from the visions, but something much deeper. She saw a quick flash of a memory. It was Eaon, but a younger, happier version of him. She couldn't tell if it was real in the present or if it was something that came directly from one of Jessie's own memories. Either way, it seemed like some form of communication from beyond.

Meanwhile, Solen readied himself to fight, but by the time he was prepared, attempting to dodge an oncoming attack, it was too late. Eaon struck Solen so hard that his body skipped across the pathway before going over the cliff and rolling down the mountainside.

"SOLLY!" Skylet shouted.

Eaon made ready to attack Skylet again with a swipe of his extremely sharp talons. His large hand was struck with an arrow from a crossbow, and Skylet batted away the hand with the cloak edge.

Eaon stomped backward with a growl and pulled the arrow out, scanning up to see where the shot came from.

Skylet kept her eyes trained on the opponent ahead of her, but she heard a voice she recognized.

"Please," the voice called out from the top of the rock formation. "I do not wish to kill you tonight. But if you harm my sister, I will." After climbing the boulder and subduing one of the soldiers, Oros claimed the crossbow and announced his presence.

King Rondal noticed as well but kept his distance, watching.

"Come and face me, hunter," Eaon called out in a voice

that sounded as though he hadn't used it in a very long time. It was like heavy rocks grinding against one another. His tone boomed, vibrating the earth beneath everyone's feet.

"Do not challenge me, dragon." Oros' voice was more alive than he had sounded in some time. "I am here to protect my family. I want no part of you." His eyes narrowed, meeting the glowing, fiery gaze of Eaon. "Nor do you want any part of me."

"A very sensible response," said a new and sharp voice. "Besides, I'm afraid this is not the young hunter's fight."

All attention turned to Henricks, who stood tall and commanding. Just behind him were Captain Holera and her men.

"Henrickssss," Eaon hissed like a scalding liquid.

"Eaon," said Henricks.

"I've been sleeping for too long... Forgotten what the blood of men tastes like." Eaon sat up straight and looked directly at Henricks as though he could shoot fire from his eyes.

Henricks became serious.

"Be thankful for your bargain with the king that states I cannot kill you."

"Roman!" the king called out, stepping out of the shadows and into the moonlight.

"Your Grace," he addressed the monarch in the distance. "My apologies for the interruption of what appears to be an important meeting. I was told I could find you up near here. I came to report."

"And? What news is there on the sea dragon?"

Before Henricks could answer, a loud flapping drew everyone's attention upward.

There was Sebastian, with Séya and Ulonae on his back. He looked majestic in the moonlit glow, highlighting his light blue skin, making it look almost silvery. It was as though he came from the moon.

"Old friend Ash," said Eaon, his tone still gravelly, but this time with a hint of a syrupy quality. "It has been a very long time."

Sebastian landed gracefully and allowed Séya off his back. "Young Solen," he said to Séya, his voice low, keeping his eyes on Eaon.

Skylet noticed and quickly rushed to the old woman. "Séya, I'm so sorry," Skylet began.

Séya waved her off and kissed her forehead. "Take her, girl, and come with me." The old woman handed the youngling to Skylet as she dashed toward the cliff.

Skylet followed and looked up to see Oros, the two of them locked eyes. In moments, Séya and Skylet jumped over the edge. Using their respective abilities, Séya's magic and Skylet's cloak, they found a way to go down the slanted cliff without hurting themselves.

Standing behind Henricks, Holera and her men noticed Séya and began whispering, recognizing her from the parchment scroll. No one moved just yet. Instead, they waited.

Sebastian scanned the area, noticing Henricks and the soldiers to his left, Eaon directly across from him, and King Rondal to his right.

He took a breath and spoke. "Eaon," he said, shaking, trying to maintain his composure.

Yet, Oros, who watched the exchange from a crouched position, had spent significant time with the sea dragon and could tell that Sebastian was barely staying calm.

"You have a great deal of pain within you, Eaon," said

Sebastian. "It has made your heart unbalanced."

"Would you care to see it?" Eaon taunted as he bowed his head. "I invite you to share in my pain. Or are you carrying your own tonight?" the dragon cackled.

"This is quite the reunion, it seems," King Rondal quipped. "Was this your doing, Roman? Did you plan to have the sea dragon meet you here to kill me? Genius! The throne would be all yours, wouldn't it?"

"No, my liege," Henricks replied. "This was not my plan—"

Eaon lashed out toward Sebastian without warning and pinned him to the ground. The impact from the fall of two large dragons made cracks in the earth and caused rocks to tumble and fall down the nearby formations.

Henricks quickly turned to Holera. "Captain, take your men and get somewhere safe. If these dragons engage in a full-scale battle, we'll all be in real trouble."

"What about you?" she asked.

"I will be fine," he said. "Get yourselves out of sight. And watch out for other soldiers from the castle guard. They are sure to be nearby."

"Be careful," she said to Henricks. "Soldiers, follow me!" They were off.

Henricks turned and faced the rolling dragons.

Meanwhile above, Oros continued to keep watch. His eyes darted from Henricks to the dragons rolling on the ground, to the king, to beyond him. That's when he noticed what looked to be an entrance into the mountain closed by a mixture of earth and a material painted to look like earth. The only reason he was able to notice it was due to the angle of the moon. It was slight, and he was thankful he happened to catch it. He was almost certain that if the other dragons were anywhere, they would be behind that entrance somewhere.

He began descending the back of the tall earth formation so neither the king nor Eaon would spot him moving. Not that their attention was on anything other than what was in front of them anyway. Still, Oros wasn't about to take a chance.

"You aren't struggling, Ash," said Eaon.

Eaon had his hands around Sebastian's neck, squeezing. His sharp talons began digging into the skin.

"Eaon..." Sebastian struggled to get the name out.

"Share my pain, brother," Eaon said, picking Sebastian's head up and slamming it back into the earth. "SHARE IT!!" Eaon butted his head against Sebastian's once. Twice. Three times. "I want you to feel the pain I feel every day!"

Henricks pulled out a projectile device that was like a single hand-held crossbow and shot an arrow at the arm of Eaon as he rested his weight on top of Sebastian.

Eaon's arm almost instantly began to tingle as he whipped his head toward Henricks. "Youuu," he grumbled. He dashed across to Henricks and delivered a backhand that caused him to slam into one of the rock formations. "Haven't you had your hands in enough loss for me?"

Henricks got to one knee and pulled out his sword.

"You've now interrupted a pleasant conversation with an old friend." Eaon stood tall on his hind legs and drew in a large breath.

Henricks got to his feet and quickly recognized what was coming next. He tried to grab something from his belt, but the dragon was ready too quickly. A split second was all it took for Eaon to unleash the full power of his fire. The heat was unimaginable and had a liquid quality.

As soon as he finished breathing all the angry fire out that he could, he was tackled by Sebastian.

Henricks found himself on the ground, patting flames off of himself. He turned around to see that Oros had pushed him out of the way of the fire and had used his cloak to take the heat. He didn't get through unscathed; the hand that held the cover to protect him was badly burned. Oros looked over at Henricks, who looked back at him. They shared a nod, signifying they had an understanding. Oros put the finger of his good hand up to Henricks as if to say, 'That is the one time you'll be saved.' Then he dashed off to try and make his way to the mountain opening.

Meanwhile, the dragons scuffled and rolled around on the mountain, making everything shake. Henricks could see them and jumped out of the way to avoid a flailing tail.

Once he got to his feet, he was kicked from behind his leg, bringing him back to one knee. King Rondal made his way around Henricks to face him and punched him down. "You made a mistake teaching me how to fight."

He went to punch Henricks again but was swept up by a clean foot trip. The monarch landed on his back.

"There happen to be some things, Your Grace, that weren't taught to you."

The king removed his crown and outer robes and prepared himself for a real fight. "Come on, Roman."

Henricks just looked at the king and shook his head.

"Fight me, or you are a traitor to the crown."

"Your Highness—"

"You brought the sea dragon here to kill me, did you not?"

"I did not."

"Then why do you protect it from Eaon?"

"I once killed a family of dragons," said Henricks. "It resulted in the loss of many lives."

The king just listened. Still ready to fight.

"I do not wish that same fate upon Ondriten."

"It is not up to you what happens to this kingdom," said the king as he rushed Henricks.

The two engaged in a dance. The monarch threw blows; the former hunter dodged and redirected the attacks.

Meanwhile, the two dragons continued to scuffle. Harder this time.

"How was it to take her from me, Ash?" Eaon struck Sebastian across the face.

Sebastian rolled with the hit and came back with a sweep of his tail that Eaon dodged and dropped the full weight of his foot upon it, crushing it.

Sebastian roared in pain.

Eaon used his functional arm to deliver punches and scratches with his talons to Sebastian's face, neck, and chest.

"I called for you, Ash. I called for you both," Eaon grumbled. "When my family was being..." he stopped and immediately went into a fire breath attack.

Sebastian quickly dispersed a water shield around the outside of his body to absorb and put out the flames. Then Eaon, delivering a devastating blow squarely on Sebastian's nose, got him to stop moving.

The two were out of breath, staring at each other.

"You've been good at keeping your mind closed," Eaon said. "Now, I want you to see the weight I've carried with me all these years since the purge."

Eaon lowered his head and touched his brow against Sebastian's, tightly holding the sea dragon's face.

In the darkness, Sebastian heard Eaon's voice. *See it. See it all.*

The images came quickly and all at once. There was no build-up. It was as though Eaon had been carrying all of the pain close to the surface, unable to bury it beneath time.

Sebastian saw Jessie and Eaon talking, and then the image shifted to when the three of them pledged to protect hatchlings and all dragon kind during the purge.

Next, Sebastian saw a family of dragons that looked similar to Eaon. And then the image shifted to that same family dead on the ground.

There was another memory of Eaon meditating, trying to call on the other Ethereans. No one came to help him save his family against the men who destroyed his home, turning him into a weapon for the kingdom of Ondriten.

Sebastian then understood why he was engaged in the fight with Eaon. He had seen images of prisoners and others who sought to bring down the kingdom killed by Eaon. He felt the hopelessness and despair in Eaon's heart; there was nothing left to live for but the next kill.

It was overwhelming for Sebastian; he shook violently. Tears streamed from his eyes. In the midst of it all, he was able to transmit one memory back to Eaon. It was the strongest one he could muster, and it pushed Eaon back, making the dragon land on his side. He tried to compose himself. His breathing became uncontrollable, and almost immediately, he cried with the force of a mighty wave crashing against a rocky shore.

"Jessie," he whimpered. "No, no. NO!!!"

Sebastian opened his eyes and looked over at Eaon, who lay curled in a fetal position. He knew his transmission had gotten through.

"I didn't know, Eaon," Sebastian said. "I had no idea you loved her too."

"She can't be gone…" Eaon suddenly sounded like a small dragon.

"Your babies, your partner," Sebastian said under his breath as he went to Eaon and put a hand on his shoulder.

"You never came back! You never came BACK!" Eaon reached up and grabbed Sebastian's throat. "EVERYBODY IS GONE! And Jessie…"

Suddenly, he heard a familiar voice.

Eaon, my dear friend.

"Jessie??" Eaon looked around and saw no one. "I can hear you!"

Close your eyes so that you can see me.

He wasted no time and did as she said.

In the darkness, he soon saw the face of Jessie and then the rest of her.

Eaon… Come. Jessie's arms were outstretched, and she embraced him with the warmest hug he had ever felt.

I am sorry… I am sorry we never came when you called. I am sorry about your family. I know how much you cared. I loved you, too. I still do. We just weren't meant to be partnered. Please understand. You are still needed here. No matter what you've done. You've no need to feel guilt or shame anymore. She held his face. You are still an Etherean.

"No… Jessie," Eaon said, his voice pained. "I am not anymore. I have strayed so far. I've killed so many… men and dragons."

A flash of some of his victims revealed itself. He saw dragons of many kinds to further the ambitions of the kingdom of Ondriten. And then there was Arca. He saw the fight they had when the kingdom's soldiers attacked Arca.

He was taken to the mountain to face Eaon. They fought heartily, and after Eaon struck a fatal blow, he flew Arca to where he would meet Oros. The image shook him. It surprised Jessie, too.

"He was your... No. You raised him," Eaon whined.

It doesn't matter. Here. Jessie came in close for an embrace. Eaon tried to fight it, but it was no use. *Feel this.*

The two embraced in silence.

This is love, Eaon, dear. It runs through everything. It is in you now. Lead with love from here onward. Please. Jessie pecked his cheek and faded away.

When Eaon opened his eyes, he found Skylet with her hands on his face. She, Sebastian, and Eaon all in tears.

***

Oros made his way to the entrance of the mountain. He pushed one of the boulders out of the way as best he could with one burned hand. He then kicked away the other bits of material that blocked the opening. He stood before the darkened entrance. The waft of dragon rushed to meet his nose. He was sure the other dragons were down there, but before he took a single step inside, he was struck in the back of the head from behind and jumped by no less than five kingdom soldiers.

56.

When Oros came to, he found himself stripped of his items and his clothes down to his undergarments. He was chained to a post inside a chamber with a single window at the very back. He noticed that his clothes were just out of reach, but his sword, which once belonged to his Uncle Servalan, made of Moonbeam Metal, lay just in front of him, shining in the moonlight.

The smell of dragons was also strong. The others were there. As he was still waking up, Oros wondered about the others on the mountain and how they were fairing.

"Poor hunter," a voice said ahead of him from the darkness of the chamber, shaking him from his thoughts. "They brought you here to die."

Suddenly, Oros saw the glowing eyes staring at him. He could just make out a large cage behind him that had been opened. This dragon was released on purpose.

Heavy footsteps made the room shake. The jangling sounds in the distance told him that they were still chained.

How long were the chains? He wondered. Then, more footsteps from another dragon to the right joined in.

"You are lucky we cannot burn you to death," the other voice said.

"That's okay, Tithla. We can play with him."

"Wait," Oros began, but he couldn't speak quickly enough to stop the hard blow from Beresay.

Chained, Oros had no way of defending himself.

"Grab his blade," said Beresay.

"Wait, I want to do one thing first."

"Please," Oros coughed, blood dripping from his mouth.

Tithla grabbed Oros with her large hands and bent down, putting his head into her mouth and closing it lightly, puncturing his chest and back.

He screamed terribly and coughed.

"You're not supposed to kill him yet, silly!" Beresay was annoyed.

"I bit him lightly!"

"Look at all that blood! Does that look light to you?"

"Sky...let," Oros managed to get out.

"What did you say, hunter?" Tithla turned her head quickly to him.

"Jessie..." Oros coughed out.

"How do you know about Jessie?" Beresay asked. "What happened to her? Is she all right??"

"She... she..." Oros' breathing was faster. "She's here..." Then he dropped from Tithla's mouth.

"How do you know about JESSIE!!" Beresay ran toward him, and as she went to grab him, she was sliced by a sword.

Beresay howled in pain and backed up, slamming into the cold chamber floor.

"Beresay!" Tithla rushed over to check on her sister. Then, she focused her attention on the culprit.

Layona had found her way to the chamber and held Oros' sword, ready to defend herself.

"I'll kill you too!" Tithla shouted as she rushed the Principal Sentinel.

In a few quick moves, Layona cut one of Oros' chains loose, twisted around, and lowered herself to get under Tithla's head, where she sliced upward just underneath the chin, which made the dragon tumble to the side. Finally, she cut Oros' last chain loose. Then she dragged him away from the post and near the chamber entrance that led back to the mountainside.

She crouched in front of Oros' mangled body and held the sword out, readying herself to defend some more. "Hear me, dragons!" Layona called out. "This man is not your enemy. Stay back, or I will be forced to kill you."

"You'll not survive against us," Tithla said seriously. "Who are you?"

"I am the one who will deliver you to your family."

"How do you mean, hunter lover," Beresay hissed. "Explain yourself!"

"I saw another dragon with no wings."

For a moment, everyone was still. Only heavy breathing and the dripping water echoed throughout the chamber as the dragons stared at Layona, taking in her words. What she spoke couldn't be true.

"Solly," Tithla whispered.

Layona slowly nodded. "He is here. And he is not alone."

"And who is this man," Beresay seemed calmer, but her tone was still hard.

"He is my prisoner. And if I can keep him alive, he will come with me and be tried for his crimes."

There was a brief silence before Layona broke it. "Your

blood. I need some to keep him alive."

"Will you free us and take us to Solen?" Tithla asked.

"You have my word."

57.

Séya knelt, tending to Solen's injuries, when the soldiers surrounded her and the dragon.

"You are the witch from the attack on Selnes," Holera said from behind Séya.

"I'm sorry?" Séya turned around to face the captain and slowly stood up.

"Stay where you are, witch." Holera drew her spear and held it out at Séya. "Keep your distance, soldiers; this dragon might spring up at any moment."

The men did as she said.

Séya just looked at Holera. "You seem on edge," said Séya. "Do you have something to ask?"

"I want to know what happened to my brother, the commander. You and your dragon friend, did you kill him?"

Séya took a moment and looked down, and then she remembered. "The commander, I remember him," Séya said. "If he was a threat at all to the girl..." Séya trailed off.

"He was like," Holera caught herself feeling emotions. "I helped raise him."

"I am so sorry, child."

"And the dragon?"

"I'm afraid she, too, is gone. Physically, anyway."

"Then you will be tried and hanged," Holera sniffled. "You will accompany us back to Selnes to await your sentencing.

"Dear," Séya began.

An explosion from the top of the mountain crashed, bringing debris and rocks down the hill.

Everyone turned their attention upward. It looked like bodies were falling from the top, rolling down the hill.

"Come in close! As close as you can!" Séya called out to the soldiers.

"What?" one of the men didn't understand.

Séya quickly sprung into action and placed her hands up toward the sky, conjuring a shield made of air to protect them against the debris and earth.

When the explosion calmed down, Séya dropped to her knees after holding the shield in place long enough for everything to finish falling.

"Séya," Solen said, holding on to her.

"I am all right, thank you, dear."

"Look!" One of the soldiers pointed up in the air.

Aria flew down, holding an unconscious Skylet in his arms.

"Skylet!" Séya cried.

"She is fine," said Aria. "We were able to catch her just before the worst of the blast."

"Where is Sebastian?" Séya asked.

"He summoned us but was nowhere to be found. Nor was anyone else."

Just then, Floren descended, holding another dark green dragon in his arms: this was Eagan. He was unable to fly due to a broken wing. The twins could have certainly used more time to recover, but with their father and new friends in trouble, they had to help, even if it cost them everything. Aria and Floren were far from strong enough to do battle, but luckily, fighting was not required of them, as capable as they were in that area. Theirs was a rescue mission.

"Eagan!!" Solen cried.

When Floren had placed him down, the two embraced tightly and began crying.

"Where are Beresay and Tithla," asked Eagan, his voice hoarse.

While all of this was happening, Holera exchanged glances with her men. They were all mesmerized by the dragons, having never seen one dragon before, let alone so many of varying colors and personalities. She knelt and thought about everything as she attempted to put the pieces together on what to do next beyond the obvious trial ahead.

58.

Back at the colony, several weeks passed following the ordeal in Ondriten. Skylet sat watching her siblings rest one evening in the infirmary. They seemed to be sleeping so soundly, a sight that brought her immense comfort. Yet, she couldn't relax. She found herself thinking deeply about the horrors they might have endured while they had been apart from her. They had been in captivity so long, and they probably hadn't realized how much rest they would need to feel normal again, Skylet thought. She wondered if they even remembered life before being taken and imprisoned.

Skylet allowed her thoughts to take her deeper, and her eyes scanned her siblings as a watchful parent might, afraid if she closed her eyes for even one moment, they would disappear. It would be as if reuniting with them were nothing more than a dream.

Séya was also awake. She made her way to the girl and sat next to her. She let out a deep breath and put an arm around Skylet. The two spoke no words; they leaned into one another and held each other.

***

Sebastian still hadn't been found. Nor had Henricks or the king. Search parties had been sent out for each, but they remained missing. Once Oros had recovered from his injuries, it was decided that he and Séya would go to Selnes with the sentinels and the soldiers to stand trial. They would visit the dragons if found innocent, but the likelihood of that was slim.

Thcy were paraded through the town to cheers and jeers on their way to central Selnes. There was outrage because neither Séya nor Oros had their hands tied up. Skylet trailed behind the carriage that had transported them. She was determined to see the whole thing through and possibly speak on their behalf.

Layona also trailed behind, beside Skylet, neither speaking the whole way there.

Once they reached the courthouse, nearly everyone had something nasty to say or throw at Oros and Séya as they exited the carriage.

Layona made her way to Séya and gently tied her hands together. Then she approached Oros, who had his hands out, ready for them to be tied.

The two of them shared a look as though no one else was present.

"A bargain is a bargain," he said to her, his face serious. He pushed his hands out to her again.

Layona stepped up and carefully tied his hands together. When she was done, her eyes went from his hands to his face. "The old merchant in Mysteya," she said. "He sends his wishes of peace for you."

Oros considered this as he met and held her gaze momentarily until he was guided away from her by a sentinel to the courthouse doors.

Off to the side, a woman surrounded by screaming spectators stood quietly near the entrance, staring at Oros. She was tall, dark-skinned, and wore a scarf wrapped over her head like a hood.

Oros had to pass her to get to the entrance. The two of them locked eyes for a moment, but Oros looked away after a second.

The woman kept staring, watching as he and Séya were escorted through the remainder of the crowd and into the courthouse. It was as though she knew him.

Skylet stood in the distance watching. She noticed the woman too, the only other person who maintained her composure in the commotion around her. She seemed almost too calm. Did she have anger and hatred for Oros too? Skylet didn't know, but she did know that the next chance she got, telling Oros how much she appreciated him would be a top priority. She wasn't sure if she was ready to love him yet, but he had risked everything to keep her safe. She would have to tell him what he meant to her as best she could. One day.

For now, though, that would have to wait. At least until the trial.

ACKNOWLEDGMENTS

This book wasn't supposed to happen. In fact, when the breath of an idea for a successive story to *Dragon Daughter* entered my thoughts, I fought it. I wasn't interested in writing a series, and yet here we are.

Kellie Kels, you were the first person to put the idea of expanding this story into the universe. Again, as with the first, I don't know that this book exists without you. After all the denying and pushing against the idea internally, I have to tell you, you were right. Thank you, dearest.

I extend my gratitude to the incredible team at Atmosphere Press. Bryce, thank you for continuing this journey with me. If this book wins in any capacity, your input and support is a massive part of that. Ms. Alex, thank you for helping tighten things up in the periphery of this project and for your enthusiasm for this work. I hope to collaborate with you again. Ms. Chris, your work on this book has been invaluable. Thank you. Thank you, Nick, for welcoming me back to the Atmosphere family and for your excitement about this story.

To my family and loved ones, always asking, "What's going on with the book," thank you. You didn't know it, but you kept reminding me to stop procrastinating and get back to work.

I thank my sister scribes in the Three Gifts Writing Group cohort. The energy and support I've found in you over the last few years has been the gift that keeps on giving in so many ways. Ms. Marguerite, you endlessly inspire me. Thank you for being a constant presence as I worked through this one. You're still the best writing partner ever.

And again, to you, dear reader, thank you for living in and between the pages of this story for a little while. Bless your heart.

About Atmosphere Press

Founded in 2015, Atmosphere Press was built on the principles of Honesty, Transparency, Professionalism, Kindness, and Making Your Book Awesome. As an ethical and author-friendly hybrid press, we stay true to that founding mission today.

If you're a reader, enter our giveaway for a free book here:

SCAN TO ENTER
BOOK GIVEAWAY

If you're a writer, submit your manuscript for consideration here:

SCAN TO SUBMIT
MANUSCRIPT

And always feel free to visit Atmosphere Press and our authors online at atmospherepress.com. See you there soon!

ABOUT THE AUTHOR

Born and raised in the Bay Area, **STEVEN ARMSTRONG** is an award-winning filmmaker, screenwriter, and author of *Dragon Daughter*. He spent several years in the non-profit world of maternal health, becoming inspired by countless stories of resilience while working as an editor and staff writer reviewing films. Steven holds a BA in Creative Arts from San Jose State University and an MFA in Writing and Consciousness from the California Institute of Integral Studies. His debut novel, *Dragon Daughter*, was released in 2021, and *Dragon of the Deep* is the next series installment. During writing breaks, he can be found on the YouTube channel C4C (Center 4 Cinephiles), talking unabashedly about movies, stress cooking, or studying stories in some form or another.